PLAN BEA

HILARY GROSSMAN

Mom-Thank you for being you.

ALSO BY HILARY GROSSMAN

I Can't Stop Loving You RomComs Series

Cop An Attitude

Cop A Plea

Forest River PTA Mom Series

Go On, Girl

Mom Genes

Mom Boss

Mom Rules

Mom Wars - The Boxed Set

Secrets, Lies, and Second Chances Series

Plan Bea

Plan Cee

RomCom Memoir

Dangled Carat

CHAPTER ONE

"Oh my God!" I jumped up from a deep sleep and turned on the light over the bed. My heart beat a mile a minute as my stomach took a nosedive. No good ever came from a call in the middle of the night. Trust me, I knew. I learned that lesson the hard way, twelve years ago.

Thankfully, the phone was on Cole's side of the bed. I knew it was probably silly of me, but when we moved into this house, we placed the phone on his side of the bed for this very reason. I wanted my husband to be the first line of defense if the police or a hospital called with an emergency in the middle of the night. I didn't think I was emotionally strong enough to experience that again.

Two rings.

Three rings.

Why was Cole letting the phone ring so long? I didn't want the kids to wake up. It would be impossible to get Harley back to sleep.

As the fourth ring began to sound, Cole thrust the phone at me. "It's for you. It's Beatrice."

"Mom. What's wrong?"

"Wrong? Wrong?" she repeated in a singsong voice as if I

was deaf. "Why do you always assume something is wrong, Annabel?"

"Um, maybe because you're calling me in the middle of the night?"

My mother let out her slow, sarcastic chuckle. You know, the kind that made you feel insignificant and so inferior. I should have been used to it by now, but sadly, I was not.

"Annabel, really? Middle of the night, aren't you being a bit melodramatic? It's what time? It's only—"

I glanced at the cable box across the room. "Ten-thirty, Mother. To you, it may not be late, but Cole and I were both asleep. With work and two kids, we're exhausted by the end of the day. Call us crazy, but we like to go to bed at a reasonable hour."

Cole was watching me. As I covered my face with my hands and shook my head in frustration, he must have realized my mother was being her usual self. He flicked off the light and rolled over. He'd be snoring in moments. I'd be lying if I said I wasn't jealous.

My mother exhaled. "I guess I can understand, although I really do think it's too early for you and Cole to be sleeping. You know Annabel; you really do need to keep that husband of yours happy. I would think you'd have other things to be doing at this time of night if you know what I mean."

"Mother, I'd love to debate our sleep patterns with you, but I guess that's not why you called, especially at this hour."

My mother and I never called each other just to talk. In fact, I didn't actually remember the last time either one of us spontaneously picked up the phone to have a little mother-daughter chat. Our calls were all business, prompted by life events, breaking family news, or just plain old forced. In fact, we have a standard fifteen minute "touching base" phone call each Thursday, precisely at eleven forty-five in the morning when my mom drove to the nail salon for her weekly manicure.

"You're right, Darling. I did have a reason for my call. I have big news for you. Very exciting news, I must add."

"Okay. I'm all ears." I said as I flopped back against the bed and pulled the covers up to my chin.

"Remember the lovely gentleman I told you about? Walter?"

"The one you met a couple of months ago when you went on that cruise with the ladies you play bridge with?"

"Yes!" She exclaimed. "That's him. Well guess what?"

I couldn't help it and I certainly didn't mean it, but a huge, loud yawn escaped my mouth. "Sorry, Mom. I don't know, and I'm too tired to play guessing games." I glanced over at a snoring Cole. Lucky bastard.

"Okay, I had such a great time on the cruise with him. If you remember, we met by the pool bar. I know everyone says the cruise line has impeccable service, but I didn't experience it. The staff wouldn't last fifteen minutes at the club that's for sure. Good help is so hard to find these days. Anyway, we both must've been waiting for the bartender for a full five minutes. Five minutes! Can you believe it? When he finally came over, we both blurted out our order at the same time. Turns out, we both ordered the same drink! We began laughing the moment the words left our mouths."

"Yes, you told me this." While my mother had no patience listening to me discuss my children, my husband, or really anything going on in my life. But when it came to one of her stories, you'd better pay attention... Well, unless Marcella, her manicurist, was waiting. In that case you got a free pass. One thing to know about my mother, Beatrice Buchanan, she has two conversational speeds. One was slow and drawn out, and the other was slower and more drawn out. There was no point in trying to rush her. So I laid my head down on my pillow and prayed I wouldn't doze off before she got to her point.

"Oh yes. I did mention it, didn't I? But it bears repeating. So after we got our drinks, we sat down together. The cruise ship had these amazing chaise lounges. They were so comfortable, way more comfortable than the ones they have at the club. Walter sat in the sun, but I was under the umbrella. You know, Annabel, I've haven't sat in the sun in twenty-five years. You should take a lesson from me if you don't want to be all wrinkled up when you are my age."

I grunted.

"So, as I was saying, once we started talking, we just couldn't stop! He was so interesting and funny. I was kind of shocked—you know most people aren't worth paying attention to. Anyway, one drink led to another and by the second gin martini, I was feeling a little tipsy, but I was having a blast!"

"I know, Mother. You told me this story already, right after you got home from the trip. Can we please cut to the chase?" I felt bad that I rushed her but I was fading fast. I feared this could go on for hours.

"Annabel, please. Let me tell my story, maybe if you stopped interrupting me I could finish."

Why did I even bother? I couldn't decide if I should stay in bed or go downstairs and brew a cup of tea. Maybe snack on some of those double-chocolate chip cookies I made this past weekend. I decided to forgo the snack, once I'm out of bed there's no chance of getting back to sleep.

My mother continued. "Where was I anyway? Oh, yes. I remember. We decided to meet up after dinner. As I ate, I wished I had arranged to have dinner with him instead of the ladies. You know I love the girls, but can they gab. I swear if I heard one more word about Miriam's granddaughter's college acceptances, I would've had to abandon ship. Stella was no better. She just couldn't stop talking about her son's promotion. And don't get me started on how Wilma kept droning on about her daughter's new house. She carried on so much you'd think she discovered a new continent, I mean really it's just a house. Some people are so self-centered."

I couldn't even reply for fear of what I would say.

"As soon as dinner ended, I ran back to the room to fix my face. The sea air really wreaks havoc on your makeup, you know. I met Walter in the lounge. We ordered an after dinner drink; it sat there untouched. There was a five-piece band, and they were playing the oldies. He asked me to dance, and let's just say that man can really trip the light fantastic. Before I knew it, it was the wee hours of the morning. I don't remember the last time I had so much fun. We were docking in Cozumel the next day. I was supposed to spend the day with the girls. But I couldn't handle being with them one more minute. Did I mention how annoying they were?"

"Yes, you did."

"Oh, well instead I stayed on the ship with Walter. Best. Decision. Ever! Let's just say for the rest of the cruise I didn't have to hear anymore about the great Harvard/Yale debate. I spent all my waking and," Beatrice paused to clear her throat, "my non-waking hours with him."

"Mother, please. Can we not go down that road, again."

"Okay, okay." She chuckled before continuing. "As I was saying before you interrupted me again, I started to worry as the trip came to an end. I didn't want to lose Walter. But, as usual, my worry was for nothing! Walter lives in Manhattan. We've been seeing each other ever since we got home. And... get ready for it..."

I stifled another yawn. "I'm at the edge of my bed."

"Walter asked me to marry him!" Beatrice screamed so loudly into the phone I was surprised she didn't wake up Cole. I glanced over at him; he was still fast asleep.

I sat straight up. "He what?"

"You heard me, dear. He asked me to marry him. And I said yes! But it gets even better; I need your help. I don't want to discuss it over the phone. Prepare dinner tomorrow night. Walter and I are coming over. I want you to meet him, and I want to go over what I need you to do for me."

"But—"

"No buts. Dinner. Tomorrow. We'll be there at seven o'clock. Oh and one more thing: no carbs. I have to watch my weight. I'm going to be a bride, you know."

CHAPTER TWO

"You're sure going all out tonight, aren't you?" Cole asked me as he snatched the practically empty bowl of chocolate frosting sitting on the white granite counter. He began wiping the spatula clean with his finger. His smile assured me the icing tasted delicious.

"Not really," I replied as I grabbed the utensil from him and rinsed it in the sink.

"You could have fooled me, Anna. It smells great in here. Believe me, I'm not complaining. I just feel bad you went to all this effort, after work no less, just because Beatrice called last night and demanded you do so."

"It wasn't like that," I lied.

"Anna, it's me you're talking to. I know exactly what happened." He arched an eyebrow at me. "Let's see if I've got this right. I bet not only did she tell you what night she wanted to have dinner, she also told you what time to have it ready, and what or what not to make."

I smirked. My mother was always on a perpetual diet, even though she'd been a size six her entire life. "Yes. She made a special point of instructing me not to have any carbs on the menu. I guess she won't partake in this cake."

"Going against Bea? That's my girl!" He leaned over and tucked a strand of blond hair away from my eyes before giving me a gentle kiss. "I don't mean to bust your chops, Anna. I just hate what she does to you. She takes you for granted and you let her do it, time and time again."

"I know," I said and sighed deeply. "But you don't understand. No matter how old you are, you always want your mother's love and acceptance. I guess I'm hoping one day I'll get it back."

He didn't say anything. He didn't have to. He stared at me with his piercing blue eyes. I read him loud and clear. Cole really tried to make a concerted effort to not express his true feelings about my mother. He didn't often put into words what he felt, but there was no mistaking his disdain for her. I couldn't blame him for his feelings. From day one, Cole had always been very protective of me, and no one had hurt me as much as she had.

I threw the dishtowel down. "Hell, who am I fooling? I'm not sure I ever had her love or acceptance."

He took the now-dry bowl and put it in the cupboard. "Remember, it's her loss, not yours."

"Have you heard anything more about the acquisition?" I asked, changing the subject.

Cole's eyes clouded. As he opened his mouth to speak, Violet came charging into the kitchen. "Daddy, Daddy!" she screamed and threw herself at Cole. At only ten years old, she was a force to be reckoned with. She didn't have a shy bone in her body. She never feared expressing herself or fighting for what she felt was right. With mischievous deep blue eyes and jet-black hair, she was the spitting image of her father. Harley, only five-years old, trailed behind his sister and waited his turn to get a kiss from his dad. I can't help but see myself when I look at him. He has light brown hair, which turns blonde in the sun, and hazel eyes.

"Guess what, Daddy?" Violet demanded.

"What, sweetheart?"

"I'm so excited! Grandma is coming over for dinner!"

Cole raised an eyebrow at me, clearly confused.

I mouthed to him, "She thinks your mom is coming." When I told her Grandma was coming, she automatically assumed I meant my mother-in-law. I didn't have the heart to tell her it was my mom, which was why I baked the cake. I wanted to have a consolation prize for the kids. I knew they would both be disappointed when my mother showed up. My children got more attention and affection from strangers then they did from her.

Cole's mother, Connie, was everything my mom wasn't. She's warm, friendly, and always made you feel wanted and special regardless of who you were. She had no airs about her. She greeted a cashier at the supermarket with the same warmth she would the CEO of a fortune five hundred company. She was incredibly thoughtful. She was always the first person I called when I needed advice, a shoulder to cry on, or just a good old laugh.

"Grandma's here!" Violet squealed as the door bell sounded. She flew out of the kitchen and ran to the front door.

"Hold up, kiddo," I yelled as I ran after her, fearing her reaction wouldn't be pretty. Of course, I was too late. Violet already had flung open the door. As soon as she saw my mother, her eyes bulged and her mouth hung open. Violet didn't even blink until she dramatically closed her eyes, shook her head, and slowly placed her hand against her cheek.

"Hello, darlings," my mother greeted us. She gave me an air kiss and patted Violet on her head. I could have missed it, but I don't think she even acknowledged Harley.

"What are *you* doing here?" Violet inquired with quite a bit of sass in her tone. Her little brother quietly stood behind her, ambivalent. Harley, unlike his sister, was the most easygoing kid around.

"Having dinner, of course. Didn't your mother tell you I was coming?" She stripped off her sable fur coat and practically threw it at Cole without so much as a nod of thanks. He obediently hung it in the closet. I could just imagine the thoughts running through his head.

With her hands firmly planted on her hips, Violet looked up at my mother. "Mommy said Grandma was coming. I expected my grandma, Grandma Connie," she clarified. "I didn't expect *you*. It's not like it's a holiday or anyone's birthday. You never come *just because*."

It took all my strength to not smile. My daughter called it like she saw it, and as usual, she was spot on. I felt like I should scold her. "Violet..." I started, but her blue eyes shined brightly and opened wide, like an idea magically popped into her head.

Inquisitively she turned to face Cole. "Daddy? Is today a holiday I don't know about? It can't be a real holiday 'cause I had school. But could it be one of those grown-up holidays?"

Cole squeezed her shoulder. "Sorry sweetie, there's no holiday today."

"Darn it! Now there is no shot of getting a present," she said with a pout.

"Do you need a gift?" My mother asked as she opened her wallet and pulled out two twenties.

Violet looked up at her grandmother but didn't accept the bills. "No, I don't need anything. I just thought a present might make tonight less *boring*. It's not like you're gonna play with us. Come on Harley. Let's get outta here."

"Not so fast, little girl," A deep voice bellowed. For the first time, I looked—really looked—at the man standing next to my mother. He was tall, about six-feet, two-inches. He was on the stocky side and had a full head of gray hair and devilish green eyes. If I had to guess his age, I'd say he was in his late sixties—

at least five years older than my mother. While she was decked out in a cream Chanel suit, he dressed casually in a long-sleeved, gray polo shirt and light blue jeans.

Violet must not have noticed him before either. "Who are you?" She crinkled her nose.

"My name's Walter. I'm a friend of your grandma. But my really good friends, the special ones who are the most fun, call me Wally. I'm hoping by the time you two go to bed tonight, Y'all will be calling me Wally too."

Violet rolled her eyes. I must have been a worse influence than I thought.

"Hey! I saw that, young lady!" Walter admonished.

Harley looked like he was about to cry. Even Violet looked taken back. Wonderful. If my mom wasn't cold enough, her main squeeze made it his business to scare my children.

Cole's jaw clenched, his body turned rigid as his eyes filled with rage.

It was clear to me he had a difficult time keeping his temper under control. Why had I agreed to this evening? Before Cole or I could say anything, Walter smiled and let out a deep laugh. He gently tickled Violet, who also started to giggle. The tension in the room began to ease ever so slightly.

"You don't think you'll be calling me Wally, huh? Hmm, okay...I guess...but an old man can hope, can't he? Did either one of you see the bag I was holding when I came in?" He gently turned his attention to my son and tickled Harley too.

"I did!" Harley squealed.

"It's over there." Violet said all businesslike. She pointed to the corner by the front door.

Walter brought the bag over to the kids. "Let's see what's inside, okay?" Walter bent down and pulled out a beautiful bouquet of white roses. "These are for your mommy. Does she like flowers?"

"Yeah!" yelled Harley.

"Good!" Walter said as he handed them to Violet. "Do me a favor and give these pretty flowers to your pretty mommy. Then come back. There might be something in this bag for you and your brother too." Violet did as she was told.

My mother had had enough of this domestic bliss. She marched into the living room; her high heels clicked on the oak wood floor as she made her way over to the yellow leather sectional against the big bay window. She tossed an abandoned Barbie doll onto the floor before she parked herself on the couch. Lila, my eleven-year-old black and white cat, rubbed up against my mother's leg and caused Beatrice to jump.

She screeched, "Can't you do something with this *thing*?"

Beatrice was never a fan of felines, and Lila sensed her dislike from day one. A few years after I'd rescued her from a kill shelter, Bea came over for Thanksgiving dinner. She kept trying to shoo Lila away. Gotta love a cat who gets her revenge by peeing in a pair of expensive Manolos that were left by the front door. My mother never took off her shoes in my house again. I think it's pretty funny that Lila always ended up running up to Beatrice as soon as she sat down—like she's trying to make up for that one little incident.

Lila, after making her point, left the room, and Beatrice picked up one of the many fashion magazines I had laying on the coffee table. She absently thumbed through the glossy pages for a second or two before calling out, "Cole, sweetheart, please be a plum and fix me a drink. A gin martini, if you don't remember. Oh, make Walter one too while you're at it."

"Yes, your majesty." Cole snickered. If my mother noticed his sarcasm, she didn't show it.

"Beatrice, please." Walter turned towards her. "Can you have a little patience for once?" Then he faced Cole. "Don't go. I've got something here for you too." He dramatically looked around the room, "Hey, where is my assistant?"

Violet raised her hand and beamed. "Here I am!"

"Good. Now you've got to be careful with this. Are you strong?" Walter asked very seriously.

"Yeah! Look at my muscles." Violet rolled up her sleeve and flexed her right arm. Walter reached down and gave her bicep a big squeeze.

"Oh really, Walter," my mother called from her perch on the couch. "Why must you make such a fuss, announcing everything to everyone. It's getting annoying. Can't you simply hand everyone their gifts and move on?"

"Oh, calm yourself, will ya? I'm trying to make an impression, Beatrice." Walter retorted. In a softer voice, he joked, "You should try it sometime." He winked at me and then turned his attention back to Violet. "Oh man, little girl! You sure are strong! Wowzers! This bottle of wine is for your daddy. I've had it in my cellar for years. I've been waiting for a special occasion, and today feels special to me. I hope your daddy likes wine!"

"They both do!" Violet said as she reached for the bottle.

"Walter!" My mother called out again. "Have you lost your mind? You are giving a 1985 Bordeaux to a ten-year-old? Are you trying to make a mess of my daughter's house?"

"Clearly you didn't check out this little girl's guns, Bea! She'll do fine. Go on, honey, give this to your dad."

I never saw Violet move so slowly or so carefully. She glowed when she handed over the bottle to Cole, who, despite Walter's request, dropped off two freshly shaken gin martinis in front of my mother.

As Beatrice sipped her drink, Walter kept turning on the charm. My children weren't the only ones smitten with him. I couldn't believe how easygoing and fun he was. I never would have imagined in my wildest dreams my mother would be capable of attracting a guy as cool as he appeared to be. I think what I marveled the most at was how he stood up to my mother and freely spoke his mind. Most people didn't act like this around her. Beatrice was used to getting her way, which usually made her difficult to be around.

By the time dinner was ready, Violet toted a new American Girl doll. Even though she pretended to have outgrown dolls in front of her friends, she secretly loved them. Harley sprawled on the floor and played with his new Lego set with Walter beside him.

"Come on into the dining room everyone," I called out as I placed a big bowl of salad on the table. The eggplant Parmesan was still in the oven on low. I was very thankful I had frozen a few extra trays a couple of weeks ago when I went on a cooking frenzy. It made preparing for tonight's unexpected dinner party much easier.

"Where should we sit?" Walter asked.

"Can Wally sit next to me?" asked Violet, grinning from ear to ear.

"No, me!" Harley chimed in.

"Walter, would you mind sitting in the middle?" I asked as Beatrice pouted.

"Of course not, it would be my pleasure."

"Walter, wouldn't you prefer to sit with me instead of the children?"

Walter ignored my mother and took a seat between Violet and Harley.

Violet turned to him. "How come Grandma Bea doesn't call you Wally? She's your friend, isn't she?"

"Of course she is. But remember, I said only the really fun ones call me Wally. Do you think Bea is one of the fun ones?"

"No!" both my children screamed in unison as my mother checked her reflection in a butter knife.

Oh man, was I glad Walter brought a good bottle of wine.

"Thank you again, Walter, for helping me get the kids to bed," I said as I filled his mug with coffee. "Your bedtime story was a real hit. I still can't believe Violet sat through it. Usually, she is," I paused to make air quotes with my fingers, "*too* old for a bedtime story. She normally prefers to read a little bit on her Kindle before drifting off. Both of them really seem to like you."

"I had fun with them this evening, Annabel. You and Cole have wonderful kids. They just get under your skin." Walter poured some cream into his cup.

"You can say that again," my mother said. Unfortunately, while she agreed with her boyfriend, I worried her interpretation was completely different than his.

Walter stirred his coffee. "They are so sweet and well behaved. You really did a great job with them."

"Of course she did. She learned from the best."

Cole coughed as he started to cut the cake. He handed a huge slice to Walter. "Beatrice, I'm assuming no cake for you. You did tell Anna no carbs." Cole handed me a piece.

"Oh, just a wee sliver, Cole. It would be rude not to taste it. After all, Annabel did go through all this trouble for us."

"Of course, you would never want to be rude." Cole snickered as he cut Beatrice the smallest slice imaginable.

I looked at Walter and said, "Since the kids are asleep, tell us a little about yourself."

"Let's see. I'm a corporate attorney, but I recently decided to cut back. Instead of retiring, I like to say I am rewiring." He chuckled at his own joke. "I'm really trying to look at life differently, you know, beyond my desk. And thanks to Bea, I think I am." He reached across the table and gently squeezed her hand.

"Are you a widower?" Cole asked.

"No, but he's had his share of losses," Beatrice interjected.

Irritated, Walter nodded to my mother. "Thank you, Beatrice." Then in a softer and kinder tone, he added, "but darling,

I'm capable of answering their questions." There was something so calming about him. Even as he scolded my mother, he didn't say the words in an angry or a mean hearted way. He seemed like he genuinely wanted to open up and get to know us.

My mother dated a bit after my father passed away. But none of the men ever took any interest in getting to know my family or me. In fact, there was one guy who she saw for almost two years who seemed to take an extreme pleasure in calling my husband, *Carl,* and me, *Anastasia.* But then again, Beatrice was never engaged before now.

"Actually, I'm divorced," Walter said. "I made a mess of my marriage. I wasn't a good husband." He took his glasses off his face and wiped them with his napkin.

"Oh, Walter. Don't say that," Beatrice said in a comforting voice, which I didn't recognize. She reached for his hand. "You know that's not true. You were faced with a very difficult situation. Most men wouldn't have been able to make it work either."

"I guess," Walter replied with a shrug. He took a bite of his cake. "Delicious, Anna. Homemade frosting?"

"Yes," I answered with a smile. It felt great for him to notice. I took a lot of pride in my baking and never used mixes or packaged frosting. I loved the way Walter automatically took to calling me Anna. My mother was the only person who still insisted on calling me by my full name.

"I hate to disagree with Beatrice," he confided to Cole and me. "I'm sure you two can appreciate it's never an easy thing to do."

Based on her pursed lips and folded arms, I think Cole and I laughed a little too hard for my mother's liking, but I couldn't help it—Walter had my mother nailed.

"Seriously, I did make a mess of my marriage," Walter continued. "Shannon and I were high school sweethearts. She was the most popular girl in the school, and man was she beautiful. I never expected her to wait for me while I went to college and then law school, but she did. The day I graduated from Yale Law was the day I asked her to marry me. I thought I loved her before, but once we were married, all the feelings I had for her magnified. I never expected to be so happy."

Walter took a sip of coffee before he continued. "We were married for three years when our daughter was born. Jessica was the spitting image of her mom. Blond curls, blue eyes, and a smile that could light up a room. She was the happiest baby. Seriously, she never cried. She slept through the night from the time she was three-weeks-old. And as happy as she was, she made everyone around her happy too. She was a little comedian. A couple of weeks before her fourth birthday, she got sick. We thought she had a slight case of the flu. Shannon never liked doctors. She would always say you go see them with one thing and come back with something worse. So she didn't bring Jessica in right away. By the time she did, it was too late. Jessica had spinal meningitis."

Walter paused to wipe a tear away from his face. "We lost her a few days later. I couldn't help it; I blamed Shannon for the death of my daughter. In my heart, I now know chances are even if she brought Jessica to the pediatrician immediately; we still would have lost her. But I couldn't stop wondering, what if? Shannon was devastated too. Jessica was the center of her world, just as she was the center of mine. She desperately needed me to comfort her but I couldn't. She knew I blamed her. I couldn't hide my disgust. I couldn't stand being in the same room as my own wife. So I started working longer hours. And then I just stopped coming home all together. We divorced six months to the day we buried my baby."

"Oh, Walter. I'm so sorry." Tears rolled down my cheeks. "I can't even imagine how hard it was to lose a child." I turned to my mother and looked her square in the eye. I was trying to gauge her reaction, but I saw nothing. Not one trace of emotion. I wasn't surprised.

"Thanks, Anna. I figured you'd be sympathetic. People always say it gets easier with time, but I am not so sure." Walter replied as he reached for my hand and squeezed gently.

"Annabel, darling, you really did an outstanding job with this cake. Cole, be a dear and cut me another sliver," my mother requested as she handed my husband her plate.

Typical Beatrice. There was not a dry eye in the room, and the woman who was anti-carbohydrates less than twenty-four hours ago was asking for more cake.

"I thought you were on a diet."

"Oh, yes. I should be." She beamed as she dug her fork into her desert.

"Did you ever remarry, Walter?" I asked.

He shook his head. "No, unless you count being married to my job." He chuckled. "Besides practicing law, I've also spent a lot of time mentoring young attorneys. I've dated, of course. But I haven't met anyone I'd consider settling down with until I met your mother."

"Well, Beatrice sure is a special lady," Cole managed to say with a straight face.

My mother cleared her throat. "Speaking of getting married —the wedding is only three months away, June fifteenth. It will be at the club, of course."

"Wow, you sure aren't wasting any time, are you, Mother?"

"Of course not. What's the point in waiting? After all, despite how great we look, Walter and I aren't getting any younger you know. And speaking of looking great, did you see my engagement ring?"

My mother held out her hand. On the ring finger of her left hand was the most beautiful ring I'd ever seen in my life. A large, super-bright turquoise square stone sat in the center. Turquoise chips, as well as small diamonds and pink stones, formed a circle around the stone, forming a mid-sized circle, and extended down around the sides of the band.

"It's beyond beautiful," I answered as Beatrice beamed.

"My Walter sure knows how to pick them, doesn't he?" Fortunately, my mother was so focused on her ring, she didn't notice when Cole choked on his coffee as he barely managed to suppress a laugh.

"I didn't want a diamond," she clarified. "They are so common. Been there and done that, you know, and besides, everyone has diamonds. So Walter found this for me instead." She held her hand up to her face and examined the ring once more. "I fell in love with it instantly. It's Paraiba Tourmaline with pink sapphires, in case you didn't know." Then she whispered, "They are extremely rare."

I would expect nothing less. "I love it, and I am very happy for you both." I glanced over at Walter and prayed he knew what he was getting himself into.

"Good," my mother gushed. "That's exactly what I was hoping you'd say. Oh, darling, I need to ask you a favor. I mentioned it last night when I called. It is the real reason why I wanted to come over here for dinner tonight," she clarified. "Although the eggplant parmesan and salad were delicious."

I took a sip of coffee. "Okay, Mother. What do you need?"

"I need you to help me plan the wedding."

"You what? You made it seem like you were all set."

"Oh, no. On the contrary, I'm not prepared at all. All I have is the venue and the date. I don't have anything else done. I need to get invitations, a band, flowers, food, cake, and, of course, the dress. Walter, take this cake. I need to be able to fit into a dress." She almost threw the plate at him. Walter didn't seem to mind as he immediately finished what was left of Bea's cake.

Focusing on me again, my mother continued, "Oh, Annabel, there is so much to do, and we only have three months to do it. There is no possible way I could do it all myself. Hence, why I need you. I just know we will make such an amazing team." She clapped her hands together for emphasis. "Doesn't this sound like fun?"

"Frankly, no. This doesn't sound like fun to me at all. If you recall, I never wanted to plan a wedding. Cole and I eloped for this very reason. I wanted to avoid the whole three-ring circus these things turn out to be."

"I know you thought heading off to the Caribbean was a good idea. But Annabel, you were wrong. A wedding doesn't have to turn out to be complete chaos, trust me. My wedding will be nothing of the sort. It will be beautiful, and I know you want to help your mother."

I didn't reply.

She placed her hand on her heart, and batted her eyelashes, "Oh come on, Annabel. Do you really want me to have to do all of this work myself? And besides, planning a wedding is a very special time in a woman's life. It should be spent with someone close to the bride. Who could possibly be closer to me than my very own daughter? But if you really want your poor mother to go it alone with no one's advice or opinions, there is nothing I can do about it. I will have to do what I have to. But know this, it disappoints me greatly that you are just too *busy* or unwilling to help me."

I couldn't believe my mother pulled the guilt card. But then again, why should I be surprised? She has made me feel guilty for practically my entire adult life. I probably should have been used to the feeling by now, but I wasn't. I hated it. I always ended up doing things I didn't want to do today just so I didn't regret not doing them tomorrow. And like it or not, if I didn't help her plan this wedding, I wouldn't be able to face myself if let her down.

"Okay, Mom. Fine, I will help," I said as I cut myself another piece of cake.

CHAPTER THREE

I quietly slid into bed after I checked on the kids one last time. I hoped Cole was already asleep. I really didn't want to talk to him.

As soon as I lay down, Cole rolled over and turned on the light. "Are you really going to do this?" He sat up and turned to face me.

"Yes, I have to." I pulled the covers up to my chin.He stroked my head. "Anna, why do you do this to yourself?"

"What are you trying to say? Do you not want me to help her?"

"Whoa, easy, killer. Don't go there. This has nothing to do with me and don't try to make it about me. She's your mother, not mine. You know I'll support you in anything you want to do. I just hate to see her use you. She has kept you at arm's length your entire life—"

"It hasn't always been this way."

"Yeah, I know, Anna. You always tell me that. But I've been with you for a very long time, and I haven't seen her treat you any other way. No, I take it back. I have seen her treat you much worse."

I sighed.

"I'm sorry Anna. I'm not trying to hurt you or make you upset. But I want you to start facing the facts. There is only one person who matters to your mother, and that's your mother. You go above and beyond for her all the time, and does she ever appreciate it? No. Does she ever make you feel like you are the amazing, beautiful, and talented woman that you are? No. She barely acknowledges our children, especially Harley. I know it has to eat you up inside as much as it does me. And all she thinks I am good for is fixing her a gin martini."

"Well, you do mix a good drink," I tried to joke.

"Anna, let's be serious here. Beatrice is one very cold woman, which is fine. But you're not. You have a heart of gold, and you are already stretched too thin. Between work and the kids you barely have a moment to yourself. When was the last time you read a book?"

"Um, I just—"

"Not a children's book." He paused, waiting for a response.

I had none. I used to be a voracious reader, but I honestly couldn't remember the last book I had read, even though my Kindle was full of books I intended to read eventually.

"Exactly," Cole smirked. "Listen. You know I have no issue with you helping your mother. I just don't want to see you put added pressure and stress on yourself. Come here." He lay back down and opened his arms. I snuggled against him. He kissed me gently. "I love you, Anna."

"I love you too, Cole," I said as a tear escaped my eye.

Within seconds, he was snoring, God I wish I had his ability to shut down and pass out. My mind raced way too fast to make sleep a realistic possibility.

I had always tried to rationalize my mother to Cole, somewhat successfully. Cole and I had very different childhoods. Every minor accomplishment in his or his sisters' lives was celebrated. For goodness sake, class picture day was cause for a Carvel ice cream cake. His parents' world revolved around their children. Connie and Patrick never missed one baseball game, school play, or spelling bee. They felt the same way with their grandchildren. Whenever Violet had a soccer game, they were always on the sidelines screaming her name at the top of their lungs. A few months back she scored the winning goal—for the opposing team. She was devastated. Patrick came over to the house a few hours later with a big bouquet of flowers for her in honor of her victory.

Violet looked at her grandfather like he lost his mind. "But I am a loser, Grandpa."

"Violet, do you know what perception means?" he asked.

"Nope," she answered with a pout.

"It's the way you see something, and there are usually many ways to see a situation. Did you score a goal today?"

"Yes," she said quietly.

"Did your goal cause a team to win the game?"

"Yes, but—"

"I know. The winning team wasn't your team, but they were still a team. And they are all celebrating right now. But they couldn't have won without you. Did anyone else score the winning goal?"

"No."

"Exactly. So you are responsible for making all those other children happy. Focus on the good you do, Violet. You don't have to be perfect; you just have to be you."

I didn't even want to think what would have happened if Beatrice was at the game instead of Cole's folks. She would have probably berated my little girl. I went through this on a regular basis; my childhood home was the opposite of my husband's. We were expected to be perfect—all the time at everything. No matter what we accomplished, my mother demanded that we do better and do more. A ninety on a test was frowned upon. She questioned why we didn't work harder and get a hundred instead.

I adored my father. He was handsome, strong, and he had the most charismatic personality. He knew how to work a room; people naturally gravitated towards him. He'd always have a joke to share, which immediately put people at ease. As I grew up, I realized he used his charm to manipulate others to do exactly what he wanted them to, which was why he was such a successful salesman. Unfortunately, he was hardly ever home. His first, second, and third loves were his office. He worked ridiculous hours and traveled a lot. In order for my brother and I to get his full attention, we'd have had to accomplish a major task, like curing cancer or some other deadly disease.

It was a difficult way to live, but it didn't really faze me too much—probably because school came naturally to me. I was a bookworm who actually liked to study. I thrived under pressure to be the best. My brother, five years my junior, struggled a lot. Brody not only had to live up to Beatrice's demands of perfection, but also the quest for our father's attention. He was constantly compared to me, especially at school, which wasn't a fair comparison.

As much as I loved school, Brody hated it. He was a free-spirited little boy who craved excitement and adventure. He loved sports, but he wasn't coordinated at all. The beauty was he didn't care. He just wanted to have fun. And boy, did that piss Beatrice off. The funny thing was, she could never stay mad at him. He made her way too happy. From the moment she brought him home from the hospital, it was clear to me and everyone else, my brother was the love of her life.

It was ironic: growing up you would have thought Brody would have been jealous of my accomplishments, but it was the other way around. I was the jealous one. I envied his free spirit. Unlike me, he never worried about pleasing anyone except himself. And it didn't take much for him to be happy.

I was never able to say no to him. I always wanted to be part of his happiness and joy. The happier he was, the happier I seemed to be. So when we were little, and he wanted to finish my ice cream, I didn't think twice: I gave my cone to him. And as we got older I kept giving. All I wanted was to make him happy.

Even though it was years ago, in some ways, it feels like yesterday. Cole and I had just gotten engaged and moved into our first apartment in Long Beach together. We were on the top floor of a recently renovated apartment building. The actual living space was quite small, but the views were amazing. We had a huge terrace, which overlooked the boardwalk and the Atlantic Ocean. I wanted to have Brody over for a barbecue to celebrate with us, and give him the chance to get to know Cole a little better. It wasn't surprising that during the two years Cole and I had dated, we'd spent more time with his family than mine. Since Brody was in college, the only time we really got to spend with him was during school breaks.

Since it wasn't a holiday Brody wasn't able to leave school, so Cole and I drove up to Ithaca instead. I expected to go to Brody's dorm, pick him up, and take him out to dinner or something. When we arrived at his dorm, I never expected we would be ushered into the frat house by his roommate. When we walked inside, the house was spotless with a fresh smell, instead of the normal stench of stale beer and sweat. Loud music was playing, and yes, there were plenty of kegs, but there were also streamers and signs that said "Congratulations, Anna and Cole."

Brody's roommate escorted Cole and me to the kitchen where my brother first engulfed Cole in a massive bear hug before he picked me up and twirled me around. Cole reached for a red Solo cup to fill with beer, but Brody stopped him.

"First thing's first," my brother said as he reached into the refrigerator and pulled out a bottle of champagne, which he opened with a pop.

A beautiful girl, as usual, stood at his side. She pulled out four flutes from a cabinet, which Brody quickly filled with champagne. "We have to properly toast don't we?" he asked with a toothy grin.

"Leave it to my brother," I smiled as I grabbed a glass.

"To my favorite sister and the man who loves her!" Brody clinked his glass into ours.

I took a sip, and Cole said to the girl, "I bet you had something to do with this party."

She shook her head. "Nah. This was all Brody's doing."

"Come on," Brody said. "Let's eat, dance, and drink. Let's celebrate! After all, this is the first, and probably the last, engagement party this frat house will ever see."

I didn't like frat parties when I was in college, and I really didn't like them now. So after about an hour I was sitting outside on the grass with a beer in my hand and Cole by my side.

"What's a matter, you no like?" Brody asked as he meandered over to us, alone.

"I can't believe you did all this for us." I smiled as I stood up. "But I was kind of hoping you'd get to know Cole a little better. I want you guys to be friends."

"Oh please, Anna. Don't be so dramatic." He rolled his hazel eyes as he spoke. "We don't have to get to know each other. How can we not get along? After all, we both love you. And I know you well enough to know you'd do anything to make both of us happy."

Cole smiled. I think he was falling for my brother's charm. I wasn't. I knew better.

"Okay, Brody. What's up? I know something is. You didn't go to all this effort to throw us a party to make me happy. You want something. Don't you?"

Brody placed his hand on his heart. "Anna, I'm shocked and offended. What could I possibly want besides your happiness? I want to know all about the wedding. I'm going to be best man, right?" Brody asked with mock indignation.

"We haven't decided yet," I crossed my arms over my chest.

Cole smiled. "Well, I only have sisters, so I don't really have anyone in mind."

"So it can be me?" Brody beamed.

Cole nodded his head. "Sure."

Cole and I didn't discuss any plans for our wedding yet. I was taking for granted the fact he'd simply go along with all of my ideas.

"Awesome. So, I'll have to write a speech, right?" Brody scratched his head.

"Yes," I rolled my eyes, "I think you'll master the task. After all, you take after Daddy. You know how to work a crowd."

"Yep, I sure do," Brody grinned. "Look how I work Bea."

"You are the master." I smiled. "I don't know how you do it. She's always like putty in your hands."

"Yeah, but before you go and get all jealous like you constantly do, I'm not always able to get my way with her."

I stared at him. "When was the last time she said no to you?"

"A couple of days ago. She can be so stubborn sometimes. It's impossible for her to see anyone else's point of view."

I punched my brother's arm gently. "What happened? She never denies you anything. Details, little brother, details!"

"Nah, it's nothing," Brody said nonchalantly. "I don't want to get into it. Tonight's supposed to be about you, not me. It's a happy occasion, remember?"

I had no doubt my brother was definitely up to something. No wonder he threw us a party.

"So let's get back to the best man duties," Brody said.

"What about them?" Cole asked.

"It's really the speech part I've been thinking about. I was hoping you'd allow me this honor. Actually, I was pretty confident you'd say yes. So much so, I already have a partial speech prepared."

"My brother, the procrastinator?" Unlike me, Brody always waited to the eleventh hour to do everything.

"When something is important you have to be prepared. Do you want to hear it?" He asked as he poked me in the shoulder.

"Sure," I said.

"It's still a little sketchy, so bear with me, okay?" He dramatically cleared his throat. "'From as far back as I remember, I wanted to have a brother. But no matter how hard I tried, Anna never transformed into a boy, although she did kick my butt in most sports. Even though I was stuck with a sister, Anna was a better sister than anyone could ask for. I know if my new brother,'" he turned to Cole and poked him in the arm as he asked, "you like that part, right?"

"Yes," Cole and I both answered in unison.

"Good. Now, where was I? Oh yeah. I know if my new brother captured my sister's heart he'd capture mine as well. He actually won my heart over when he and my sister made me the happiest man alive by loaning me the money I needed to make my dream of owning a motorcycle come true.'"

"What?" I asked.

"Do you need me to repeat, Sis?" Brody smirked.

"No." I shook my head. "I heard you the first time. I just don't know what you're talking about."

"I found the most perfect Harley Davidson bike in the whole world. It's used but in mint condition. It's exactly what I've been looking for. What I've always wanted!" The volume of his voice increased as his excitement grew. "Only problem is I don't have enough money saved. I'm five-K short. I really don't know why we have to wait until we're twenty-five to get access to our trust funds." He groaned. "But that's beside the point. I start work right after graduation, so it won't take me long to make the money. Problem is I need the money now. I can't wait until summer to get the bike. It's going to be gone by then. So you'll help me out, right?" Brody kneeled down on the ground and looked up at Cole and me with puppy dog eyes.

"Is this what Bea said no to?" I asked although I knew the answer.

"Yeah. Apparently, *your* mother is totally against the idea."

"Why? Does she think it's dangerous?" Cole asked.

"He doesn't know Mother too well, does he?" Brody turned to me.

"How can you tell?" I chuckled.

"What? What'd I miss?"

"Bea not wanting Brody to have the motorcycle has nothing to do with safety, unless you count the safety of her reputation. She doesn't want any of the ladies at the club to see her son riding around on a motorcycle. What would they think? He must be some hoodlum or something. First a bike, then what?"

Brody chuckled.

I continued, "He might do something completely crazy, like getting a tattoo or something. Then what would happen? I shudder at the thought." I placed both my hands over my heart.

"But Anna, you have a tattoo on your ankle," Cole commented.

Brody choked from laughter. "Yes. I know that. You know that. And even my brother knows that. But do you think my mother knows about it?"

"How much do you need again?" Cole asked, beating me to the punch.

"Five thousand," Brody answered.

"By when?" I asked.

"Next week," Brody replied.

"Done!" I exclaimed as Cole smiled.

I wired my brother the money as soon as we returned home. He picked up the bike two days later. I didn't remember ever seeing my brother happier. It was funny; even though Cole didn't fully understand then how difficult my mother could be, I think he truly bonded with Brody over our frustration with her. Unfortunately, soon after Cole found out my mother's snobbery was the least of our concerns.

I glanced at the clock. It was already three o'clock in the morning. I rolled over onto my stomach and buried my head in my pillow in a futile attempt to drown out my husband's snores. There were only three hours left before my alarm would sound. I really hoped I could manage to sleep just a little.

I sat up and grabbed my iPad that was charging on my night table. I sent a quick email to my best friend and co-worker, Cecelia, and asked her if she was available go out to lunch tomorrow. I really needed to tell her about tonight and what I had gotten myself into.

I knew I should close my iPad and try to go to sleep, but instead I logged onto Facebook and headed over to my former best friend and college roommate, Michelle's page. All these thoughts about the past made me feel sad. I scrolled through her pictures and marveled at how great she looked. She really hadn't aged at all. I liked a bunch of her more recent pictures. I felt bad I allowed our friendship to drift apart. We used to be so close, and now our relationship was pretty much limited to social media. I wrote her a private message about getting together one of these days for lunch or a drink. But I didn't hit send. Too many years had passed with too little communication.

CHAPTER FOUR

"Good morning, Annabel," my mother said as I answered my cell phone early Friday morning, a little over a week after her big announcement. Since we'd already had our "scheduled chat" the day before I got a sinking feeling in my stomach she was finally going to enlist my help in her wedding preparations. I didn't know why I got my hopes up, but after over a week of not hearing one more peep about the wedding, I really thought there was a chance she would switch plans and forgo this whole idea and just dash off to the Justice of the Peace, or something equally sensible.

"Hi Mom," I said as I hit save on the Power Point presentation I was working on.

"What are you doing today?" she asked, clearly forgetting I had a full-time job.

"Working," I answered as I tried to ignore the email from a client that popped up on my screen.

"But it's Friday. Aren't you off on Fridays?" she asked, perplexed.

"No, Mother." I sighed. I was so tired of explaining this. "I'm not off. I work from home on Tuesdays and Fridays."

"Like I said, you're off."

"No, Mother, just because I'm home doesn't mean I'm off. I still have to work all day." I rolled my eyes and started to walk into the kitchen to refill my coffee cup. "Why doesn't anyone ever realize when you work from home you still have to work?" I said, exasperated.

"No need to get testy, Dear. A simple 'I'm busy' would have sufficed. I can appreciate you have things to do. After all, my day is pretty jam packed too. I have a hair appointment in a little over an hour. I'm thinking about adding some low lights to my hair. Everyone is blonde these days, you know covering up the grays and all. I don't want to look like everyone else... Especially for the wedding."

"You would probably look very pretty darker. I remember when you were a brunette. I liked it." Over my lifetime my mother has had every color hair imaginable. I had no clue what her natural shade was. I wondered if she even remembered.

"Oh yes. I was mahogany brown when Brody graduated middle school," she let out a deep sigh. "Those were the good old days, weren't they?"

I smiled as I thought back, "They sure were, Mom. Do you remember—"

Before I could continue, she cut me off. "Good. So you agree. Low lights are the way to go. Then after my hair, I am going to Walter's apartment in the city to help pack up. He is officially moving in with me tonight. Isn't it exciting?"

"I guess." I didn't know how I really felt about it. On the one hand, Walter seemed like a very nice guy. But they were moving extremely fast. After all, they had only known each other a few months.

"He isn't going to give up the apartment, of course. What a location!" My mother exclaimed. "It has magnificent views of Central Park. We will weekend there, of course. It's the perfect get-a-way!"

"Sounds lovely." I stirred some half and half into my coffee.

"I don't remember the last time Cole and I had a weekend in the city," I mused. Before we had kids Cole and I would spend at least a weekend a month in Manhattan. Sometimes we'd catch a show, but more often than not we'd just walk around, pretending to be tourists. It was amazing, despite living your entire life on Long Island, like Cole and I both had, you never seemed to experience all the sights. In fact, I was actually almost twenty years old when I went to the top of the Empire State Building for the first time.

"You two should go one of these days then. I don't understand why you don't."

"You're right. We should go. I'm sure Connie and Patrick would gladly take the kids for a weekend. I hate to impose, but really I'm sure they wouldn't mind. After all, they're always begging to have the kids stay for an overnight."

"You should take them up on it," she replied. Although I expected the response it still stung me like a hard slap across the face. Just once I wished my mother would offer to spend time with my children. What grandmother didn't want to dote on her grandbabies?

But rather than express the hurt and disappointment I felt, I opted to just abort the call. "Okay, Mom. I gotta go. I have to get back to work, and it seems like we resolved your hair conundrum."

"Yes. Thanks for your help. But that wasn't why I called. Today I am tied up, and you apparently have work to do. So I guess that leaves tomorrow. We really need to pick out invitations for the wedding."

"What?" I asked.

"Invitations. Annabel, the wedding is in three months. We have to begin planning, time is running out. I don't know how long they will take but I want to send them out in sufficient time. I don't want anyone to think they were on the B list. There is nothing worse than being an afterthought invitee."

"You need my help in selecting invitations?" I asked as I sat back down in front of my computer.

"Of course, I told you all of this already. Really sweetie sometimes I think you don't listen to a word I say. I need your help with all of this. I'm in way over my head. I love Walter so much. I want this day to be perfect. I don't want to mess anything up. So yes, I want your help. No, I need your help. Come by my house at one o'clock and we will drive over to the store together."

I took a deep breath. Tell me again, why did I say yes to this? But I wasn't going to back out. "Sure, Mom," I answered unenthusiastically.

"Great. Oh, before I let you go. Guess who called me to offer congratulations?"

"Who?" I asked.

"Cole's mother, Connie. She was so sincere. Like a breath of fresh air," Beatrice gushed. "Oh, what a delightful woman. Okay, well I'll see you tomorrow," she said as she hung up not waiting for me to reply or say goodbye.

I pulled the phone away from my ear and stared at it. Did my mother really just compliment Connie? Although my mother-in-law was phenomenal, I was shocked at my mother's comment. In all the years Cole and I had been together my mother had never tried to get to know her. Even when Connie included my mother and invited her to family functions or holidays, Bea just kept to herself.

I remembered the first time Connie invited my mother over. It was Cole's birthday, the first one after we got engaged. Connie and I had already bonded. We basically became insepa-rable during that first summer. I would call her multiple times a day, more often than not, crying hysterically. No matter what she was doing, she would always stop and listen to me. I don't know how I would have made it without her.

I was shocked when Connie called me up to tell me she had

invited my mother to join us for Cole's birthday dinner. "Why did you do that Connie?" I asked.

"Because she is your mother and he will soon be her son-in-law. She should be invited. It was the right thing to do," Connie stated matter of factly.

"But she won't come," I replied. I wondered if I wanted her to accept or not.

"She may change her mind later, but she accepted my invitation," Connie spat out.

"She did?" My voice was barely a whisper."You seem shocked, Anna."

"I am. After everything that has happened... After what she said to me...I didn't think she'd want to be around me." My mother's vicious words haunted me, even months later.

"Anna, regardless of what you think, regardless of what Beatrice said to you, you are still her daughter. You are a wonderful woman and she loves you. It would be impossible for her not to," Connie tried to reassure me.

"But—"

"But nothing. I know you don't understand now. One day you will have children and then you will. And Anna, I know you don't want to hear this, but your mother is suffering too. She is hurt, she is upset, and she is in pain. She needs to heal as well. We all handle situations differently. I'm not saying what she said and did was right. I am not saying I agree with her. All I'm saying is I can put myself in her shoes, and I can understand what she must have been feeling. I think you need to try and do the same."

The night of Cole's birthday dinner I was incredibly excited to see my mother. It was going to be the first time I saw her in months. I allowed myself to dream that when she saw me, she'd engulf me in her arms, apologize for what she said, and tell me how much she missed and loved me. Well, that didn't happen!

I was in the small kitchen with Connie, and Cole's sisters

Shannon and Denise, when the doorbell rang. Cole's dad answered the door. It was the first time Beatrice was invited to their house. She handed Patrick a bottle of wine and the first comment out of her mouth was, "Oh, thank goodness you are wearing regular clothes. With all those Halloween decorations out front I feared I was walking into a costume party. I didn't realize people who had children over the age of six still decorated their homes. I guess you learn something new every day."

The night went downhill from there. "Mom," I exclaimed as I ran over to her. "I'm so glad you came!" I embraced her tightly. She barely lifted her arms from her sides.

"Annabel. It's," she paused to clear her throat, "good to see you. Oh, Cole," she gushed, moving away from me as quickly as she could. "Happy birthday, darling. I have a little something for you." She reached into her Louis Vuitton hobo bag and pulled out a matching purse. From there she removed a card that I was sure either contained an overly generous check or a gift card. Beatrice's way to get into people's hearts was through her pocketbook.

"Thanks so much, Beatrice. Why don't you have a seat." Cole pointed to an open bottle of wine on the coffee table in the living room and asked, "Would you like a glass of wine or maybe something a little stronger?"

"Mother," I chimed in. "Cole and I bought your favorite gin. Cole can make you a martini. I know it's your favorite drink."

My mother looked around the room. "No need to go to any trouble, Cole. Everyone is drinking wine. I'll have a glass."

"It's no trouble, Mom," I said as I grabbed the gin. "Cole won't mind."

With disgust in her voice, my mother replied, "Annabel, I said I would drink the wine, please don't make a scene."

Every time I opened my mouth, Beatrice took offense to what I said. Every time Connie tried to draw Beatrice into the conversation she was rebuffed. Shannon and Denise kept trying to distract me, but their attempts didn't work. If all this wasn't bad enough, Beatrice barely touched her dinner, which to a gourmet cook like Connie, was such an insult. Instead of tasting, she pretty much just moved her food around her plate like a petulant child. By the time the dinner dishes were cleared off the table, Beatrice had bailed. She didn't even stay long enough to watch Cole blow out his candles.

That was the night I decided I wanted to run off as quickly as I could with Cole and get married. I needed to feel loved and wanted. I wanted a family.

CHAPTER FIVE

I pulled into the wide circular driveway and parked behind my mother's Mercedes, near the front door. I took a deep breath as I grabbed my handbag and stared at the large brick house I used to call home. It seemed like it was a lifetime ago when Brody and I would sit here on the driveway making chalk drawings before racing to the back yard to jump into the in-ground Olympic size pool. Our Golden Retriever, George, was at our sides the entire time.

My mother lived in Old Westbury, which was a very affluent town on the north shore of Long Island. I think the happiest day of Beatrice's life was when Business Week dubbed the town New York's wealthiest suburb. She bought at least fifty copies of the edition and had one strategically placed on her coffee table for over a year.

Keeping up with expectations of the town, her house was huge, twelve thousand square feet to be exact. Growing up Brody and I didn't have our own rooms. Instead, we had our own wings complete with a full bathroom, large walk-in closet, and a playroom. Sometimes we communicated by walkie-talkie if we had friends over or were feeling lazy. In addition to a living room, complete with a baby grand piano, which no one ever played, there was a den and a formal dining room with a Swarovski crystal chandelier. The office was for my dad, and was where he spent almost all of his time at home. There was a media room, which was set up like a movie theater, complete with reclining chairs. A billiard room that contained a pool table, foosball, a pinball machine, a ping-pong table, and two arcade games. There was also a library. Not surprisingly, most of the space was hardly ever used, except for maybe the billiard room. Brody and I always spent hours together there with our friends.

It was sad. The house was so beautiful, but it never felt like a home. It always seemed way too large for a family of four. I had no idea how my mom was able to live here all these years alone. I never could decide what troubled me more, the thought of her keeping the house or her selling it.

I was about to ring the doorbell when the front door opened.

"Annabel! I saw you pull in! I'm so glad to see you! How are you?" Walter greeted me before pulling me into a bear hug.

"I'm doing well, and you?"

"I'm great! How is that pretty friend of yours?"

Earlier in the week, Walter stopped off at my office to give me some wedding band demo tapes to listen to and evaluate. He said he was in the neighborhood, but I knew my mother made him run the errand for her. She would have simply dropped off the recordings with the receptionist before dashing away. Walter on the other hand, really took an interest in seeing where I worked. He sat in my office and chatted with me for about fifteen minutes. Cecelia had popped in. When I introduced them and explained she was also my best friend, he insisted on taking us both out to lunch.

"She was delighted she had been in the office when you were visiting me. She really liked you."

He smiled.

"So, I heard you moved in yesterday."

"Yep. I did. Well, I moved in what Beatrice allowed," Walter chuckled. "But I'm not worried. Little by little there will be some of my personality present in this place."

"Be careful my friend. Beatrice is very particular, and not only about her home."

"Yeah, I know. I don't know how I passed the test. Do you think she'll ever allow me to display my comic book collection in the living room?"

I arched my eye at him and shook my head.

"Yeah. I thought so. But I'll probably try anyway."

I smiled at him. "If anyone can get her to change her mind, my money is on you. Speaking of the queen of the house, where is she anyway?"

Walter's face lit up. He flashed me a huge grin as he replied, "She's in the kitchen."

I was about to say something snarky, but instead, for the first time, I realized I smelled a familiar scent.

"Is she baking?" I asked as I took a deep breath, allowing the aroma of sugar and chocolate to fill my nostrils.

Walter smirked. "Let's go see. Come on."

We walked through all the familiar rooms to the back of the house where the kitchen was located. The kitchen had floor to ceiling windows that overlooked the pool and cabana. Although the pool was closed up for the winter, it still provided a breathtaking view.

My suspicion was confirmed. I watched in shock as my mother took trays of chocolate chip cookies out of the double Viking oven. "Hi, darling!"

"You're responsible for this, huh?" I asked Walter, who reached into the Sub Zero refrigerator for a container of milk and a bottle of Perrier that he placed on the white marble center island. He then reached into one of the island's drawers and pulled out three crystal glasses.

"You betcha!" He answered as he sat down on a stool at the island. There was no doubt he eagerly awaited his treat.

"Hi Mother," I said as I walked over to the stove where my mom put the cookies on a large silver-serving tray. I air kissed her. "You're baking? This sure is a blast from the past."

Growing up, at least once a week, my mom would bake cookies with Brody and me. It was one of our favorite things to do together. We all had our roles. My mom would chop up our favorite candy to add to the cookies to *spice it up*, she'd say. I did all the measuring and Brody did the mixing. Sometimes he managed to avoid batter hitting the walls, but usually not. As the cookies baked, Brody and I would dip a non-chopped piece of candy into the remaining batter before Rosie, our house-keeper and babysitter, snatched the bowl to wash.

"Yes. Walter loves sweets. When I told him how I used to bake all the time he begged me to make a batch of cookies. I don't think he believed I could actually do it."

"Do you blame me? When I first met her, I was positive she would be one of those women who stored sweaters in the oven. I never dreamt she'd know how to use anything in this state of the art kitchen of hers. I figured everything here was for show. Let's be realistic now; it's not like she's a domestic goddess, if you know what I mean. Well, she fooled me alright," he clari-fied. "She made a batch about a month ago and, wow! It was totally not what I expected. Truth be told, I thought she was going to do a switcheroo with bakery cookies. But she really made these from scratch. I made her do it in front of me the second time, just to be sure. Oh boy, the candy pieces were sheer genius!"

My mother flashed a loving smile Walter's way before turning her attention to me. "Speaking of candy, here you go Annabel," my mother said as she handed me a Butterfinger bar, my all-time favorite candy, and a bowl that had some remaining batter in it.

I couldn't say a word. Tears filled my eyes. Memories came flooding back as I dipped the piece of chocolate into the batter and popped it into my mouth. It tasted like my childhood felt. Oh, how I wish Brody could be here next to me, dipping a Snickers bar into the bowl.

"Don't cry, Sweetie," my mother said as she reached over and wiped a tear away from my cheek. "Just enjoy." Her eyes were a little misty too. Walter must have noticed because he walked over to her and hugged her tightly before he grabbed two cookies.

"Thanks, Mommy," I said as Walter handed me one. I realized I hadn't called her that for many years.

She walked back to the platter of cookies and wrapped half of them in aluminum foil. "You'll take these home with you," she said to me as she handed me the foil packet. "I can't have all these cookies in the house. I can't eat any of them with the wedding and all. And I certainly can't trust Walter with a full batch. I need to make sure he can fit down the aisle! Besides, I am sure Violet and Harley will enjoy them."

The first time since my children were born, she sounded almost grandmother-ish. Could there be hope for her I wondered as I replied, "They sure will."

"Good. Are you ready to leave? We should head over to the stationery store."

———

Two hours passed and we still didn't select an invitation. I wondered if the search would ever end. While I didn't expect this to be a quick task, I didn't anticipate it to be an all-day affair either. I swore my mother was determined to look through each and every book. I already had found ten invitations I thought would have been perfect. Every time I showed her one she'd just hand me a sticky and instruct me to mark it for later. She wanted us to narrow down our favorites.

"Excuse me?" I asked the bored-looking girl behind the counter. "Exactly how many more books of invitations do you have?"

She paused for a second. "You're in luck. There are only five more so you're only looking at another hour or two before you can leave here."

"Thank you." Turning to Beatrice, "Mother, we need to speed up this process. I don't have another two hours to sort through all these books."

"Why? Do you have somewhere to go? A plane to catch or something?" she asked, her eyes never left the books.

"Mother, it's already a quarter to four. I have to get home and prepare something for dinner, so I can feed the kids."

She cocked an eyebrow, "Isn't Cole with them?"

"Yes, but cooking isn't exactly his specialty."

"Really?" She said as she continued to flip pages of the book. "I pegged him for the cooking type. He does make a marvelous martini, you know. Walter, on the other hand, sure knows his way around the kitchen let me tell you! It's probably from all those years he lived as a bachelor. He's an excellent cook. He makes the most amazing shrimp scampi with just the perfect amount of garlic. He's completely the opposite of your father. Do you recall your dad wasn't even capable of making toast? He tried to once and nearly burnt my house to the ground."

"Yes, I remember mother." At first, I wasn't going to say anymore, but then anguish filled my heart. I stared at her. "Don't you think that it's sad I've been married to Cole for almost twelve years, yet you barely know anything about him? He makes a good martini because he had to work as a bartender in order to pay for college. Connie and Patrick didn't have money to send him to school. He worked his ass off in order to get his degree. He was so determined to become an architect. In fact, as a little boy, he drew blueprints for fun. Connie once showed me some of his drawings, she saved them you know. They were amazing. He was so cute..." I paused as I pictured the little boy my husband once was. "His dad was doing the plumbing for a nursing home that was being built, and he took Cole to the site almost every weekend. Cole was fascinated by the building and started drawing his own blueprints. They were so detailed." I smiled. "But the really cute part was while he was able to do such intricate work, he titled the drawing *senior citizen home* and spelled citizen s-i-t-e-z-e-n."

She marked another invitation. "That's sweet," my mother muttered, without so much as a glance in my direction.

"Well, nothing was going to stop him from his dream, especially a lack of funds. When he graduated, he was so in debt he continued to bartend for years after on weekends just to pay them off. Which is why he makes such a mean martini."

Beatrice didn't comment so I continued, unable to keep inside what I had kept bottled up for so long. "Of course you didn't know any of this. After all, you never once tried to get to know him. You never made any attempt to get to know anyone important to me. Whenever you've been with Cole's family, you barely manage to be civil. I wonder if you even know his sisters' names. Do you have any idea how hurtful this is to me?" I bit my lip in an attempt to hold back my tears.

"Oh, Annabel. Don't be so dramatic."

"Dramatic? I'm just trying to express my feelings, Mother. You know, I have feelings too." I sighed. I felt so defeated.

"Mmm, hmm."

The girl behind the desk no longer looked bored. Her gaze was fixated on us as I debated if I should say more. For far too long I've held my tongue, the words I wanted to say stuck in my throat. They choked me. I finally had to get my feelings out in the open.

"How do you think it makes me feel knowing you have no interest in my children?" I closed the book of invitations in front of me with probably more force than was needed. "You never spend any time with them. Forget about going to one of their sporting events or recitals; you've never even played a game with them. You have no idea if Violet plays baseball or soccer. You don't know what Harley's favorite food is or that he's allergic to strawberries. The fact that you don't know any of this, Mother, is what is tearing me apart inside."

"Are you done with this little outburst?" She asked as she tucked a caramel colored lock of hair behind her ear.

"You know what Mother? Yes. I'm done. I have been done for years. I don't know why I didn't realize it sooner. But I guess better late than never. I'm sorry." I reached into my pocketbook and pulled out my car keys. "I've got to go. I wish you all the best picking out your invitations. I hope you find happiness with Walter. He really does seem like a lovely man. But I can't do this anymore. I can't continue to walk on eggshells around you hoping and praying to gain your affection and your forgiveness. I've done nothing to be forgiven for, despite what you may think." I got up from the stool and started to put on my coat. As I zipped it, I remembered my car was parked in her driveway. Leave it to me to ruin my grand exit with a lack of transportation. I really hoped I would be able to catch a cab by the train station down the block.

"Wait. Don't go," Beatrice said. Her voice was quiet.

"What?" I opened my arms in defeat.

"Shannon and Denise... Cole's sisters' names."

"Congratulations, Mother. Bravo," I said sarcastically as I softly clapped. "Do you want a medal?"

"No, Annabel. I don't, but I do want something. Despite what you think I don't want our relationship to be like this forever. I want to try and change things, improve things between us. I want to get back some of what we once had. I realize our relationship can't change overnight, but I want it to change, and I am willing to work on it. I want to get to know you and your family better. This is why I wanted you to be part of my wedding preparation."

I didn't know what to think. The sad thing was when a relationship deteriorates as much as ours had; it was hard not to think the worst. Was she telling me the truth or just desperate for some premarital help?

"I don't know Mother," I answered honestly and stared into her gray eyes for clues.

"I don't expect you to believe me. But I do hope you are willing to give me the benefit of the doubt and see if I am sincere." She clapped her hands, "I know! How about we finish up here and then Walter and I will take you out to dinner."

"While it's a lovely thought, Mother, there is no way I can get a babysitter on a Saturday night with no notice."

"But—"

"Before you ask no. I'm not going to call Connie and impose on her either, if that was what you were going to suggest. The woman does so much for me already."

"I know she does. You're lucky to have her. I was going to suggest the kids come along too. They really did seem to take a liking to Walter."

"They did like him," I said, amazed at how they were already so much closer to this man after one evening than they were to my mother who they knew their entire lives.

"So what do you say? Dinner?" She asked.

And because I desperately wanted to believe her I said *yes*.

"Wonderful. Why don't you call Cole and let him know? I'll finish looking through this book and then we'll select an invitation from what we already have narrowed down. I think we can skip the remaining books, don't you?"

I put my keys back in my bag and removed my phone. I walked outside the store to call Cole and gave him the play by play. To say he was skeptical about Beatrice's intentions would've been an understatement. However, he did agree to go, probably because he was getting hungry.

When I walked back into the store Beatrice and the girl behind the desk giggled like two schoolgirls. I didn't even want to think about what they were discussing, so I didn't. I just resumed flipping pages.

"Here are my five favorites," my mother said to me about fifteen minutes later. "As she pointed to several invitations. Which ones are yours?"

Feeling much calmer now than I did before I replied, "Mine are totally different than yours. You're going traditional. I'm not. Here, this one is my favorite," I said as I pointed to a thick square invitation, which was ultra modern. The background was white, but there was a thick black border around it that was framed first in a brushed gold and then in brushed silver. The couple's name was very prominent in a large bold font with minimal calligraphy.

"You like, that one?" Beatrice asked as she scrunched her face in disbelief. "It doesn't look wedding like at all. Shouldn't it be eggshell and ornate?"

"Are you a virginal bride, Mother?"

"Excuse me?" She asked as she clutched her chest and looked mortified.

"Mother, you are not exactly twenty-five years old anymore, and neither is Walter. Do you really want to have a totally traditional wedding? Don't you think perhaps you should be a little more flexible? Maybe you should think of it more like a party to celebrate your new beginning."

"Don't be absurd! I don't want people getting my invitation in the mail and thinking they are getting invited to some random party or something. I want them to see it and wonder who is getting married."

My mother thrust the most cliché looking invitation in my

direction. "Look at this invitation, Annabel. This is what I am talking about. This screams wedding. Don't you agree?"

"No doubt about that," I replied, sarcastically.

"Great! So we're decided!" She turned to the girl behind the counter, "I will take two hundred of these, please."

"Very good, Ms. Buchanan. Now we just have to decide on the wording."

Blissfully my mother replied, "It's already all done." She reached inside her Prada bag and pulled out a folded sheet of paper. "Here you go. This is how I want them to read."

The girl scanned the paper and smiled. Beatrice put her American Express card on the counter, and the girl walked away with it.

CHAPTER SIX

"Well, dinner went better than expected, didn't it?" I asked Cole as we cuddled in bed.

He let out a slow chuckle in response. "Yeah. The night could have gone downhill fast after your daughter made her little comment."

"My daughter, huh?" I asked as I gently punched him in the ribs. "Why is she always my daughter when she's snarky?"

"Are you seriously asking me that question?"

I answered with a smile, "What were Violet's exact words again?"

He picked up on our daughter's inflections perfectly. "She said with an exaggerated eye roll, 'Oh man! Why didn't I wear a dress? Grandmother 'fess up. Come on. Is there a TV crew hiding in the kitchen? We gotta be on a reality television show or something because dinner with you twice in a couple of weeks can't really be real.' Did you see your mother's face?"

"I did. She bit her bottom lip so hard I was shocked she didn't draw blood. I can only imagine what she would have said. Thankfully she kept her mouth shut."

"No, thank goodness for Walter. He diffused the situation quickly. I loved how he poked fun at Beatrice, and she let him do it. She even seemed to enjoy it. She's so different when she is around him."

"I know.... Maybe there is hope for her yet."

"As crazy as it seems, I think he really loves her," Cole stated, as he gently rubbed my back. "At one point while you were talking to your mother about something or other, I couldn't help myself. I asked Walter if he takes the pink pill or the blue one."

"You didn't?" I gasped.

"Yeah. I did." Cole chuckled.

"And what did he say?"

"Good thing you're laying down," he snickered.

"Tell me," I whined as I sat up to stare at him.

"He said he doesn't need either. All he has to do is hold her hand."

"Aww... That's so sweet."

"I thought so too. But is that even possible? I say we test it out for ourselves," he said salaciously as he grabbed hold of my hand. Without skipping a beat, "Yep, it's possible!" He pulled the nightshirt I was wearing off my body in one swift, fluid motion before he gently pushed me down on the bed, and kissed me passionately. He removed his own tee-shirt before he tenderly, but forcefully, rolled me on top of him, so my back was on his stomach. I was clearly able to feel exactly how possible it was.

FROM THE FIRST time I met Cole, I felt safe and protected, which wasn't surprising considering how we met. I was driving to my boyfriend's house after work. Mitch and I had been dating for about nine months, and I was running late, as usual. I had interned at my firm over the summers while in I was college, but technically I just started my career in marketing and hated to leave my office too early. I learned from watching my father if you wanted to succeed in business you couldn't be afraid to put in lots of hours at the office. Considering how much Mitch cared about his own career, he had no interest or respect for mine. Especially if my schedule interfered with his plans, as was often the case.

Mitch was a third year associate in a patent law firm. He had scheduled dinner for us with one of the senior associates and his wife. It took Mitch months to secure these plans. He was desperately trying to impress this man, and I knew it. I felt bad I didn't leave my office earlier, but right as I was about to leave an upset client called me. I had to take the call. Fortunately, I was able to calm him down and resolve his problem. Unfortunately, the call took over a half hour.

I was less than a mile from Mitch's house, driving in the middle lane of a busy street, right behind a landscaper's truck when it happened. A mid-sized plastic bucket rolled off the truck, right into my lane. I wanted to swerve to avoid, it but there were cars on both sides of me. I couldn't stop short, since there were also cars behind me. All I could think to do was slow down and pray I would somehow manage to hit the side of the bucket and push it away from my car.

Well, that didn't happen. I ran right over the bucket, and the thick plastic got lodged under the front of my car. I managed to pull to the side of the road, while the bucket scraped the road underneath. I got out of my car and assessed the damage. "Crap," I muttered to myself as I tried to pull the bucket out. It wiggled, but I wasn't strong enough to free it. I went back in to my car and called Mitch.

"Where are you?" He snapped.

"About a mile away. I need your help. I sort of had an accident."

"For God's sake Annabel," he spat out. "Can't you be careful? We have dinner with Carl Peterson and his wife in half an hour!"

"Thanks for your concern, Mitch. I really appreciate it. I'm fine. Thank you so much for asking," I said, not trying to hide my anger.

"Sorry," he muttered. "Are you okay?" He managed to ask although I could clearly tell by the tone of his voice his only concern was if we would be able to make our reservation in time.

"Yeah, I'm fine. I ran over a bucket, and it's stuck. I can't drive like this. I'm just down the road. I need you to come and help me get it out."

"You want me to pull a bucket out of your car? Have you completely lost your mind? You know we have dinner with the Petersons. I'm already dressed. In a brand new suit," he clarified. "And you want me to get all dirty?"

"I want my boyfriend to help me when I have a problem," I replied as a tear trickled down my right cheek. "I don't think it's too much to ask."

"Annabel, you have Triple A precisely for times like these. You pay them a yearly fee so they can help you. Call them. I'm sure they can send someone properly equipped over to help with your little situation."

I said nothing. I couldn't speak. My mouth hung open in disbelief.

Mitch didn't seem to notice or mind my silence. "You know where dinner is, right? Meet us there. I'll make up some excuse for the Peterson's as to why you're late. Who runs over a bucket anyway?"

If I had any doubts about Mitch before, his last comment squelched them. "No, Mitch. Come up with an excuse as to why I will not be at dinner."

"Annabel, you can't be serious. You know how important

tonight is for me. How can you do this to me? Come to dinner; you can have your little temper tantrum later tonight."

I didn't reply. I simply hung up the phone.

I was halfway through dialing Triple-A for assistance when there was a knock on my half opened window. I looked up and saw an incredibly handsome man outside my car. He was tall, definitely at least six-feet, with slightly overgrown jet-black hair and the bluest eyes I had ever seen.

"Are you okay?" He asked sounding concerned. "Do you need any help?" He pointed, "I was stuck at the red light on the other side of the street. I saw what happened." He clarified.

"Um, I'm okay," I answered. "I was just calling roadside assistance. The bucket is stuck," I explained.

"Did you try to get it out?"

"Yeah," I answered. "I can't budge it, which is why I am calling for help."

"Let me try." He said as he proceeded to walk to the front of my parked car.

"No. Don't be silly," I answered, as I opened my door and got out.

"You will be here hours waiting for them. I'm here now. Come on. Let's see what we can do."

He squatted down and looked underneath the front of my car. "You did a good job, here," he joked. He took off his suit jacket and placed it on the hood of my car. He bent back down and started to reach for the bucket. I stopped him.

"You are all dressed. You don't have to do this. You'll get dirty."

"Big deal. There is this great invention called laundry," he joked as he started to tug at the bucket. His tone turned serious. "Wow, you weren't kidding. This bucket is really stuck. But don't worry; I think we can get it out. You up to helping?"

"Sure," I answered as I squatted down next to him.

"Cool! I will grab the right. You grab the left and on the count of three we pull with all of our might. One. Two. Three…"

It was hard to focus on pulling while being this close to him, but I managed to concentrate, and together we freed the bucket.

"Oh my God! Thank you so much," I gushed. "I don't know how to thank you."

"I do," he smirked. "Come out to dinner with me?"

So I did, and I had the best time.

I'd like to say I never spoke to, or saw, Mitch again, but that would be a lie. He called me early the next morning. I wanted to let the call go to voicemail, but instead I answered it. He apologized profusely; he sounded so sincere. I think he realized how upset he made me and was rightly afraid he'd lose me. I agreed to have dinner with him that night. He acted like the Mitch I first started dating, the one who I had fallen in love with.

I found it difficult to stop seeing him. After all, Mitch had so many good qualities. He was funny, smart, and incredibly charming. When he wanted to, he knew how to make me incredibly happy. Unfortunately more times than not, he was inconsistent in his affection and often his actions didn't feel sincere. Eventually, I began to realize he didn't really love me, he loved the idea of me—a pretty girl on his arm to help him impress others while he fulfilled his own needs. In a lot of ways, I realized Mitch reminded me of my father.

As I sorted out my feelings for Mitch, I also spent time with Cole. I think hanging out with both men gave me a clearer perspective. I slowly realized when I was with Mitch I walked on eggshells. I was always concerned about his moods and reactions. I constantly tried to be the perfect girlfriend. With Cole, however, it was completely the opposite. I always felt like I could just be myself. I didn't worry about how I looked or what I said. I was so comfortable around him, and I felt like I could tell him anything. Our relationship was easygoing and fun. He made me realize I wanted comfort and compassion out of life, not turmoil and drama.

Looking back I really wish I'd made a clean break with Mitch the first night I met Cole. I'm sure I would have been much happier if I was one hundred percent open to starting a new relationship with Cole. But I was scared to give up what I had known for so long for the unknown.

CHAPTER SEVEN

"I'll get it!" **Violet yelled** as she raced to the front door. Since I wasn't expecting anyone, I trailed behind her. My mother was waiting on the other side of the door.

"Oh, you again," Violet said with her hand on her hip, and head cocked to the side. "You're coming around a lot lately. Are you planning on moving in or something?"

"You sure got your mother's mouth, don't you, darling," Beatrice replied.

"Yep! I do! I call 'em how I see 'em," Violet answered, unfazed.

"What are you doing home anyway? Shouldn't you be in school?" Beatrice asked sounding annoyed more than concerned.

"Strep!" Violet had yelled before she ran back into the den to resume playing with Harley, who was also under the weather.

"Is she contagious, Annabel? I can't be getting sick you know. There's too much to do with the wedding right around the corner."

"You'll be fine, Mother. It's not like you were planning on kissing or playing with her. Besides, she's on antibiotics."

"If you say so, I guess I'll have to trust you." She removed her coat and handed it to me. "But if I get sick, you will be to blame."

What grandmother acted like this, I wondered. Connie had always been the complete opposite. I remembered the first time Violet got sick. She was six months old and had a fever of one hundred and three. I didn't know what to do. Connie was the first person I called. She went to the pediatrician with me and then even slept over just in case we needed anything. She never worried about herself. She just wanted to help nurse her grand-babies back to health.

"If you're not comfortable being here Mother, there is no reason to stay. We can talk on the phone."

"No, no. I'll be okay, I'm sure. I have hand sanitizer some-where in this purse."

"Oh, good," I answered as I tried to keep my sarcasm under control. "What are you doing here, anyway?" I asked as I pulled my hair into a ponytail. "I wasn't expecting you. I'm working from home today."

"I know. Which is precisely why I came by. I figured since you were home you'd have time to go over the guest list."

I bit my tongue as I followed her into my kitchen. It was pointless trying to explain to her work is work regardless of where I'm performing it. She was never going to understand because she didn't want to. "Do you want some coffee?"

"Only if it's fresh."

I filled two cups and joined her at the kitchen table where she already had a stack of papers sitting.

I took a sip of my coffee and picked up the papers. "There are a lot of names here," I remarked. "How big is this shindig gonna to be?"

"I'm trying to keep it under three hundred and fifty, but that's easier said than done. Between Walter and myself there are just so many people we have to include," she answered before she took a sip of coffee. As soon as she swallowed her face puckered up as if I gave her poison. "I thought you said this was fresh, Annabel." She dramatically moved her cup to the side.

"It is. I made it only about an hour ago. And besides, I like it," I answered as I took another sip. "Do you want me to make you something else? Maybe a cup of tea?"

"No. I'm fine. Let's just get down to business, so you can continue your day." She handed the handwritten pages over to me, "Here's my preliminary list. Walter has his own, of course. I didn't bring that one. You won't know anyone on it, I'm sure. But I did want to check if you or Cole wanted to include anyone I missed. After all, your mother doesn't get married everyday!" She beamed.

I scanned the names. On the bottom of the very last page, and written in a different color ink, clearly indicating an after-thought, were Cole's parents and sisters' names.

"Figures," I muttered.

"Did you say something, Annabel?" She asked as her steel gray eyes peered into mine.

"No. I'm glad to see you managed to include the O'Conner's."

"Of course I did," Beatrice smiled. "I knew you wouldn't want it any other way."

"Is it safe to assume my kids are invited or would you prefer I find a random babysitter?" I asked.

"Annabel, really. Was that comment necessary?"

I didn't reply. I knew my tone indicated my frustration, but really, was it such a far out question given how close my mother was to my children?

"Of course they're invited," she answered, not missing a beat. "I want them to be my ring bearer and flower girl. They are my grandchildren after all. But it probably would be a good idea for you to arrange to have a babysitter come along too.

You do want to make sure they stay occupied and out of trouble." She reached for the undrinkable cup of coffee and took a sip. "Why do you always think the worst of me? Seriously, Annabel, it would be nice if just one time you could cut me a little slack."

I blurted out, "Slack, Mother? Really? You've got to be kidding. What do you think I've been doing all these years?" Speaking my mind was addictive. The more I did it the more, I wanted to let out everything that has been troubling me for so long.

"If that's what you want to tell yourself, fine. But you know what? You can lie to others, but you can't lie to yourself. I'm not afraid to admit it; I know I made a lot of mistakes. I know I handled a lot of situations extremely poorly," she said, as she made sure her caramel chignon was in place.

"You can say that again," I mumbled, a little louder than I planned to.

"Yes, I know I did. And I'm not the only one. You have been far from perfect yourself." She said pointedly.

"What do you mean?" I asked, confused.

"Let's take your little destination wedding for instance, shall we?"

"What about it?" I asked, not sure where she was going.

"I could understand given everything that had happened why you wanted to dash off to St. Kitts rather than have a proper wedding and reception. I could also understand why you wished to marry Cole alone and keep the ceremony intimate."

I swallowed hard but didn't say anything.

"I would even be able to accept it, but that wasn't what happened, now was it?" Beatrice snarled.

I took a deep breath but remained quiet.

She didn't take her eyes off me, "I asked you a question, Annabel. I deserve an answer."

"What are you getting at, Mother?" I asked as I pushed my cup of coffee away. I no longer had any interest in drinking it.

"You know damn well what I am getting at. And you still haven't answered my question."

My mind reeled. Could my mother have possibly known what really happened on the island? When I had told Connie my plan she tried to make me change my mind. She begged me to reconsider, in fact. But I was too stubborn. I didn't want to heed her advice. She warned me I was playing with fire and I couldn't keep the secret forever. I didn't want to believe her. Who was I trying to fool? I think at the time I truly hoped my mother would learn the truth. Part of me wanted to hurt her just as much as she had hurt me. But now I am no longer dealing in hypotheticals, and I felt sick to my stomach. I had secretly felt guilty about this decision for years. For so many reasons, guilt has been my constant companion.

I removed the rubber band that was securing my hair in place and nervously ran both my hands through my hair, scratching my scalp hard in the process. "I don't know what to say," I replied softly. "You clearly already know the answer."

"Yes, I do. And you want to know how I know? I know because I was there."

Shocked I whispered, "What?" I got up and looked out my kitchen window, and stared at my backyard without seeing anything.

"Get back here and sit down." She ordered. I did as I was told.

"You heard me correctly. I... Was... There..." she answered slowly. "I wanted to respect your wishes, but I also wanted to see you on your wedding day, even if from afar. So, a couple of weeks before you were scheduled to dash off, I called the hotel you were staying at. I spoke to the wedding planner, what a delightful woman. Flora was her name, wasn't it?"

I nodded.

"Well, I told her I wanted to have flowers and a nice bottle of champagne delivered to your room an hour before the ceremony, so I needed to know the time, date, and location. She was extremely cooperative. I arrived on the island the day of the wedding. I made sure to spend most of the day in my room, tucked away. But when the service started I was on the shoreline. I looked like any other vacationer, just enjoying the sunset with a frozen drink in my hand. But under my oversized hat and sunglasses, tears were falling from my eyes. I watched you and Cole exchange your rings and share your first kiss as husband and wife. I stayed on the beach just long enough to see you embrace Connie right afterward. You were holding onto her so tightly with such affection. It was like a knife to my heart." Beatrice wiped her eye with the back of her hand.

I opened my mouth to speak, but Beatrice held out her hand, pointing a long French manicured fingernail at me urging me to stop.

"Don't speak. Listen." She commanded.

I nodded slowly and closed my mouth.

"I am not surprised Connie and Patrick attended the ceremony."

"You're not?" I asked.

"Hffmpp," she scoffed. "Not at all. I know how close you and she were. I saw it the night I went to their house for Cole's birthday. You were practically joined at the hip. The two of you were exchanging glances across the table as if you were communicating a secret language. I knew she had become the one you confided in. And it hurt me. Badly. Why do you think I couldn't wait to leave their house the night of Cole's birthday dinner?"

"I thought you didn't want to be with me," I answered quietly.

Beatrice took another sip of her coffee. "You weren't completely wrong. I didn't really want to be with you. It was too soon, and I wasn't ready. But I also didn't want not to be with you. I'm not sure if this makes any sense."

"It really doesn't," I answered honestly.

"I don't expect you to understand. Maybe another day, let's get back to the wedding, shall we? Connie and Patrick being there made sense to me. I wasn't mad about it. I wasn't even surprised Cole's sisters were there. But when you brought along," my mother paused and made the finger quote gesture with her hands, "that friend of yours, I was very hurt."

"What was wrong with Michelle being there?" I asked. I then used all the force I could muster to hold back a tear, which threatened to escape as I continued, "Brody couldn't be there. I wanted... No, I needed someone who loved me at my side. I didn't want to be alone as I started my new life with Cole. Michelle was like my sister. She was my best friend!"

Michelle and I met in college our sophomore year and became instantly inseparable.

"Friend? Is that what she was?" Beatrice spat.

"Yes," I said a little too loudly. "You never liked her, did you? Every time I brought her home with me, you gave her the cold shoulder. You never made her feel welcome."

"I know. It was intentional." My mother admitted. She picked up her cup again but placed it back on the table without taking a sip. "I saw right through her act. She was a user. She never cared about you. Not one bit!"

"What are you talking about mother?" I was outraged. Why was she saying these horrible things?

"Annabel, for a smart girl you have always been so naive. Don't you think it was odd how she latched onto you so quickly as soon as you two met? How everything you liked she liked too. She wanted what you had and the only way to get it was to be at your side, constantly, especially when it came to men. She slept with all of your boyfriends, you know."

For about the hundredth time this morning I said the only word that seemed to be able to come out of my mouth. "What?"

"You heard me. She had quite the appetite! Thomas, Daniel, Mitch. All of them."

"I didn't even sleep with Thomas," I said. "How do you even know this? Did she tell you?"

"Of course not. I know her type, unfortunately all too well. I can spot someone like her a million miles away."

Dumbfounded as the realization of what she said slowly hit me, I asked, "Did you cheat on Daddy?"

"Jesus, Annabel. You're not really asking me that question, now are you? I guess it shouldn't surprise me. You always think the worst of me. Believe what you want, you always do. Here keep the guest list." She thrust the pieces of paper at me. "I have a photocopy of it at home. You may find your answers on these pages," she explained.

With that, Harley came charging into the kitchen and ran right up to my mother. He had one hand behind his back. "Hi, Grandma! Violet said you were here! I made you present!"

"Oh, how sweet. Thanks." Beatrice replied barely making eye contact with him.

"It's a neck-a-wace. See?" He held it up to her face and practically smacked her in the nose with it.

"Oh yes. It's very pretty. You are very crafty," she said dismissively.

"I'm not crafty!" He said proudly. "I'm just a boy who made a neck-a-wace with beads and a pattern. I'll put it on you!"

"No, no. It's okay. I'll put it on later," my mother replied, appalled.

Harley paid her no mind. He dragged another kitchen chair closer, stood on it and placed it over her head. My mother grimaced. Then he sneezed.

"Are you sick too?" My mother squealed and jumped back.

"No. I'm perfect except my smell is broken," Harley replied, and I laughed. My mother, however, wasn't amused.

She reached into her bag and removed her bottle of hand sanitizer, which she generously applied to her palm. "Annabel, I have to go. Be at my house Sunday at eleven o'clock. We need to go to the florist, and then maybe we'll do lunch."

CHAPTER EIGHT

"You look like crap. Are you going to tell me what is going on?" Cole asked as he handed me a glass of red wine and sat down next to me in the den. Ever since I tucked the kids into bed, my mind had been racing. My hair was standing on end, and I feared my nails were one bite away from falling off. The television was on, but I had no idea what was playing. I couldn't focus. My cat was curled up in my lap, sleeping. I absently petted her.

I leaned over and grabbed the remote control and turned the television off. "Bea came for a visit today," I answered, solemnly.

He smiled. "Well, all the pieces fall into place. What did the queen demand now?"

"Nothing. It was something completely different." I started picking my cuticle, drawing blood. My voice barely a whisper, "She was at our wedding."

"Excuse me?"

As he stroked my hair, I repeated what Beatrice had told me. When I was done, he asked, "Are you okay with knowing she was there?"

"Yes. No. Maybe. I don't know." I took a sip of wine. "I think in a way I'm relieved she knows what we did. Keeping the secret all these years was exhausting. I no longer have to worry about the truth slipping out. I just can't imagine what she must have felt like being on the sidelines the way she was, watching us from afar. What if Violet…"

Cole gently squeezed my knee. "Don't even go there, Anna. It will never happen. You are nothing like your mother. You would never treat Violet or Harley the way she treated you."

I stared into his eyes, urging him to continue, and he did. "Sweetheart, yes in retrospect, we didn't handle everything perfectly, but we didn't have much choice now did we? Don't forget it was your mother who started it. She caused this, not you. You simply reacted."

"In my head, I know you're right, but I still feel bad." I took a large sip of Pinot Noir, "She brought up Michelle too."

I couldn't tell if it was real or if I imagined it, but darkness passed over Cole's eyes at the mention of her name.

"Why did you kill our friendship with her?"

He took a sip of wine. "I don't know what you are talking about."

"Come on, Cole. I'm not stupid. Something happened, and I just don't know what. We used to hang out with her all the time. When we first got engaged, we'd have dinner with her at least once a week. At first, I thought you didn't like her boyfriend."

"You mean Bobby? I didn't. He was a pompous idiot."

I smiled. "Yeah, he sure was. But there was something else. There had to be. After all, she broke up with him right before we went to St. Kitts. And almost every time I made plans you found a reason why we should cancel. It was months after the wedding before we spent time with her."

"We had a lot going on, Anna. And we were at different places in our lives. You and I didn't have much free time, and the time we had I wanted to spend with you." He leaned over and kissed me for emphasis. I wasn't buying it.

"Come on, Cole. We had plenty of time to spend with other people. But every single time I mentioned getting together with Michelle you always nixed the idea. You'd either," I made air quotes with my fingers, "remember you made other plans for us with someone else or you'd convince me that we needed some alone time."

He ran his fingers through his hair.

"Isn't it true?" I demanded.

After a moment softly he said, "Yes."

"Why? My mother said..." I paused. I couldn't bring myself to say the words. I knew I needed answers, but I was petrified of what they would be. Fear and repulsion had been haunting me ever since Bea left the house.

"What did your mother say, Anna?" His tone was impatient.

I took a deep breath. "She told me something about Michelle. Something awful." I swallowed hard. "She said she slept with all my boyfriends. Cole, did you and her ever..."

His eyes bulged, "How can you even ask me that question, Anna?"

"Cole. I—"

He banged his fist on the coffee table. "Damn it, Anna, don't." He stared straight ahead, and breathed deeply for a moment before he turned to face me.

"You know, I really don't understand you sometimes. Have I not shown you day in and day out how much I love you? Have I not always been right at your side, no matter what? Have I ever given you any reason not to trust me?"

I started to cry. "No," I whispered.

"So how could you think I would sleep with your best friend behind your back?"

I sniffed. "I didn't think you did."

"Really, Anna? If you didn't think it why did you ask me?" He picked up his glass of wine and took a gulp.

"I don't know, Cole. My mom came over and told me all these things about her. Then I remembered how strange you acted back then. I couldn't help but wonder why."

"But asking me if I slept with her, Anna? Really. I haven't been with another woman since the day I met you. Do you know how hurtful your question is?"

I squeezed his thigh. "Yes. And I'm sorry, Cole. I know you'd never hurt me. But there has to be something more." I stared at him. "Please, I need to know. What did you really have against her? What aren't you telling me?"

He got up and walked to the window. I didn't move. He stared at the backyard for a few minutes before he sat down next to me. He took another sip of wine. He bit his lower lip. "You're right, Anna. There was more. And I probably should have told you years ago."

My stomach cramped. "Told me what?"

"She tried to sleep with me."

"I don't understand."

"You know, she always was a flirt. But I never paid any attention to it, especially since she did it right in front of you."

"She didn't flirt with you." I had no idea why I was defending her, but I felt like I had to.

"Yes, Anna, she did. A lot, but in a very laid back joking way. And, since you didn't seem to mind, I figured it was harmless. After all, some girls are just that way."

I took a sip of wine. "So what happened to have changed your mind?"

"The little bachelorette party she threw for you happened, and she took things too far."

I thought back to how she arranged for all of our college friends, most of whom I hadn't seen since graduation, to get together about a month before our wedding.

"What happened?"

"Do you remember anything about the night?"

I scrunched my face. "Not really."

"I'm not surprised. You were so trashed when she brought you home. I've never seen you so drunk, ever. It was bad; I was worried about you. I got you into bed. I thought she left, but she didn't. When I came out of our room to get you some water to leave by the bed, I found her sitting on the couch. I asked her what she was still doing here, and she said she wanted to talk to me about the wedding. I sat down next to her. She started asking me some lame questions about the trip. I realized, unlike you, she was stone cold sober."

Cole reached over and picked up the bottle of Pinot Noir, which was sitting on the coffee table and topped off our glasses. He took a big gulp before continuing. "So one minute she was asking about airline shuttles and the next she was practically sitting on my lap. She kissed me. It happened so fast. I pushed her away."

My mouth hung open, but I didn't speak.

"I was shocked and repulsed. She was your best friend, and she didn't take the hint." Cole started to shake his head from side to side, "She tried to straddle me. I literally pushed her onto the floor. I screamed at her. I asked her what she was doing. And she told me she was tired of waiting."

"What?"

"You heard me." He sighed. "She said she knew I wanted her from the day we first met. I told her she was crazy. She laughed, but the laugh sounded evil. It was then I understood why you were so drunk and she wasn't. She planned everything, seducing me was her main goal for that night."

"I can't believe this."

"Believe it. She was cocky and so sure of herself. In fact, she patted me on my chest and said my head was fighting but deep down my heart knew what it wanted. If that wasn't bad enough, she also said I'm going to change your mind just like I have done with all the other guys. Then she left."

Tears streamed down my face. "Why didn't you tell me this? How could you have kept this from me all these years? I should have known what she was really like a long time ago. If I did, I never would have brought her to St. Kitts with us."

Cole walked across the room where there was a tissue box. He handed me one and I dried my eyes and blew my nose.

"Anna, I didn't tell you because I wanted to protect you. You were already hurting. You were practically hanging on by a thread. I was afraid you wouldn't be able to handle anymore. We were so close to the wedding. I didn't want to have to tell you what your best friend was really like. I wanted you to have a little happiness. You deserved it."

He ran his hands over his face. "I planned to tell you, really I did. But since I was able to get you to spend less time with her, I didn't know what telling the truth would accomplish. The friendship died a natural death, and you didn't get your heart broken. I'm so sorry." He leaned over and wiped a tear away from my cheek before he gave me a small kiss.

"I'm so angry," I answered as I got up and paced the room. "And I'm so confused. I wish I'd known the truth, but you're right. I don't know if I could have handled knowing it then. Does anyone else know? Did you tell Connie?"

Cole chuckled as I sat back down. "What do you think? Do you think I would've been able to come up with this plan on my own? I'm not that bright, baby."

I smiled, my first real smile of the night. "Well, yeah. That's true." I snuggled against him, and we were both quiet for a few minutes. "Should I call Michelle? Confront her?"

"What's the point?" Cole asked as he gently caressed my back. "The past is the past. Why cause stress in the present and add aggravation to the future? What are you trying to accomplish?"

"I don't know," I said as my voice cracked. "I'm so angry, and hurt. I thought she was my friend. How she could have done this to me?"

"I don't know, Anna. I doubt we'll ever know. She isn't going to come clean and explain now after all these years. Look at it this way you, learned a lesson. But addressing this now, so many years later..." he paused, "I just don't know how it helps you. For all you know she thinks I told you the truth years ago. She's the one with this on her conscience, not you. Besides, you have already gotten even with her."

"How?" I asked, confused.

"By being happy. By having me love you. She always was and will be, a sad little girl searching for love. That is why she did the things she did. She was jealous of you. You had what she longed for in so many ways."

CHAPTER NINE

"**D**amn it!" **I muttered** to myself as I pulled into the circular driveway of my mother's house and glanced at the clock on my dashboard. Eleven-fifteen. I was late, and I knew from experience my mother didn't tolerate tardiness well. We bicker enough as it was without me adding fuel to the fire.

I could just picture the scene inside. I would bet my favorite pair of shoes she was sitting on the couch in the living room, with her purse on her lap, glancing at her Rolex every ten seconds while muttering about how disrespectful I was to Walter. Then for the rest of the afternoon, there would be an added undercurrent to every word out of her mouth, reminding me how I had derailed her perfect day by not being on time.

I exited the car and walked quickly to the front door. It was unseasonably warm outside, and I was enjoying every second of the heat. We've had a very long, cold winter, and the sun felt beyond amazing on my face. As I approached the front door, I noticed it was open, so I walked inside. "Hello! I'm here," I called out from the center hallway.

Walter's robust voice greeted me back, "Hey there, Anna! Come on in! I'm in the living room."

Do I know my mother or what?

Apparently not!

Instead of walking in on an impatient and upset Beatrice, I found a sweaty Walter, clutching a water bottle staring out the window. My mom was nowhere in sight.

"Hey, Walter."

He turned and when he saw me he flashed me his big boyish grin. "I'd give you a hug, but I think you are better off passing." He joked.

"I'm not afraid of some sweat, I'm a mom, remember?" I replied as I gave him a quick hug. I glanced at my watch. "I know I am late. I'm sure my mother has been chewing your ear off about me for the past fifteen minutes."

"Nope. She is running late too," he said with a chuckle.

"Is she okay?" I asked, concerned. "I don't think my mother has ever been late for anything, in her life."

"Don't worry, she is perfectly fine. We decided to take advantage of this delightful weather and went for a really long bike ride, and we sort of lost track of the time. She is showering now."

"My mother, on a bike? Are you sure we are talking about the same person here? My mother is Beatrice Buchanan," I joked. "I don't think she even knows how to ride a bike." My mind flashed back to my childhood. Rosie, our housekeeper and babysitter, taught Brody and me how to ride our bikes. She was the one who would accompany us on bike rides. I never saw my mom even so much as sit on a bicycle let alone ride one unless you count the stationary ones at her country club's gym.

Walter took a swig of his water. "There is a lot about that lady you probably don't know, Anna. There is even more she's slowly learning about herself as well. Here, look at this picture I took of her today."

Walter pulled his iPhone from the pocket of his shorts and scrolled through a few photographs before handing me the device. "Look closely at it," he said as he beamed.

I gazed at the picture and then made it larger. My mother was standing next to a bright red bike. Was she wearing a pair of ratty sweatpants? I didn't think she owned anything that wasn't a designer brand. On one hand, she held a helmet almost the exact shade of her bike. On the other hand, there was a water bottle that she was drinking from. Her hair was not in its usual chignon; instead, it was loose and blowing in the wind. Her eyes were twinkling with delight, and she was glowing. But something definitely seemed off. Could it be?

Walter had his eyes on me as I surveyed the picture. Walter chuckled. "I guess you spotted it," Walter stated as he sat down on the sofa.

I sat down next to him. I really need to work on my poker face. "Am I seeing this correctly?" I asked him. "Is she really not wearing any makeup?" I asked in disbelief. "I don't think I have ever seen her without makeup in my entire life. Even when I was little, I remember waking up in the middle of the night, feeling sick, going into her room. I swear she had mascara and lipstick on!"

"I know, but naturally she's something else, isn't she?" He didn't wait for me to reply. He continued, "It took a lot of work on my part but slowly she is coming around and going bare. In fact lately, when we are home alone, she doesn't have a lick of makeup on. Now I haven't been able to get her to go out of the house without it, but I am not giving up." He winked at me. "When we first started dating I called her makeup her war paint. At first, I thought it was just a joke, but I soon realized that was exactly what it was to her. It was a self-preservation method. She keeps her real self and emotions hidden under the mask she has created."

Before I could say anything, my mother appeared in the room, dressed in a black Chanel pantsuit and fully made up. Walter and I exchanged silent grins. "I'm dreadfully sorry I'm late, Annabel. I know it was quite inconsiderate of me, but time just got away." She glanced at her Rolex, "Oh my. We need to get going. Come on; I'll drive."

Neither one of us said much as we drove the short distance to the local florist. Instead, we just listened to the classical music that played on the car radio, both of us seemingly lost in our own thoughts. Beatrice found a parking spot right in front of the florist. As soon as we entered the mid-sized store, I turned to the right and smiled. They still had the huge wall of photographs of all the baseball teams they had sponsored.

Since the florist was in business for over thirty years, the wall was crammed full of pictures. Despite the number of pictures displayed I immediately spotted the one I was looking for. I traced my fingers along the face that belonged to my six-year-old brother. Brody was so excited the year he played baseball, and he looked so precious in his uniform. He was far from the best player, but he loved the game. I turned around, and my mom was standing behind me looking at the same picture.

"He was so adorable, wasn't he?" Without letting her reply, I continued, smiling. "Do you remember the time he hit the ball way out into the park? His hit probably could have been a home run, but he ran the bases so slowly." I smiled as the memory came flooding back. "When he finally got back to the dugout, the coach asked him why he was running so slow and he replied his shoes were super fast but his legs weren't." I laughed as I finished.

My mom didn't even smile. Instead, she pursed her lips and crossed her arms over her chest. "Let's not take a trip down memory lane. Please, we don't have time for it. We have floral arrangements to pick out, and we are already late for our appointment. Come on. Let's get to work. Suzanne is waiting on us." She marched to the back of the store. I lingered a few moments longer and stared at my brother's face. I was always amazed how much Harley resembled him.

After ten minutes with Suzanne, I felt like I was back at the stationery store picking out invitations. Suzanne showed us every possible type of centerpiece style. The possibilities seemed endless, and we didn't even discuss flower types yet. I feared this was going to be a very, very long day.

"There seem to be so many options. Don't you think it would be better if we just tell you what we are looking for and go from there?" I asked in the hope of speeding up the process. I really did want to spend some time with my kids today. Walter got me in the mood to go for a bike ride.

"Well, I guess that is one way to do it," my mother answered, unenthusiastically. "What do you think, Suzanne?"

She tucked her shoulder-length gray hair behind her ears and said, "That's the way I usually work, but you mentioned when you called you wanted to see everything. So— "

Before she could continue her thought, Bea butted in. "You're right. I'd like to see everything, so there are no doubts that we made the right choice. If I don't see everything how will I be sure? This is my wedding after all. I want," my mother placed her right hand on her chest for emphasis, "I mean, I need everything to be perfect." With a roll of her eyes, she continued, "You know how those country club ladies can be. They are just so judgmental! And they talk so much!"

"You mean your friends, Mother?" I couldn't help ask.

As if she didn't hear me she continued her rant. "I want to make it impossible for them to find fault with anything we choose. I want them to be green with envy over all of my selections. They're going to eat themselves alive that they didn't think to get remarried this year too!"

Suzanne looked worried as she asked, "So you really want to see every floral arrangement we have prepared, Beatrice? You are aware we've been in business for thirty-two years."

"I just thought we'd need ideas and pictures would help. But I guess, maybe, my daughter has a point." My mother looked pained as she pointed this out. "How about I just tell you what I want?"

"Yes!" Suzanne and I both answered in unison.

"I want something big and bold, with lots of white roses. I want the centerpieces to really grab everyone's attention when they walk in the dining room for the reception. Something that will make the ladies gasp. Don't you agree, Annabel?"

I rubbed my eyes. "Honestly, no, Mother. I think something smaller and more delicate is the way to go. I like the idea of a round bowl, similar to a goldfish bowl, with cut white tulips or mini calla lilies in it. You know, something simple and elegant. And besides, if you keep the flowers small people can see each other and talk at the table rather than having to peek around the centerpieces."

"Small? Goldfish bowls? Annabel, are you crazy? Where do you get these cockamamie ideas anyway?" My mother asked as Suzanne flashed me a sympathetic smile. "That is so minimalist. I don't want anyone to think I had to scrimp on the flowers. I can see the rumors flying now. No bridge game would be complete without a comment from those gossips. Everyone will think I have to sell the house next. Or worse, that I married Walter for his money!"

I tried unsuccessfully to suppress my laughter. "Where do you get these thoughts?" I asked. "Simple doesn't have to be a bad thing?"

"Your daughter has a point, Beatrice. More and more people are opting for basic arrangements," Suzanne chimed in.

"Well, I am certainly not going to be one of them," my mother huffed. "I want the flowers to make a statement. Show me a picture of your biggest, most expensive arrangement," Beatrice ordered.

Suzanne went behind the counter and grabbed yet another book. She flipped through the pages until she found a picture of the most enormous and gaudy arrangement I had ever seen in my entire life. There were so many layers of flowers it almost looked like a wedding cake."

"I love it!" Beatrice gushed and clasped her hands in joy. "This is perfect!" She exclaimed. I rolled my eyes, again. "Now I don't know the final count, but I'm sure I will need at least thirty-five of these. I have time I assume to give you the final count?"

"Of course," Suzanne answered as she reached for her order book, under the counter.

"Wonderful," my mother replied as she removed her American Express card from her Bottega Veneta wallet. "Now, as for the bouquets, since my daughter and granddaughter will be the only two accompanying me down the aisle, let's make her happy, shall we?" My mother turned to me and flashed me one of her phony smiles. "Suzanne, make two small and simple calla lily bouquets, one for my daughter and one for me. Oh, and I will also need a basket of white rose petals for my granddaughter to toss down the aisle." My mother squeezed my forearm, "See Annabel, I am taking your opinion into consideration. Now, be a plum and run next door and get us a table while I finish up here. I'm parched; make sure to order me an iced tea. It needs to be unsweetened, remember. I have to watch my calories!" She sighed deeply.

CHAPTER TEN

Catching up on work e-mails was my least favorite thing to do, but it seemed that every time I had a few minutes to spare, there I sat sorting out the mess that was my e-mail account. I swear emails are like gray hairs. You get rid of one and five more came in their place.

My mother approached the table at the small cafe next to the florist and snickered, "On your phone again? I don't understand why everyone is so addicted to those things these days. It's really getting out of control. Did I tell you what happened on Thursday when I was getting my nails done? Marcel interrupted my manicure to read and reply to a text from her daughter. I was dumbfounded!" My mother paused to take a sip of the iced tea that I dutifully ordered for her. "And then, to make matters worse, she kept the phone on the table the entire time she was doing my nails. She couldn't stop peeking at it. I couldn't believe the gall. I was paying for her services, and her attention was elsewhere. She even clipped my cuticle and drew blood." My mother shoved her right index finger in my face for me to examine, but it looked perfectly fine to me. "If I hadn't used her for fifteen years I would have been forced to make a change right then and there. What kind of customer service is that?"

"Did you ever think maybe her daughter had a problem, Mother?" I was pretty sure the concept never even dawned on her. Despite the fact the woman gave birth to my brother and me, I often was left wondering if she had a maternal bone in her body. If she did, I sure haven't witnessed it lately.

As if I didn't ask a question, she continued, "Walter is the same way, though. He checks his phone several times a day, too."

"Several times a day?" I laughed. "That's clearly not an addiction," I replied. Fortunately for Walter he was in the process of retiring. My mother clearly wouldn't be able to understand with today's technology your workday never really stopped. Clients expected immediate answers to their questions all hours of the day and night.

My mother tilted her head to the side in contemplation. "I guess you're right, but it's still distracting. Did I tell you he wants to get me a smartphone? Can you picture me, texting?" She asked as she took a long sip of her iced tea.

I cringed. Getting a weekly play-by-play of Bea's poor customer service experiences was bearable. But now I will be bombarded with updates as they happened. One cheating move by one of her friends in a game of canasta or bridge - my phone may explode! But on the bright side, I will never miss a shoe sale at Nordstrom's again.

"Hi, I'm Amy, and I will be your server. Would you like to hear the specials?" A perky twenty-year-old girl asked with a huge smile.

I was about to say sure. Even though I hardly ever ordered a special, I loved to know what was available.

Bea beat me to the punch, "No, thank you. I know exactly what I want. I'll have the chopped salad, and make sure it is chopped finely. Last time I was here it wasn't, and I had to send it back. I don't want any onions on it either, you know sometimes a sliver or two gets in. I don't want that. If I find any onions in it I will have to send the salad back. Also, please put the tomatoes on the side. Sometimes they are too ripe and runny, ruining the crispiness of the entire salad. I want grilled chicken in it too, and pay attention, this is important. I need the chicken to be cubed and not in strips. Oh, and it must be dry. I don't want it sautéed in a ton of oil or butter. I'm getting married in a couple of months, and I have to watch my figure." She offered the poor girl a smile, which wasn't reciprocated. "Oh and as for dressing, I'd like your low-calorie raspberry vinaigrette, but on the side, of course."

The now weary waitress turned to me. After all my mother's demands, I felt bad asking her about the specials, especially since I already knew what I wanted to eat. "I'll have the Cobb salad, with ranch dressing. Thank you very much."

As soon as she was out of earshot, my mom chimed in, "Ranch dressing, Annabel? Are you serious? You do know how many calories there are in it, right? You might as well have ordered a cheeseburger?"

"I almost did, Mother, but I figured if I ordered one you'd have a meltdown, and it seems like Amy already has enough to handle as it is."

Not wanting to get into another argument, I quickly changed the subject as we waited for our food. I filled my mother in on the conversation I had with Cole a few days earlier, which confirmed her belief that my former best friend indeed had slept with all my boyfriends. Shockingly, for the first time in more years than I could remember I really felt like she was focused on my story. She seemed to truly care about what I was saying, as opposed to just waiting to turn the conversation back to her.

It was a wonderful feeling, to have some of her attention again. While my mother was far from being the loving and affectionate mother every daughter wanted, she wasn't always as cold and distant as she is now. In fact, I remember when I was in middle school; she'd pick me up from gymnastics and she'd always ask me about my friends. She loved hearing all the drama. Often she shared stories of her own teenage years. I used to love those car rides. Man, I really missed those days.

When I finished my play by play of the conversation she simply said, "I'm really sorry you had to find out, but I am so thankful you married a man like Cole. There aren't many guys like him around. He's one of the few good ones."

Before I could comment the waitress was back at our table. "Here you go," she said as she placed our salads in front of us. I held my breath as my mom thoroughly examined hers. Fortunately, the presentation passed because she simply thanked the waitress.

"Did you get a chance to go over the guest list, Annabel?" She asked as she slowly drizzled the dressing on her salad.

"I did, and it looks fine to me. I just think you missed inviting one person." I answered right before I popped a piece of avocado into my mouth.

"Who?" My mother asked as she placed a few tomato cubes into her salad.

"Mindy, she wasn't on the list."

My mother let out a huff. "Oh, omitting her wasn't an oversight. It was intentional. I have nothing to do with Mindy, and I haven't for many years."

I took a small bite of my salad. I was confused. When did my mom stop speaking to her, and why wasn't I aware of this? Mindy was always a huge part of my life. She was a beautiful and vibrant woman, you know the kind who could light up a room with just her smile. She was always so kind to Brody and me. When we were little, every time she came to the house, which was practically every weekend, she always had a little something for us. When I entered my teens, and I was confused about boys, she was the one I went to. She gave me dating advice and answered all my questions about sex. I found her so much easier to talk to than my mother, probably because she was only about fifteen years older than me. I think in a lot of ways I thought of her as the older sister I didn't have.

"What happened with you and Mindy?" I asked. Mindy and my dad worked very closely together. In fact, they were pretty much partners. My dad was in sales and he and Mindy traveled all over the country together. Mindy would demonstrate the product and go over the basics with the prospective client. Then my dad would negotiate the terms and close the deal.

"You really don't have any idea, do you?" Bea asked as she nibbled on a piece of lettuce.

I took a sip of my Diet Coke and shook my head. Most weekends the two of them would be huddled up together, in my dad's study, as they strategized for the upcoming week's meetings. There were many times Mindy would join us for dinner afterward. She was always a part of our family.

My mother dabbed her lips with her napkin before announcing, "I have nothing to do with that woman because she had an affair with my husband."

It took every ounce of willpower I had not to spit my soda at her. I struggled to swallow my beverage as shock washed over me. How could this be? Hoping I misunderstood, I asked, "What did you just say?"

"You heard me." My mother answered and then she took a deep breath. "Your dad and Mindy were involved. They were intimate together. And, I'm afraid, for more years than I care to admit to you or myself."

"But I don't understand. How? When?" I stammered as images of my childhood and my teen life passed before my eyes like a bad movie.

My mother put down her fork and reached across the table and grabbed both my hands in hers. She squeezed gently. "Oh

Annabel, I have struggled for so many years wondering if I should tell you this. I was determined to keep this situation a secret. It was a very private matter to me, as I'm sure you can appreciate. But Walter has encouraged me to open up more. He told me I couldn't continue to keep everything all bottled up. It's not easy for me to share my feelings and experiences, but despite the difficulty, I think he may be right. I do feel much better when I finally open up."

"You told Walter about Daddy and Mindy's affair?" I asked, dumbfounded. Why didn't she ever tell me?

"Of course, darling."

"This is unbelievable. You're always so closed mouthed."

"Yes, I know. But there's just something about the man." Her face lit up. "He's so easy to talk to. I've told him everything there is to know about me." Then, with a smile that didn't quite reach her eyes, she added, "And for some strange reason none of it has stopped him from loving me."

I took a bite of my salad and chewed slowly. Her words made me feel sad. Did she realize how difficult and distant she was? Did she think of herself as unlovable? Did I think she was unlovable?

"Walter is a great guy, Mom."

"Yes, he sure is."

"I'm glad you met him," I said, honestly.

"Me too. Although, I'm not completely sure I deserve him. But hopefully, he doesn't realize that anytime soon. Now, let's get back to your dad and Mindy, shall we? It's not a pleasant subject for me to talk about, so I'd rather just get it over with if you don't mind."

I nodded.

"So, I'm not exactly sure when the affair started, but I have my suspicions. If I had to guess, I'd say it probably began about a year before Brody was born. But I'm not one hundred percent sure. All I can be sure of was I didn't like the way your dad looked at Mindy. And I didn't like how they spoke to each other either. There was always a very strong connection between those two. I hated the fact that she was always over at the house, preparing for sales meetings with your father. With the number of hours he put in at the office and the number of days he was traipsing across the country with her, they had more than enough time to prepare for a meeting without them needing to work together every single weekend, in my house no less! I mean, give me a break. Your dad and Mindy were the highest-ranking sales team the company ever saw. They didn't need practice. They could close deals in their sleep."

"Did you talk to him about it?" I asked. My mother had to be wrong. If I was honest, I wasn't surprised to learn he had an affair. He and my mom weren't overly romantic with each other. I never saw a spark between them. In a lot of ways, they seemed more like roommates than lovers or even friends. But I couldn't imagine he would be cruel enough to bring his mistress home on a regular basis. Nor could I believe his mistress was Mindy.

"Of course I did, Annabel. He told me I didn't understand how the business world operated. He would pontificate about what obstacles and difficulties he was up against each and every day. He sang me a river. And then, he would rub in my face the fact I never had a career to speak of. He stripped away my confidence and made me feel so useless and so insignificant. Which, by the way, was the reason why I pushed you so hard in school. I didn't want you to feel the way I did all of my life."

"I questioned him time and time again if he and Mindy were involved. He always denied it. Part of me wanted to believe him, but the bigger part of me knew I couldn't. You have no idea how difficult it was to live with someone you fear is in love with another woman. It was a miserable way to live. My heart died a little every day. I was practically positive my husband was unfaithful to me while I had to plaster on a phony smile as I entertained his mistress."

A memory suddenly hit me, and I dropped my fork into my salad bowl. "Oh my God," I said more to myself than to my mother. "Could Brody have been right?"

"What are you talking about, Annabel?" My mother asked pointedly.

"I never believed him," my voice was barely audible, as I gently shook my head from side to side.

"Are you going to tell me what you are talking about?" my mother demanded.

"Brody. It was a long time ago. He was probably around eight years old at the time. Remember when he was obsessed with the Hardy Boys? He was constantly trying to manufacture mysteries so he could solve them."

Beatrice smiled at the memory but didn't say anything, so I continued. "He was always snooping around spying on us, hoping to catch a case. Well one, day when Daddy and Mindy were working together he hid in Dad's office. I don't remember where you were, but you weren't home. I knew what Brody was up to. I let him stay in there for about an hour, but after that I was worried he'd have to go to the bathroom or something, so I manufactured a problem. I knocked on his office door and told them I thought something was wrong with the dog."

"Good thinking. I always felt your father preferred the dog to everyone else in our house."

"I think you're right," I said with a small, sad smile. "Dad and Mindy came rushing out, which allowed Brody time to escape. They found George fast asleep curled up on the sofa in the living room. I lied and said a few minutes ago he was walking strangely. Well, that was all Daddy needed to hear. He was panicked. He nudged the dog to wake him up, strapped on his leash, and made a beeline for the front door with Mindy right behind him. As soon as they made it down the driveway, I rushed upstairs to find Brody. He was sitting on his bed, cross-legged, as pale as a ghost."

I paused to take a sip of my soda. "I asked him what was wrong. He said he saw something really bad, but he didn't want to tell me. I kept pestering him to spill it, and finally he told me he saw Daddy and Mindy kissing like they did on Dynasty."

"He said what?"

"Yeah, those were his exact words. I told him he had to be wrong. But he kept telling me he wasn't stupid and he knew what he saw. I didn't believe him. I honestly figured he was trying to create a situation so he could utilize his awesome investigative skills. I was so angry with him for lying. I made him swear never to say anything about it. He didn't want to, but after I told him how mad you'd be at him, he reluctantly agreed. And as far as I know he never mentioned it again."

"He certainly never said anything to me," Beatrice said before sighing deeply.

"I didn't think he would have. At first, he was so afraid of what you would do. Then when he got older, he probably realized how hurt you would be if you knew what he saw. He'd never be able to intentionally hurt you." Brody always was very in-tuned to our mother's feelings, much more so than me. I decided we'd probably be better off if I moved the conversation away from my brother and what he told me he saw. I asked, "Did you ever think of leaving Daddy?"

"Of course I did. But what would I do? What would everyone think, especially my father? I couldn't handle facing everyone and admitting my marriage was a failure, so I just pretended everything was okay. I was always pretty good at lying to myself anyway," my mom said with a small, sad chuckle. "Weekend after weekend Mindy would come over to *work* with your dad, and I'd invite her to stay for dinner because that is what he expected me to do. Mindy was very lucky we had Rosie doing the cooking. If I had to prepare the meals myself, I might not have been able to control myself from adding some special ingredients," Beatrice flashed an evil grin. "It's funny, I should have known better, but every time she accepted my invitation to dinner I was shocked she decided to stay. I can't imagine it was comfortable for her to sit opposite me at a table either. But then again, maybe she took pleasure in it. She probably thought I was such a fool, not that she was wrong, of course. I was idiotic and cowardly."

"Are you one hundred percent sure the affair happened? Couldn't you be wrong?" I asked, hopeful. I didn't want to believe the worst of my father. Having an affair was one thing. It was terrible, I know. But to add insult to injury, he involved his mistress in his children's lives and waved his relationship in my mother's face! It was inexcusable.

"Of course I could have been wrong. I kept telling myself that, day after day." My mother explained as she crumbled her paper napkin and tossed it in her barely touched salad bowl. "It's amazing if you try hard enough you can force yourself to believe your own lies. When your father died, however, there was no denying their relationship."

My mother reached into her bag and pulled out a red lipstick. Using her butter knife as a mirror, she applied the makeup. How she could be worried about her appearance at a time like this baffled me.

I pushed my salad bowl towards the center of the table. My appetite was completely gone. "I don't understand," I said, "What happened after Daddy died?"

"Suffice it to say your father didn't die the way I told you and Brody." Her words hung in the air as she caught the waitress's attention and asked for two glasses of pinot grigio.

As far as I knew, when I was away at college and my brother was spending the night at a friend's house, my dad was in Boston with Mindy, on a sales call. They had a late dinner scheduled with a prospective client. As soon as the appetizers were delivered to their table, my dad clutched his chest, keeled over and fell to the ground. He passed away from a massive heart attack right on the restaurant's floor.

"What do you mean Daddy didn't die the way you told us he did," I asked, as Amy dropped off the wine and cleared away our barely touched salads. "How could you have lied to us?" I asked quietly.

"I couldn't tell you and Brody the truth. I couldn't tell anyone the truth. It was just too," Beatrice stopped talking and stared up at the ceiling. I wasn't sure if she would go on or if she'd just clam up, never to reveal the truth. She sat silent for several moments. I was afraid to say anything, so I just remained quiet, my eyes glued to her.

When she returned her attention to me, tears were streaming down her face. I reached into my giant mommy bag and handed her a packet of tissues. She accepted them silently and removed one from the packet. She blotted her eyes first and then her face.

"Sorry," she said softly. "This is just so hard to say out loud, especially to you. I know how much you loved your father, and how much you looked up to him. But I really think you should know the truth."

"I need to know, Mom," I managed to say despite the fact I was choking on my own tears which I was desperately trying not to shed.

In a robotic voice, Beatrice continued, "Not everything was a lie. Your dad had a dinner meeting scheduled with a prospective client from Boston. That much was true. But instead of him and Mindy heading to Massachusetts to meet with the client as he told me, the client came to New York City. Your father and Mindy never made it to the restaurant, though. An hour before their reservation, your dad had a massive heart attack. He was having sex with Mindy at the time."

"No!" I exclaimed as I grabbed my stomach. I felt like someone sucker punched me.

"You heard me." My mother said as she stared straight into my eyes. With venom in her voice, she elaborated, "He died while he was fucking that slut."

My mouth hung open. No words came out. My heart was beating so fast, and my face felt flushed.

My mother had waited a moment before she continued. With sympathetic eyes, she said, "I know you can imagine how hard it is to receive a call telling you someone you care about has been hurt. Can you imagine what it was like to get a call from a hotel manager telling you he believed your husband passed away in one of their suites," she snickered? "I kept arguing with the poor guy, insisting he had to have dialed the wrong number. I was adamant my husband was in Boston and not on the upper east side of Manhattan. He must've thought me the fool."

Beatrice took a sip of her wine. "The manager was a patient man; that's for sure. I probably would have never continued the call if I was him. But he wasn't going to let me hang up. He kept on providing me with information about your father until I had no choice but to come to terms with the fact he was indeed telling me the truth. He wouldn't give me any details about what happened, but he did give me the name of the hospital where they brought your father."

My mother took a deep breath before continuing. I hung on her every word. "I don't know if you will believe it or not given what I just told you, but despite everything, I cared deeply for your father. In many ways, I loved him. I didn't give his lies a moment of thought. I just reacted. I rushed out to my car and drove to the city. My mind was racing as I tried to process everything."

My mother picked up her glass of wine but put it back down on the table without taking a sip. She seemed in a trance as she spoke. "I knew it was going to be bad. After all, if your dad were okay, the hotel manager wouldn't have told me he thought my husband was dead. I don't know how I got there so quickly, but I made it to the hospital in about a half hour. I threw my car keys at the valet attendant and ran into the emergency room. Mindy was there, pacing. She raced over to me and engulfed me in her arms. I hugged her back, in fact I clung to her." My mother started shaking her head at the memory.

In a soft voice, she continued. "Mindy whispered into my ear 'He's gone, Bea.' Then she started running her hands up and down my back in an attempt to try to soothe me. While she was holding me, she said, 'Don't worry, Beatrice I don't think he felt any pain.' She tried to comfort me, can you believe that?" My mother banged her fists on the table before she took a large gulp of white wine. I reached for my glass as well.

"It was a very strange moment, Annabel. It was completely surreal. For a moment or two, we held onto each other, our cries becoming one. We were both lost in memories of the man he was, the man that we both cared about. Then the realization hit me like a ton of bricks. I pulled away from her; I didn't want her embrace or her sympathy. In that instant, I noticed what she was wearing."

"Do I want to know?" I asked.

Beatrice shook her head. "Probably not, but I'm going to tell you anyway. She was wearing the skimpiest bathrobe I have ever seen in my entire life. And, to tell you the truth, I don't think she had anything on underneath it. If I had any doubts about your father, they instantly disappeared. As I stared at her half naked body, the pieces of the night quickly fell into place just as the puzzle that was my life instantly became crystal clear to me. I didn't utter another word to her. You have no idea how hard it was for me to control my tongue. I wanted to rip her to pieces. I wanted to curse and scream at the top of my lungs. But I didn't. Instead of vocalizing all the bitterness and anger I felt inside, I slapped her across the face with everything I had. She looked dumbfounded, but for the first time in a long time, I felt great. She stood there in shock clutching her face with her hands. She didn't utter a word either. Unable to handle the sight of her for one more second I found a nurse who compassionately confirmed my suspicions. At least Mindy was truthful with the hospital. She explicitly explained to them exactly what your father was doing at the time of his death..."

I reached across the table and grabbed her hands and squeezed them tightly. "Oh, mother I can't even imagine what you felt like. I'm sorry."

"Thanks, Darling." My mom held onto my hands for a moment, and then she continued her story. "Mindy came to the funeral. I expected she would show up, how could she not? Fortunately, she had enough brains to stay away from me. She didn't speak to me, which I was thankful for. She simply sat in the last row of the chapel with the rest of the people she and your father worked with. It was funny all these years everyone thought I married your dad for his money. The truth was he married me for my father's. Sure, your dad was successful, but without my father's connections, he never would have had his job in the first place. After the funeral, I went to his office to pick up his personal belongings. I filled his boss, my father's longtime friend, in on Mindy's extracurricular activities. Needless to say, Mindy didn't remain at the firm long after. I heard she moved to California where she had some relatives. I haven't seen her since the funeral."

I chewed on my bottom lip. I wasn't sure what do. But my mother was being honest with me; I felt I owed it to her to be honest as well. I took another sip of wine. "She did move to California, but she only stayed there for about nine months. She met a man at a work conference who lived in Seattle. A long-distance relationship wasn't working for her, so she moved there to be with him. They were married about a year later, and they adopted two little girls from China."

"How do you know this?" my mother asked. She looked so hurt.

"I stayed in contact with her. She was always so nice to me." A tear trickled down my face. "I'm sorry. I thought she was my friend. I had no idea she did what she did. Oh God, I wish you would have told me this before."

CHAPTER ELEVEN

Monday **mornings** were always the worst. No matter how hard I tried I was never able to get Violet moving, which was pretty ironic considering how much my child loved school. In fact at the beginning of the school year, she requested to sit directly in front of her teacher. When I went to the first parent teacher conference of the year I feared she was sitting there because she did something wrong. I never expected it was her choice.

Without fail, week after week, I barely had enough time to scrape together lunches for everyone. I usually managed to end up with some kitchen related injury. Today I sliced my thumb when I put the knife I used to cut celery and carrots in the dishwasher. Leave it to me to hurt myself while not actually using the knife. I always vowed to plan better the following Sunday, but I never did. I could never bring myself to get a head start on the week.

Today was no different. I had no idea how, but I somehow managed to get both my children to school on time. I on the other hand was late for work, as usual. I was lucky though. I've been working at the same company since right before I graduated college. I started as a marketing intern and now supervise a team of five. My boss is the most understanding and supportive woman imaginable, probably because she has four grown children of her own, so she understands my struggles as a working mother. Despite, or maybe because of, her sympathetic nature I always felt guilty every time I arrived late.

"Finally! You're here," Cecelia said as she stood outside my office door.

"Very funny. I actually have been here," I paused and looked at the gold bracelet watch that I was wearing, "a whole fifteen minutes."

"Then my timing is perfect. You need a break." She announced.

I rolled my eyes.

"Oh, come on. Don't be so serious, Annabel. Besides, I've got muffins!" She dangled a bag from the bakery down the street. The smell of fresh blueberries filled the air.

"Well in that case, why are you still standing in the doorway?" I asked, as my stomach growled.

Cecelia closed the door behind her as I shuffled the many manila folders on my desk to the side to make room for her to sit and eat. While my desk always looked like a war zone, I knew exactly where everything was, well most of the time.

"Did you happen to see the email from McGrevor yet?" She asked, concerned.

John McGrevor was one of our newest and most difficult clients. He was the managing partner in a mid-sized CPA firm that was founded by his grandfather. He hired my company to help him modernize the image of the company, which currently screamed 1942. My team and I were working on his branding. We were trying to create a new logo for them as well as come up with some catchy tag lines for him to use in his brochures and business cards. We were striving to create something that would bring the firm's history into the present day. Cecelia and her group were working on launching a website for the firm, as well as helping them create a blog so he could update his clients on new tax trends. Practically our entire company was involved in some manner, shape, or form with the account, and he had been horrible to every person he has come in contact with. When we sent our staff photographer to his office to take photos for the website he had the poor girl in tears. She was so traumatized by his belittling she missed an entire week of work. I was positive she was going to quit as a result.

"No. I didn't get to check my emails from home this morning," I said as I pushed my muffin to the side and wiggled my mouse to remove my screen saver.

"If you didn't see it yet, it can wait a few minutes. Come on. Don't let him spoil your appetite. Eat your muffin first. Then we can deal with him."

I was dying to see what McGrevor's issue was this time, but I also wanted to put off the inevitable just a little longer. I had sent him some logo mockups over the weekend and what I was able to gather from Cecelia was that he wasn't happy with them. I was disappointed because I really liked some of them. My personal favorite was, *For decades you take the credits and we process the debits.*

"Well if you insist." I smiled and picked at the bottom of my muffin. I always ate the bottom first, saving the top for last.

"So, I've been dying to know. Did you call Mindy?"

I had been debating on whether or not to reach out to her. Connie and Cole had been trying to convince me not to call. Cecelia on the other hand practically dialed the phone for me several times last week.

I bit my lip. "Yeah. I called her yesterday morning."

"And?"

"Cee, it was awful!" I ran my fingers through my hair. "She sounded so happy to speak to me. She was asking all about the kids and told me about the trip she and her husband just took to Mexico. After about fifteen minutes of small talk, I told her that my mother finally told me the truth. I asked her point blank how she could have had an affair with my father, parading herself around my house, pretending to be my and my brother's friend."

"What did she say?"

"She laughed," I said as I brushed some muffin crumbs off my desk.

"You're joking?"

"No, she laughed and then she asked me why I was acting like she did something wrong."

"She did not!" Cecelia sounded outraged.

"Oh yes, she did. Then she had the audacity to say she was proud of everything she did. She said that my father was the love of her life, and she was more of a partner to him than my mother ever was. She also said Brody and I were lucky to have had her in our lives. And then, if all that wasn't bad enough, she said if she had her life to live over she wouldn't change a thing."

"Wow," Cecelia shook her head in disbelief.

"But you know what hurt me the most?" I asked as I nervously twirled a strand of hair.

"No."

"She said that she was positive Bea told me about the affair years ago. And when I kept in contact with her she just assumed I felt the same way. She thought I would have been happy my dad had her to love him. How could she think I would ever feel that way? My mother is far from perfect, but how could I want someone to hurt her? How can she think I was so cruel? Do you think I would have felt that way, given everything?"

"Oh, Sweetie. Don't go there, and don't let her get to you. She's just trying to rationalize her actions."

I gave her a closed mouth smile. "I know. But I still feel

guilty. Anyway, that's enough about me, how was your weekend?"

Cecelia smiled, "Well, now that you've asked, you'll never believe—"

She was cut off by the sound of my ringing cell phone. I quickly reached for it fearing it was the kid's school. Fortunately, it wasn't.

"Do you need to take the call?"

"No, it can wait," I replied as I clicked ignore and tossed my phone back on my desk. "Go on."

"Okay. I'm not sure if I mentioned it, my sister has been pretty bummed out lately. Even though she was the one who broke up with Gary, she has been second guessing her decision ever since they split."

"How long were they together again?" I asked.

"Um... Nine months maybe more. I'm not really sure. She's hard to keep up with. I don't think she misses him that much, actually. They were totally wrong for each other, and she knew it. But she hates to be alone. I think this may be the first time she ended a relationship without having someone waiting in the wings."

"Oh, she is one of those," I said with a smile.

Before Cecelia married her husband she was never without a man in her life, even though most of her relationships were over before they started. I liked to credit her marriage to my awesome matchmaking skills. Even though Bryce was the fourth friend of Cole's I had set her up with, I didn't think I could take credit for the nuptials.

I was actually shocked when she came into work, four years ago, sporting an engagement ring. I never expected their relationship to have lasted. I figured, like all the men who came before him, she'd date him a couple of months before finding a fatal flaw, then end the relationship. I hated to admit it, but I always wondered what was different about him that made her want to get married. I really hoped she fell madly in love with him, but I always have wondered if she was just tired of being alone.

Catching my innuendo, Cecelia picked up a paperclip on my desk and tossed it at me. "Yeah, smart ass. It must run in my family. And, do I need to point out you're not one to talk either, big shot. If I recall correctly, didn't you tell me you kept Cole at arm's length while you were deciding if you should give him a chance because you were afraid to risk losing some safe but jerky guy? What was his name? Oh yeah, Mitch?"

"Point taken," I said.

"So as I was saying," Cecelia continued. "My sister has been down in the dumps, so I decided to leave Bryce home with the twins and take her out for a night on the town."

Once again my cell phone rang. After a quick glance at the caller ID, I hit the ignore button again.

Cecelia barely paused and kept talking; "We went to this cute little bar on the upper west side. Oh my God, they had the most amazing lychee martinis! And you will never guess who was there!"

"Who?"

"Remember that girl, Christy?" Cecelia asked as she popped a piece of muffin into her mouth.

"The out of control flirt who worked here about two years ago?"

Cecelia nodded her head slowly.

Memories came flooding back to me as I said, "Yes! She was assigned to the Dawson account and wouldn't leave poor Tim alone. Remember she drove him crazy? He complained about her constantly barging into his office and interrupting him, calling him all hours of the day and night with silly questions. I think he also said he felt like she was following him. Then the next thing I knew she was fired."

"That's what we thought," Cecelia clarified. "But I think we got the story completely wrong. Tim Dawson was with her and guess what. They're married."

"Shut up!"

Before Cecelia could reply my intercom sounded. "Excuse me, Annabel," Mary, the receptionist, announced. "Your mother is on the line, and she says it's an emergency. Shall I put her through?"

"Yes," I replied and sighed.

"I'll give you some privacy," Cecelia said, as she looked concerned.

"No, don't go."

Once Mary transferred the call I answered the phone on the first ring.

"Annabel, I keep calling you on your cell phone, and you're not answering it," Beatrice said in a scolding tone.

"I know Mother. I'm in a meeting and couldn't. Is everything okay?"

"Really, Annabel. What is the point of having a mobile phone if you refuse to answer it."

"Like I said Mother, I'm at work and in a meeting. I can't always answer my phone. What's the matter anyway? Mary said it was an emergency."

"It is!" She exclaimed with glee. "Walter and I need to pick a song for our first dance, and I don't know what to choose. What do you think?"

"Are you kidding me?" I asked as I rubbed my face. Cecelia stared at me and looked worried. "Selecting a wedding song is your emergency?"

Cecelia snorted out loud.

"Yes, Annabel. This is a serious issue. I've no idea what song I should pick. It's extremely troubling." As my mother attempted to rationalize her actions, I opened the McGrevor email and skimmed it.

Anna,

The tag lines you submitted were an embarrassment. What is wrong with you that you possibly thought I would use something like that to represent my company? Seriously, my sixth grade daughter could have come up with something better than our strength + your numbers = decades of success. Call me before noon.

JM

HIS HARSH WORDS caused my heart to beat fast and my face to turn red.

"Mother. I can't have this conversation with you right now. I told you, I am in a meeting. I'll have to call you back."

"When?" She asked disappointedly.

"I don't know. When I can. Most likely tonight when I get home from work and after I put the kids to sleep."

"Annabel, that is simply not acceptable."

"What do you mean?"

"We need to discuss this now. I need to get this resolved."

I took a deep breath. "I told you I can't talk now. We have a very angry client on our hands. We have damage control to do. Besides, I don't understand what the rush is."

Cecelia watched me intently for a few moments before she got up from her seat. "I'm going," she whispered. "Buzz me when you're done."

"Annabel, if your client is already angry another couple of minutes won't make much of a difference, now will it," My mother, the stellar businesswoman, asked?

I put my head on my desk. I knew there would be no way I would be able to deal with McGrevor until I first dealt with Beatrice.

"Fine," I said completely irritated that my mother wouldn't let this go.

"Great!" She exclaimed, clearly not picking up on my tone. "I knew I could count on you. I have breakfast with the girls

and then this afternoon Walter and I have a dance lesson to go
to. We need to have our song all picked out so we can coordi-
nate our moves. I didn't think I'd be able to convince Walter to
take the lesson, but I made him an offer he couldn't refuse if
you know what I mean." She chuckled and I tossed the
remnants of my muffin into my trash. There went my appetite.

"I'm confused," I said. "I thought you said Walter was an
excellent dancer. Didn't you spend your first night with him
dancing into the wee hours of the morning?"

"Yes, sweetie. We did. But dancing alone on a cruise ship
isn't the same thing as having a first dance in front of three
hundred and fifty of our closest friends and family. I need this
wedding to be perfect, and I can't risk us clumsily moving
around to the music while everyone stands by, silently judging
us. But that's enough about the lesson, I don't want to waste
your time, you are at work, after all. Let's just stick to the matter
at hand. If you were picking a song which one would you
select?"

I thought of the song I would have chosen if Cole and I had
a big wedding instead of eloping. "I always liked 'In Your Eyes'
by Peter Gabriel."

"Oh Annabel, please be serious," Beatrice scolded.

"I was," I answered as I wondered what she found so offen-
sive about my choice.

"Well, that song won't work for me. What other ideas do
you have?"

"What about James Taylor's 'How Sweet It Is to Be Loved By
You.' It's a great song everybody loves."

"True, but it is a little fast, don't you think?"

"Not really," I replied as I googled first dance wedding songs
and prayed for a winner. "How about 'Here and Now' is that
more your style?"

"Hmm, you're probably getting closer. But I'm not sure. Do
you have any other ideas?"

I started to tap my fingers on my desk as my patience level deteriorated. "I'm getting a strange feeling, Mother, we can debate songs all day long. And I don't have all day. Did you ask Walter what song he wanted? Don't you think his opinion matters more than mine?"

"You may have a point. He likes Ella James's 'At Last,' what do you think of that one?"

"I think it's perfect. Yes! You should go with it. Enjoy your dance lesson. I've got to go." Today was sure off to a stellar start. I hung up the phone and turned my full attention to Mr. Picky Pants, the man who would never be pleased.

CHAPTER TWELVE

"Hey guys. I'm home!" I called out as I kicked off my boots and left them by the front door. I had spent the day with my mother, and I was really looking forward to spending some quality time with my family. Too bad only Lila greeted me. I bent down to pick her up. I carried her with me. I gently stroked her head, as I walked into the den where my kids were engrossed in a movie. I kissed them hello and then headed into the kitchen in hopes of finding Cole.

He was ending a telephone conversation, and his mouth was set in a firm line. He barely made eye contact with me as I entered the room. I went over to where he sat and kissed the top of his head before I opened the refrigerator and pulled out a bottle of water.

I took a long sip as Cole put his cell phone down and rubbed his forehead. I sat down next to him. "You wouldn't believe the afternoon I had," I wasn't sure if I had Cole's full attention, but I continued speaking anyway. "When my mother asked me to go to the club to go over food options for the wedding, I expected we'd look at a menu or two, make a few selections and then move on. But no! That didn't happen. We had to taste samples of everything. Of course, she's on a diet, so she made me do all of the tastings and then describe everything I ate in painful detail. I sampled so much my stomach is killing me."

"Hmm," he muttered. He was facing me, but not really looking at me.

"And if that wasn't bad enough, we then spent over an hour and a half selecting tablecloths and napkins. I don't understand all the fuss. I mean really! Who's even going to notice the linens?"

"Hmm."

"But here is the crazy part," I poked him for emphasis. "You're never going to believe this. She is making the whole wait staff get fitted for special tuxedos. Isn't it the craziest thing you have ever heard of?"

"What?" Cole asked sounding annoyed.

"Have you not been listening to me?" I asked as I smirked. I really couldn't blame him for tuning me out. Most of my outings with my mother were agonizing. I could understand him not being fascinated with the play by play of my day, although he did usually humor me.

"Actually, Anna, no, I haven't been. I hate to break it to you, but there are other issues in the world besides your mother and her wedding."

"Whoa," I sat up straight in my chair. "What's wrong with you? Why are you so angry? I thought you were okay with me helping her."

"Yes. I'm fine with you helping her. I've told you a thousand times I was, didn't I?"

"Yeah. So then why are you acting this way?"

He pointed to his phone that was laying on the table. "I just got off the phone with Nicholas. He wanted to give me, and all the directors for that matter, an advanced warning. He signed the papers this afternoon. He sold the firm to Eastridge." Cole ran his fingers through his black hair. "The acquisition went through."

"Well, you kind of knew it was going to happen," I said softly as I grasped his arm.

"Yeah. I did." He muttered as he moved his arm away. "Although, I really did think he was having a change of heart. It probably was just wishful thinking on my part. I was counting on him changing his mind." He banged his fist on the table. "In the end, he just couldn't turn down the money they offered him; not that I can blame him. He's going to stay on for two years to help with the transition."

"That's good," I said enthusiastically.

"Yeah, good for him."

"What do you mean? Why are you so upset?"

"You don't get it, do you?" Cole glared at me.

I was afraid to say anything. He was not acting like himself.

"Chances are I am going to lose my job."

"But why? Nicholas is still there; you just said so."

"Anna, Nicholas isn't going to have any say in the company's direction come Monday. He's just going to be there to help with the transition. Eastridge is huge. They have a team of project directors across all channels. Hell, their retail division has one hundred people in it alone. They won't need me."

I tilted my head to the side. "Don't you think you are over-reacting?"

"No. When companies are acquired people are made redundant and they lose their jobs. Those people are usually managers like me. Nicholas so much as told me the next few months are going to be extremely difficult for everyone. There are going to be a lot of changes. He said he doesn't know what Eastridge's plans are exactly, but all of us directors should plan for the worst."

"Okay. So you'll brush up on your resume," I said noncha-lantly as I took another sip of water.

"You just don't get it, do you? With the changes in the industry, and Eastridge snatching up all the mid-sized architectural firms, my position will be practically impossible to find. I'm going to have to start over, from the bottom up."

"Well, you always loved drawing. You always say you miss it," I tried to comfort him.

"Yeah. I miss it, but I don't miss the salary!" he yelled. Then he slowly walked to the window.

I walked over to him and rubbed his back. I chuckled. "You're upset about money? Come on Cole. You know we have nothing to worry about. We have the money my grandfather left me."

Cole spun around so fast. His eyes were full of rage. "You know how I feel about that money, Annabel. It's wonderful you have it, but I don't want to live off of it. I refused to accept money from you when I was paying off my student loans. We didn't touch a penny when we bought this house. And I am certainly not going to take a cent of it now to survive on when I lose my job."

"Cole, I didn't mean—"

He cut me off. "I know you didn't mean anything, Anna. But you just don't get it. You've had everything handed to you your entire life. Rather than appreciate it and being thankful for what you have, you dwell on what didn't go your way. You've gone through a lot of difficult situations, trust me I know that better than anyone else. But come on. Who hasn't? So many people have had it far worse than you, and I don't think you even realize it."

"Cole," I said as tears streamed down my face. "I—"

He didn't give me a chance to speak. "You know what, Anna. I think I've already said enough."

"But..." I reached for his arms, but he pushed me away.

"I've got to go talk to my dad about the acquisition and the layoffs. He understands what I'm feeling. I'm taking the kids with me."

"Wait. I'll come too," I said as my voice cracked.

"No. I think it is best if you don't. I think some time alone may do us both some good." As he walked out of the kitchen, he yelled out, "Violet, Harley. Get your coats. We are going to Grandma and Grandpa's house."

My children squealed in delight while I was left sobbing at my kitchen counter. I wondered what the hell just happened.

CHAPTER THIRTEEN

"**I 've got wine,**" I announced as Cecelia opened her front door. I had called her about twenty minutes after Cole stormed out of the house. Part of me wanted just to curl up and cry on my couch, but the bigger part of me didn't want to be alone. I needed to talk to someone. I was thrilled she and her husband didn't have any plans tonight.

My friend gave me a small smile as I stepped inside her home. "From the looks of it, you could use something stronger." She then pulled a bottle of tequila out from behind her back.

I followed her to her kitchen and placed the bottle of wine I brought on her counter as she filled two glasses with ice. "I sent Bryce out to the park and told him to take the twins out to dinner afterward. This way we'll have some alone time."

I sat down at her table. "I'm sorry."

"Don't be. I'd rather have a girl's night anytime. Even though the boys are only two, there's already too much testosterone in this house. Oh, and I ordered a pepperoni pizza too. The delivery guy should be here in about an hour." She stated as she squeezed a little lime in both of the glasses.

"Thanks," I muttered, even though I didn't have much of an appetite.

She poured a generous helping of tequila and handed me a tumbler. "Come on. So you had a fight with Cole. Big deal. I'm sure it wasn't the first one you two have had."

"Of course it's not." I sighed. "But he has never stormed out of the house like this before. He was so angry at me."

Cecelia raised her glass and held it out to me. I unenthusiastically clinked it with hers, and we both took a sip, well I took more of a gulp.

"Tell me everything that happened," she urged.

By the time I finished my story the pizza was already delivered, and we were working on our second glass of tequila.

"Cee, so what do you think?" I asked as I picked off a piece of pepperoni from my slice and popped it in my mouth.

"Truth?" she asked as she put her long red hair into a ponytail.

"Yes. Of course." I didn't expect anything less from her. She tended to be pretty blunt most of the time. Unlike me, she never feared to speak her mind.

She took a sip of her drink. It seemed like she was stalling.

"Anna, I love you, you know that. But I think he has a point."

"What?" I asked as I put my pizza down.

"Think about it. You get home, and you can see he is clearly troubled by something. Since when does he basically not acknowledge you when you walk into a room? Hell, the guy idolizes you. But tonight, he clearly had other things on his mind. You didn't pay any attention to his mood. You didn't question who he was on the phone with, or even ask if he was okay, did you?"

I bit my lip and shook my head no.

"You just launched into another Beatrice Buchanan ties the knot tale. Which, is fine, I guess. But it would have been nice if you showed him some interest, some concern."

"I was trying to entertain him, make him laugh. My mother

was so over the top today." I smirked as I tried to defend my actions.

"Come on, Anna. It's me you are talking to, remember? Did you really think he was going to crack up over hors d'oeuvres and table cloths?" She arched her eyebrow, and I looked away. She poked me in the arm. "You just wanted to vent to him because your mother annoyed you, yet again. Isn't that right?"

I took another gulp of my drink, emptying it. "She was so irritating today," I whined.

"Yes, I know, Anna. She is always grating on your last nerve, but yet, for the last month or so you are right there at her side whenever she calls you."

"I promised I would help her," I tried to defend myself.

"Yeah, I know you did. But what really was your motive? Are you really trying to help her or are you just looking for more ways to find fault with her? Sometimes I wonder if you egg her on so that you have something to complain about."

Her words stung. "What are you talking about?" I asked as I pushed my slice of pizza away.

"Listen, Anna. You and I are very different people. You wear your heart on your sleeve. You discuss your feelings and emotions easily. I don't. I keep things bottled up. I don't talk about my past, nor do I share my worries and fears with others, not even with Bryce for the most part. You're the opposite. And I admire you for your openness and honesty. But sometimes you take it too far."

"What do you mean?"

She leaned over and reached for the bottle of tequila and poured some into her glass. "More?"

"Nah. I won't be able to drive home."

She rolled her eyes. "You're not driving home as it is. You'll sleep over or Bryce will drive you home. Your choice."

"He won't mind?"

She glared at me and shook her head. "Mind an opportunity to drive his midlife crisis? I don't think so," she joked.

"Um, I think I should go home tonight, I don't want to make things worse," I answered as I held out my glass for her to fill up.

"Good choice. Okay, where was I? Oh yeah, taking it too far." She took another sip of her drink. "I'm going to be blunt, so don't go getting mad at me. You know I love you, and I want to help. Okay?"

I bit my lip and fought back tears, "Okay."

"We've known each other for about ten years, and for that entire time you've complained about your mother. A lot. You're always bitching about how she hurt you and how she makes you feel inferior. And from everything you've told me, I understand completely why you feel like you do. Honestly, if I were you, I don't think I would be able to have any kind of relationship with her. I would have made peace with the situation and moved on with my life severing all interaction with her. You, on the other hand, are the opposite. You are constantly trying to keep the relationship alive. You talk to her on the phone every week like clockwork. You're always seeking her approval. You do everything she wants you to do whenever she wants it done. She walks all over you, and you let her. You never stand up to her, and you never tell her how you feel. It's almost like you want her to treat you the way she does."

"You're crazy."

"No, I'm not. Hear me out. You have allowed the way she treated you to define you. You have made yourself out to be the poor little girl whose mother doesn't love her. There is way more to you than that!"

"I know..." I sniffed.

"You say you do, but I am not so sure." She grabbed my arm and squeezed it. "You dwell on your relationship with her rather than focusing on the fact you have a husband who would do anything for you. You downplay that your mother-in-law is made out of gold. Seriously, by the way, most of the civilized world including me would kill for a mother-in-law like her. You also have two beautiful children, a lovely home, an amazing job, and of course the most perfect best friend in the world." She chuckled. "Seriously, Anna, I don't think you realize how lucky you are. So you have a cold mother who has a cruel streak. Big fucking deal. You have everything else going for you. You've lived a charmed life, my friend. A life most people would be jealous of."

I buried my head in my hands and cried because I knew she was right.

"Look at me," she commanded. "I'm not done yet."

I slowly raised my head and met her gaze. "There's more?" I asked as I reached for my glass of tequila. "Remind me again why I came over tonight. I thought you were supposed to make me feel better."

"No," Cecelia patted my leg. "I'm here to help you not pacify you."

"Placating would be nice though," I joked.

"Yes, but it wouldn't accomplish anything" Cecelia pulled another slice of pizza out of the box and put it on her plate. "I don't know your mother. I think I met her once or twice, but I don't think I've ever had a conversation with her. My opinion on the woman is based solely on what you have said to me. So don't go getting offended by what I am about to say. She's selfish and unforgiving, isn't that right?"

I didn't answer right away. I felt bad to speak the truth. She was still my mother after all. Why is it we could complain easily about people important in our lives, yet we get offended when others voice the same opinion of them?

"Yes," I whispered.

"Again, Anna, I'm not trying to hurt you. I'm trying to help you." She studied my face. "You have a lot of those very same traits. I just don't think you see it." She took a bite of pizza and chewed slowly as she allowed me to digest her words. "You were incredibly selfish and insensitive tonight. You wanted Cole's support for your difficult day, yet he was faced with a major issue, and you blew it off like it was insignificant. You know how much his career matters to him. And you also know his pride is huge; he hates having to accept help from anyone, including you. What do you do? You brush off his concern about losing the job he loves, the job he worked so hard for. And then, if that's not bad enough, you throw the money your grandfather left you in his face? How do you think you made him feel?"

"I was trying to make him feel better. I didn't want him to worry about money."

"I am sure you meant well, after all, I know how much you love him. But Anna, you insulted him."

I rubbed my eyes. "I didn't mean to."

"I know that, Sweetie. I'm sure as soon as he cools down he will realize it too."

CHAPTER FOURTEEN

"Violet! Come on! We have to go, NOW!" I screamed from the bottom of the staircase as I tossed my cell phone into my pocketbook.

Cole walked over to where I waited and wrapped his arms around my waist and pulled me towards him for a small kiss. It had been a rough week.

I was pleasantly surprised by how calm Cole was when Bryce drove me home last Saturday night. But then again, I was numbed by tequila. I apologized for my actions, and I told him all about the conversation I had with Cecelia. He didn't admit it right away, but after some prodding, he agreed with her assessment. The truth really hurts, especially when you begin to see characteristics you hate in someone else creep their way into your own personality.

I knew whatever advice his dad gave him helped. It hurt that he found the need to go to his father for comfort instead of me.

The new owners met with all the directors this past Wednesday and then the full-staff on Thursday. Apparently, they were going to begin reviewing everyone's roles in order to find where cuts needed to be made. Most likely it would be

months before any changes would take place, although two
senior directors announced their early retirement on Friday.
The uncertainty was making Cole very nervous, but he was
trying not to let it consume him, which I really admired.
Although I did worry he was simply putting on a brave face for
my benefit.

"You'd think she'd be excited to look at dresses," Cole said.
"After all, she is your daughter."

"Hey, I am not that bad," I said with an innocent smile.

Cole cocked his head to the side and raised his eyebrow.

"Fine. I do have a lot of clothes, but it's only because I want
to look beautiful for my husband at all times."

"Oh, that's what it is?" He asked as he swatted me on my
rear end.

"Yes. As a matter of fact, it is. What other reason could it
possibly be?" I giggled. I took a deep breath and yelled for my
daughter once again. "VIOLET come on, TODAY!"

Turning back to Cole I said, "If it were just the two of us
we'd be at the store already. I made the mistake of telling her
we were meeting my mother. I don't think she is looking
forward to a shopping trip with Beatrice." I laughed nervously.

"Can you blame her?" Cole asked as Violet finally appeared
at the top of the staircase.

"I guess not," I answered honestly. "But Cole, I feel bad."

"About what?"

"Even though weeks have passed since she told me, I can't
stop thinking about my dad and Mindy. I can't believe she had
to live like that, for so many years. I don't know. There was
something about her opening up to me. It was almost like her
confession humanized her. I think for once I saw her as the
person that she is instead of just the woman she always
pretends to be."

"Meaning?"

"A few weeks ago when I went over to her house, Walter

made a comment about her hiding behind her makeup. Do you think it's possible that she isn't as cold as she lets on?"

"I guess anything is possible, but if she's been acting all these years she definitely deserves an award." He snickered as Violet finally began to meander down the stairs dragging her feet like she was marching to her own execution.

"Yeah, I guess. But I still can't imagine how she survived all those years knowing what she knew. And I can't believe how cruel and inconsiderate my father was to her. The more I think about it, the angrier I get at him."

Cole opened his mouth to speak, but Violet didn't give him a chance. "It's not fair, Daddy! Why do you and Harley get to spend the day with Wally while Mommy and I have to be with Grandma Bea? Wally is so much more fun," she whined as she zipped up her jacket.

"Boys need tuxedos, Sweetie, and girls need dresses. Your brother and I would look very funny in dresses, don't you think?"

"Yeah, but I'd look great in a tuxedo," Violet confidently stated pulling at the collar of her jacket. "Can't I go with you and get a tuxedo instead? Please?"

"Like your mom, you'd look great in anything," Cole said as he patted her head. "But you're the flower girl. Flower girls can't wear tuxedos. They need dresses."

"I don't want to be the stupid flower girl anyway," she said with a pout.

"Sorry, munchkin, but you've got to be. You love dressing up. Try to make the best of it, okay?"

"Fine," she answered reluctantly. "I'll go with Mommy, but for the record, I am not happy about it." Slowly she opened the front door and walked to my car with her head cast down.

As I pulled out of the driveway, I smiled at my daughter and said, "So you never told me about Stacey's birthday party. Did Jamie end up going?" Violet had slept over her friend's house last night after the party and Cole picked her up a few hours ago while I was at the park with Harley, so I didn't get to talk to her yet.

"Yes," Violet answered, quietly.

I smiled. "So they made up after all?"

"Yeah." She mumbled.

For the past few weeks, Violet has been talking none stop about a huge fight her two best friends had. Jamie had accused Stacey of stealing her birthday party idea. According to my daughter, Stacey swore she didn't know anything about Jamie wanting a spa party when she arranged for all of her friends to go to a local salon for manicures, pedicures, facials, and a massage. Violet couldn't wait for the birthday party to see if Jamie would end up coming, especially since Jamie vowed she wasn't going to. Violet feared if Jamie didn't show up, Stacey would never forgive her. Violet kept on coming up with scenarios as to who, if either, would apologize first and how.

"So what ended up happening?" I was seriously dying to know.

"They. Made. Up."

"Yes, you said that already. But what happened?" I glanced over at her and grinned. "Come on, Violet. Don't hold out on me now. I need details."

"I don't want to talk, Mommy. I just want to get to the store and get this dress shopping over with." Violet then reached over and turned the volume up on the radio. She turned her head away from me and stared out the passenger window.

I unsuccessfully tried to make conversation again, before finally giving into my daughter's request for silence. My mind raced as I drove. It broke my heart that my little girl dreaded spending time with my mother. This wasn't the way it should be! As soon as I felt myself letting go of some of the anger I had towards my mother something happened to make the pain begin again.

I hated the way I've been feeling. I've been on an emotional roller coaster for weeks. One minute I felt horrible for not being forgiving enough towards my mother. But then, just as I decided I should cut her some slack, I was painfully reminded that she was the one who caused the rift in our relationship.

"We're here," I announced cheerfully as I parked the car right in front of the shop where we were meeting Bea. I put two dollars' worth of quarters in the parking meter while Violet made her way out of the car. I swear if she moved any slower, she'd be going in reverse.

As soon as I opened the heavy wood door and glanced around at the numerous racks, I realized the store was one hundred percent Beatrice. While I didn't spot my mother right away, I noticed all her best friends were present and accounted for—Coco Chanel, Roberto Cavalli, Donatella Versace, Christian Dior, Yves Saint Laurent, and Giorgio Armani, just to name a few.

"Violet, there she is," I said as I pointed to my mother who was sitting in the center of the store on a small hot pink couch. She held a small bottle of San Pellegrino with a straw as she talked to a saleswoman.

My daughter glared at me but walked over to my mother. "Hi Violet," Beatrice said as she patted the couch. "Have a seat, are you ready to pick out a dress for my big day?"

"I guess so," Violet said with a shrug as she sat down.

"Oh, come on. This will be fun. What little girl doesn't love dresses? Your mom always loved to get dressed up when she was your age." Turning to me, she said, "I got here early and already picked out my dress! I can't believe how easy it was. They had exactly what I was looking for. Sophia, be a plum and show my daughter what I picked out, would you?"

A gorgeous girl, with straight platinum blond hair down to her lower back, came up to us looking like she belonged on a runway instead of working retail. She grabbed a garment bag and removed a stunning cream-colored beaded Chanel dress. It was simple but extremely elegant.

"Wow, Mother, the dress is beautiful."

"I know. And I look amazing in it. It was as if it was made just for me, darling! I know Walter will love it. Let me go try it on for you, so that you can see for yourselves. While I'm dressing why don't you and Violet start looking around. Maybe you can figure out what you would like to wear."

"I don't understand. What are we looking for?" I asked. I fully expected my mother to give us a very clear and precise description of what was acceptable for her big day.

"Anything you like! You're the ones wearing them not me. You both can pick the style and the color you like. You won't hear me say this very often Violet, but this time anything goes." With that, she got up and walked away.

"Did someone switch bodies with Grandma?" Violet asked. "She is acting very strange today."

"You got me. But let's not question it. Let's take advantage of it!" I pointed to the back of the store. "The girl's dresses are over there. Why don't you pick out a few you like, and I will do the same."

Once turned loose, Violet was in her element. By the time my mother emerged from the dressing room Violet had ten dresses in her arms. "Wow, you look pretty, Grandma," Violet said as she struggled to hold onto the dresses while looking my mother up and down. "You sparkle and shine. You're dazzling!"

"Thanks, Sweetie. It looks like you have found some dresses you like as well. Let me see what you've got there." My mom took the dresses away from Violet and held each and every one up as she nodded her head. "You picked some great ones here." My mother handed the dresses to the saleswoman. "Start a room for my granddaughter, please." Returning her attention to me, she asked, "How are you making out Annabel?"

"I'm still looking."

"Okay, you keep at it. Violet, how about I help you try on the dresses while your mom continues to look around?"

I expected Violet to hesitate but instead she replied "sure" and followed my mother into a dressing room. Cole was right. She was so my daughter, and there was nothing retail therapy couldn't fix.

The store was small and intimate so as I milled around I was easily able to hear chatter and giggles coming from the dressing room where Violet was trying on dresses.

I handed the five dresses I selected to the saleswoman so she could set me up in a dressing room of my own. Before going in to try them on I wanted to check on Violet's progress. "How's it going in there?" I asked as I stood right outside their door.

"Great!" Violet and my mother answered in unison.

"Can I see?"

"Not yet!" Violet answered as she cracked open the door sticking just her head out. "We are narrowing it down. You'll see our favorite ones. What did you get?"

"Two can play this game. You'll only see my favorite ones too," I answered as I headed into my own dressing room. I tried on dresses as my daughter and mother continued to laugh. The sound was like music to my ears. I had no difficulty picking out my favorite. It was one shoulder, A-line dress in a beautiful shade of wine. It was form fitting around my waist but had a long flared bottom, which reached my ankles.

"I'm ready!" I said as I emerged from the dressing room.

My mom was once again sitting on the sofa in the center of the store sipping her drink. "Annabel, you look beautiful. Twirl around for me, would you?" she ordered.

I did as instructed. "You approve, Mother?"

"Most definitely! It is perfect for you. Just let Sophia check it out to see if any alterations are needed."

Sophia measured every single aspect of the dress. She strategically placed pins where she felt improvements were needed. Personally, I felt the dress fit wonderfully as it was, but I knew better than to argue. After all, Beatrice always strived for perfection.

"Can I come out yet?" Violet asked as she once again poked her head out of the dressing room.

"In a second," Beatrice instructed as she stood up and walked over to Violet's dressing room door. Turning to me she said, "I know that we said we'd show you our favorites, but like you, we found the perfect dress. Without further ado, I introduce the one, the only, the most beautiful Violet."

My mother opened the door, and Violet emerged glowing. Imitating a runway model she strutted her stuff. She walked a few feet away from my mom. Then she stopped, put her hand on her hip, spun around in a circle, paused again and marched back to where my mother stood. Clearly, they planned this routine. She looked amazing, just like a princess. The dress was pale pink. It was sleeveless with a round neck, the bodice was sequined, and it had a tulle-overlaid skirt.

"You sure did find the perfect dress!" I exclaimed. "Violet you look gorgeous!"

"You don't look too shabby yourself, Mommy."

With that, Sophia took her pins to where my daughter stood and focused her attention on Violet's dress. I put my clothes back on and then sat down on the couch next to my mother as I waited for Violet to finish up.

"It was great seeing you two having so much fun together."

"I know! I've always gotten a kick out of her. But today... Annabel, I had a blast. She's such a wonderful girl, and so funny! She really is a character. You did a great job with her. You sure have yourself an amazing daughter."

Although her words should have made me feel happy, they had the adverse effect on me. Despite the fact that my mother didn't offer praise often, there were a few rare occasions where she had complimented my daughter. Don't get me wrong. I was always thrilled when she praised Violet. But the problem is while she sometimes complimented my daughter; she's never had one positive thing to say about my son.

"She is an amazing girl," I replied. "I am very fortunate. I have two amazing kids. My son is equally outstanding."

Beatrice opened her mouth to speak, but no words came out. She ran her fingers through her hair and rummaged through her purse. When she finally did speak all she said was, "I better go pay for the dresses."

CHAPTER FIFTEEN

I stood at the stove, early Saturday morning when the telephone rang. Without having to glance at the caller ID, Cole said, "That'll be my mom." He walked over to me and reached for the spatula I had in my hand. "Give it to me. I'll finish scrambling the eggs for the kids. Go. Answer the phone, and talk to her."

I slowly reached for the phone and headed out of the kitchen. Without fail, Connie never forgot the anniversary. She always made sure to call me first thing in the morning every year. Her soothing voice and kind words always encouraged me and helped get me through this difficult day. The conversation was never long. She knew I preferred not to talk about it. She just wanted to reassure me that she was thinking about me and loved me. This year, she spoke to me a little longer.

"Have you called your mother today?" She asked, pointedly.

"No," I replied as I nervously twirled a lock of hair around my index finger.

"You are going to, aren't you?"

I took a deep breath. "I don't know, probably not. I don't normally call her on this day. I try to avoid her, actually. I never know how she is going to act. I can't handle her taking her frustrations out on me." And then as an afterthought, I quietly added, "Again."

"I know Anna, but don't you think this year should be different? After all, you've been spending a lot of time with her. Much more than you ever have before, isn't that right?"

"Yes, but—"

Connie cut me off before I could continue. "But nothing. Today is just as hard for your mother as it is for you. In fact, I would bet it is probably harder for her. I think it would be really nice if you called her today."

"I don't know, Connie. Part of me really wants to, but the other part of me is worried." I nervously picked at a cuticle as I spoke.

"What are you worried about?" She didn't give me a chance to answer; she kept on speaking. "You're making a big deal out of nothing. After all that has happened with you and your mother, what do you really think would be so bad? Come on, don't be a wimp, Anna. Just do it, call her." Connie hung up the phone guaranteeing she got the last word.

I didn't stop to think. I just acted. I really did long to speak to my mother today. I wanted to somehow comfort each other. It was possible, wasn't it? I dialed the number to my mother's home phone quickly. After a few rings, I was greeted by Walter's deep voice.

"Hey, Anna. How are you doing today?" Walter asked, compassionately.

"As well as can be expected," I answered honestly as I stared out of the den window. Not wanting to make small talk, I quickly asked if my mom was around.

"No, I'm afraid not. You just missed her. She left for the cemetery a couple of minutes ago."

"She did?" I asked, surprised. I haven't gone in years, so I guess I automatically assumed she didn't either.

"Yes. She often goes actually. Usually, I go with her, but

today she wanted to go by herself, so I stayed home. You should head over there and meet her. I'm sure she'd appreciate you coming."

"I'm not sure, Walter." I walked back to the sofa and sat down.

"Why not? I think it may do both of you some good."

"She may be gone by the time I can drive over there. After all, you guys are closer than I am."

"I doubt it. She usually stays for quite a while. I'm sure she'll still be there. What's the worst that could happen if you miss her? You can always go visit your brother while you're out that way."

I took a deep breath. I thought for a moment and then replied, "You've got a point, Walter. I think I'll take a chance."

"Oh, that's wonderful, Anna." He answered, sounding very pleased. Then, in a softer tone, he added, "Hang in there, sweetie. Every year it gets easier. Trust me, I know."

It only took me a few minutes to throw on black slacks and a lightweight sweater. When I reentered the kitchen. Cole was sitting at the table with the kids buttering a piece of toast for Harley. "You okay?" he asked as he placed the toast on our son's plate.

"Yeah. I'm okay. I'm going to take a ride. I'll be back in a few hours. Beatrice is at the cemetery, and believe it or not I'm going to join her there." I walked over to the stove where I had abandoned my coffee cup earlier. Despite it now being ice-cold, I grabbed it and took a big gulp before placing it in the sink.

"Did you speak to her?" Cole asked as he got up and stood next to me.

"No, she wasn't home. I spoke to Walter. He told me where she was. It was actually his idea for me to join her."

Cole put his hand on the small of my back and whispered in my ear. "Do you really think to show up there today, unannounced, is a good idea?"

I looked in his eyes and answered honestly. "I don't know."

"I'm not sure I like the idea of you going there alone. Why don't I come with you? We can drop the kids off at my parent's house."

"Thanks, but that isn't necessary. I'll be fine. I know I could be making a huge mistake, but I feel like I have to go. And I have to go now," I joked, "Before I change my mind."

Cole combed his fingers through his hair. "Fine. I'm not going to stop you, Anna. You are a big girl. You need to do whatever you feel is right. I just want you to have realistic expectations. Be happy if you're met with a warm reception, but prepare yourself for the opposite. And please, promise me you won't let anything your mother says get you down. Remember, regardless of what she says and thinks, you are the most amazing woman in the world. Don't let her fog up your clarity. You are smart, beautiful and have a heart of gold. You are the best thing ever to happen to me, and you have brought so much joy into so many lives." He then kissed me.

As I MERGED onto the parkway and drove towards the eastern end of Long Island where the cemetery was located, flashes from the past kept coming to the forefront of my mind. I truly couldn't believe how naive I used to be. They say ignorance is bliss, and I could attest to that fact. I should have known better, but late night telephone calls were never any cause for alarm. They were usually humorous. I hated to admit it, but Cole and I loved getting them. It usually meant one of our friends or siblings found themselves in a precarious situation where booze was often involved. Also, the best dating drama always happened in the middle of the night. I remembered that night like it was yesterday. When the phone rang around two thirty in the morning, after glancing at the caller ID and seeing my brother's cell phone number, I mouthed to Cole, who was my fiancé at the time, *this should be good*. I answered using my generic middle of the night greeting, "Annabel's advice line, how may I help you?"

But instead of my laughing brother, Brody, on the other end, an unfamiliar, but strong, male voice replied, "Excuse me?" He didn't sound amused. And he didn't give me a chance to reply. "Are you related to Brody Buchanan?" he asked.

"Yes," I said, quietly as I sat up straight in bed. I immediately sensed something was off. My heart started pounding. "Is something wrong?" I felt all the color drain from my face. "Who is this?" Cole sat up at the sound of my voice. His eyes were glued to me. "I'm his sister," barely made it out of my mouth. I paused almost forgetting my name, "Anna... Annabel."

"Annabel, I am Officer Davis. I'm very sorry to have to inform you, but there has been an accident. Your brother was riding his motorcycle on Long Beach Road and was hit by a drunk driver."

"What?" I asked out of reflex even though I had heard him crystal clear. I found it hard to breathe. I managed to mutter, "Is he okay?"

"He is in an ambulance on his way to Mercy Hospital right now. I suggest you and your family come as quickly as you can. I'm sorry, but it doesn't look good."

I buried my face in my hands as he continued. "I'll be at the hospital when you get there. But Annabel, like I said before, please hurry."

"Oh... Okay. Um... Thank you, Officer," I said, robotically.

"Anna, what's wrong?" Cole asked.

I didn't answer him. Instead, as tears streamed down my face, I dialed my mother's phone number. She answered on the third ring.

She didn't say hello when she answered. Instead, sounding

irritated, she asked, "Do you have any idea what time it is, Annabel?"

"Not now, Mother. You need to get to Mercy Hospital like five minutes ago. It's Brody. He's been in an accident. A drunk driver hit him. The police just called, they said he's really hurt." I then proceeded to parrot back everything the officer just told me.

"I'm on my way," Beatrice simply replied before the line went dead.

I dropped the phone and put both my hands over my face and sobbed. I was frozen. I couldn't move from my bed, and I didn't want to.

"Come on, Anna," Cole, who had already managed to get dressed, gently coaxed me. "You gotta get dressed. We can make it there in twenty minutes if you hurry. Try not to worry, sweetie. He'll be fine."

"But what if he isn't?"

"Don't think that way. Come on baby you have to get up." Cole picked up the jeans I had casually tossed on the floor by the bed a few hours ago and handed them to me. I was shaking uncontrollably as I put them on.

As Cole sped through the dark and semi-deserted roads, he held onto the steering wheel with his left hand while his right hand tightly grasped my frigid fingers. I was so afraid for my baby brother. Nothing felt real, not even my fiancé's touch. After all, I was just with my brother a few hours ago. Brody joined Cole and me for dinner and then he came back to our apartment to watch a movie. We had a great time, and when he left, he was planning on meeting up with some friends.

"Anna. Look at me. Now!" Cole insisted. He maneuvered the vehicle around several police cars.

I didn't listen.

"Don't do this to yourself just look away," Cole whispered as he tried to cover my eyes with his right hand. I pushed him away. I didn't want to look, but I couldn't resist. There, in the middle of the road was my brother's mangled motorcycle, and what looked like too much blood.

I opened my mouth to speak, but no words came out, just sobs.

"Hang on. We are almost there, Baby." Cole said softly as he extended his arm. I nestled next to him and closed my eyes for the rest of the trip. Fortunately, the hospital was only about fifteen minutes away from the site of the accident.

As soon as he pulled up to the emergency room entrance, I flung open the door and raced inside. I didn't even give Cole a chance to put the car into park. I immediately spotted two police officers standing off to the side holding cups of coffee. I ran over to them. "Officer Davis?" I asked as I glanced back and forth between the two men.

The taller and rounder of the pair slowly nodded his head. "Yes. Are you Annabel?"

I nodded as Cole appeared by my side. "He's in with the doctors, but I am sure they will let you see him," he said as he exchanged a look with one of the nurses.

"My mom is on her way too," I explained.

"That's good. My partner will stay here. He will look out for her. Come on, let's go."

I don't know what I expected to see when they pulled back the curtain surrounding the bed where my brother laid. But the image that greeted me was far worse than anything I could have imagined in my worst nightmares. His head was wrapped in thick gauze; blood was seeping through the bandages. His left eye was gashed and swollen. His left arm hung lifelessly at his side while his right leg was suspended in the air in traction. He had tubes coming out of numerous body parts, and a respirator assisted his breathing.

"Family I presume?" the tall, balding doctor asked.

"Yes, I am his sister, and this is my fiancé," I said, swallowing down the lump in my throat. I couldn't take my eyes off my brother. My legs started to wobble. Cole must have noticed because he put his arm around my waist to steady me.

The doctor squeezed my arm gently as he replied, "Okay, I'll give you a few minutes, but then we have to move him to ICU."

I went around to the right side of the bed and took his hand in mine. I looked over at the doctor. "Can he hear me?" I asked. The doctor nodded his head, affirmatively, before walking out of the room.

"Brody, buddy? What happened to you?" I asked, as Cole gently rubbed my back. "I've got to admit I've seen you looking better. But don't you worry, I know you're gonna pull through." I don't know who I was trying to assure more, him or myself. By the way my voice was cracking, I knew I wouldn't be able to keep it together much longer.

Cole, whose mother was a nurse, leaned over and whispered into my ear, "Really talk to him, Anna. He just needs to hear your voice."

I nodded my head at Cole, and whispered, "Okay. I'll try." I took a deep breath as I tried to hold back my tears. I rubbed my brother's good arm and said, "Oh, Brody. You are the same prankster you always were. You were just saying a few hours ago how you didn't want to go to work on Monday, well it sure looks like you found a way to get out of that one." I looked up at Cole for reassurance and he gave me the thumbs up, so I continued. "You really pulled out all the stops, didn't you? Hey, do you remember the time when you had that big math test? I think you were in fifth grade, and—"

I was cut off by the sound of my mother screaming as she barreled her way over to Brody's bed. "Oh my God! My baby. MY BABY!"

The beeps of his heart monitor quickened. "Mom, I think we should stay calm around him. I don't think it is good to agitate him," I said as my eyes studied the jumps of his monitors.

With venom in her voice, my mother answered. "Don't tell me what to do or how to act, Annabel. I'm his mother. You've done enough already, don't you think?"

I had no idea what she was talking about. I was about to ask her when the doctor reappeared. Two nurses also entered the room and rushed over to Brody's bed. Clearly having overheard the exchange.

The doctor chimed in, "Your daughter is right. I know this is difficult, but it is very important you all try to stay as calm as possible around him. He can pick up on your emotions, and we don't want his heart rate to become any more elevated than it already is. It's time we move him to intensive care. His room is ready now. The nurses are going to bring him upstairs. Please come with me. I will fill you in on his condition while the nurses take him to his new room."

Before leaving, I leaned over and kissed Brody. Cole squeezed his shoulder, and we both started to follow the doctor out. My mother lingered behind but soon met us in the hallway.

Glancing first at me then at my mother, the doctor said sympathetically, "As you can see, Brody is in very bad shape." He looked down at the clipboard he was holding and elaborated, "He experienced blunt force trauma. He has a brain hemorrhage, and there is bleeding around his lungs. His left arm is broken. So are most of his ribs. He has a thigh fracture, which is causing internal bleeding in his legs. I am afraid there is also damage to his heart, liver, lungs, and spleen."

My mother buried her face in her hands. In a barely audible voice she said, "It can't be. I can't do this again." I had no idea what she meant, but I wasn't about to ask. I had questions to ask the doctor instead.

"Will he be able to walk again?"

The doctor squeezed my forearm gently. "I'm sorry. I don't think you understand the severity of your brother's situation. Walking is the least of your brother's concerns. I hate to have to tell you this, but he may not make it through the night."

Cole grabbed hold of me. He stopped me from falling. I felt like the world was spinning out of control. My brother and I went through so much together. He was such an important part of my life. There was nothing I wouldn't do for him. And now he could be dying? How was that possible? He was only twenty-one, too young for it all to end.

The doctor continued. "Give the nurses a few more minutes to settle him in, and then they will come get you and bring you upstairs. You'll be able to see him. He's sedated so he isn't in any pain. We're going to do everything we can for him. Giving up is not an option, so stay strong. Pray for the best, but prepare yourselves for the worst." He looked over at the policemen and gestured for them to come over. "While you are waiting, the police will fill you in on how the accident happened. I'm going to be here all night. I will see you in a little while. I have some other patients to check in on."

I reached for Cole's hand. "Who cares how the accident happened?" I said as the doctor walked away and the police began walking towards us. "Brody could be dying."

Cole put his arms around me and engulfed me in a hug. He squeezed me tightly and kissed the top of my head. "We need to know what happened," he said calmly. "Come on, Anna. You need to be strong. For your brother." My mother didn't say a word. She glared at me; her gray eyes were ice-cold.

Officer Davis did the speaking while his partner stood silently at his side looking down at his shoes. "We have several witnesses that came forward who saw the accident, so we have a very clear picture of what happened tonight. Brody was driving northbound on Long Beach Road. He was stopped at a red light at the border of Island Park and Oceanside. The light turned green, and he started to accelerate. He barely made it through the intersection when he was hit head on by a forty-five year old woman in a Lexus SUV. She was driving approximately seventy-five miles per hour and was going in the wrong direction. She hit Brody head on. The impact caused his body to become airborne. When he landed, he hit the ground hard. After slamming into your brother's motorcycle, the driver swerved her car back into the correct lane and came to a complete stop. She was clearly intoxicated. In fact, her blood alcohol level was three times the legal limit. She was unscathed and was arrested at the scene."

"You've got to be kidding me," my mother exclaimed. She looked like she wanted to punch the cop, a wall, or me. "She does this to my son, and she just walks away without a scratch on her? Where is the fucking justice? I hope to hell she rots in prison. I could kill that ignorant bitch with my own bare hands."

Cole let go of me and tried to put his arm around my mom. "Get the hell off of me," she pushed Cole away. "I don't need your comforting. Who the hell do you think you are anyway, some white knight? You think your calm, soothing words are going to make a difference here? My son is in intensive care. He very well may be dying. And you think a hug will make things better? Unbelievable." She shook her head in disgust. "If you feel the need to hug someone, hug her," she said as she pointed at me.

There was something about the way she said it. It sounded so vicious. I had no idea why she seemed so hateful towards me, but it didn't really matter. All that mattered to me was my brother.

A nurse approached us and told us we could go upstairs and see Brody. I held onto Cole's hand. My nails dug deeply into his palm. We all rode up the elevator in silence. When we got to the intensive care unit only my mom and I were allowed to see Brody. Cole had to stay behind because they didn't want to overwhelm Brody, and technically he wasn't family.

If Brody looked bad before, he looked worse now. There were tubes and monitors everywhere. His face was as pale as the hospital gown draped over his body. Despite the fact he was almost six-feet tall, he looked tiny and helpless in the hospital bed. Memories of our childhood came flooding back to me. I remembered when my parents first brought him home from the hospital. I held him constantly, always wanting to feed him and change his diaper. I would pretend he was my baby. When he was two, he grabbed my hand and put it next to his face. I felt so much love for him, thinking he was returning my affection until he used my finger to pick his nose. I didn't get mad. I never could. I still couldn't. The memories kept coming at a fast and furious pace, just as tears slid down my face. I stood by the left side of his bed and held on tightly to his shoulder. As if silently praying, I kept repeating in a barely audible voice, "I love you Brody, please come back to me," over and over again.

My mother had pulled a chair over to his bed. She was leaning over and was whispering into his left ear. I think she also was reflecting on his childhood. I couldn't hear most of what she said, but I did hear her say "little boy" and "remember when" a lot of times.

Brody was the light of my mother's eye. In her world, the sun rose and set over her son. She adored him, and always favored him to me. I was never jealous, probably because I recognized how special he was.

We stayed at his side for at least an hour. We only left because a nurse asked us to step outside for a few minutes so they could tend to him. She urged us to go home and get some rest. But her words fell on deaf ears. Neither my mother nor I could fathom leaving Brody alone.

We walked to the waiting room in silence. In fact, my mother didn't say one word to me the entire time we were with my brother. Cole sat in an oversized chair absently thumbing through an upside down magazine. Before we entered the waiting area, I grabbed my mom's arm and spun her slightly towards me. "I need to give you a hug, Mom," I said. "I am so scared."

I tried to put my arms around her but she pushed back. "Not now, Annabel. I can't hug you. I can barely look at you right now. Please just sit with your fiancé. I'll be on the other side of the room. I need to be alone." And with a huff, she walked to the furthest corner of the waiting room.

"What was that all about?" Cole asked me as I sat down next to him.

"I've no idea. She told me she could barely look at me? Why would she say that to me?" I asked as another tear rolled down my face.

He used the back of his hand to wipe my tear away. "I don't know, Baby. I don't know." He put his arm around me and held me tight. "Don't worry about your mother now. Focus your energy on your brother. I called my mom when you were inside. She used to work at this hospital before she retired. She knows Brody's doctor quite well. She said he is one of the best. She offered to come and stay with us, but I told her I thought it was best if she stayed home, especially given how your mother is acting. She agreed but assured me if we needed help she'd come right over."

"I don't know if I feel better or worse knowing Connie's opinion of the doctor. I mean, I'm glad she thinks highly of him. But I want his diagnosis to be wrong."

As soon as those words were out of my mouth, there was an announcement on the hospital's loudspeaker. "Code Blue, ICU. Code Blue, ICU." I watched in shock as doctors and nurses with a crash cart went running into the ward.

I buried my head in Cole's chest. "Oh my God. What if it's Brody," my voice was barely a whisper through my tears.

"Shhh, Anna," Cole said as he gently stroked my hair. "We don't know anything. He's not the only person in the ward. Look around. There are plenty of other people in this waiting room. Everyone in intensive care is very sick. You have no way of knowing the code is for your brother."

In my head, I knew Cole had a valid point, but my stomach and my heart told me otherwise. I tried so hard to stay positive, but it was practically impossible. I held on to Cole so tightly. Every second that passed felt like an eternity.

Eventually, a nurse came to the waiting room. One by one, like a domino effect, each and every head snapped up, eyes like saucers red with grief stared at her. No one said a word, and I held my breath. The ticking of the clock on the wall was the only sound to be heard. A television was playing, but someone must have turned off the sound. I was sure, everyone there was praying the nurse was not there for them, I know I sure was. We were all desperate to know our loved one was spared.

In a soft and compassionate voice, she asked, "Is Brody Buchanan's family here?"

Cole replied we were. Then the three of us slowly rose from our seats.

"Come with me," she said, and she started walking down the long hallway. We followed her in silence. She opened a door and brought us into a small room. There were several seats, but not one of us sat down.

She closed the door before addressing us. "The emergency we just had was for Brody. He went into cardiac arrest. We tried everything we could to resuscitate him but his heart just wasn't strong enough. I'm so very sorry, Brody didn't make it."

My mother screamed "No" and sunk to the floor. The nurse squatted down next to her and engulfed her in her arms. She guided my mother to one of the chairs. I remained standing but buried my head into Cole's chest and sobbed uncontrollably. My brother was dead?

I had no idea how much time passed. It could have been a moment or an hour? What was time when the world you knew was ending? Eventually, the nurse broke the silence. "Let me know if you want to see him and say a final goodbye."

"I can't," I said. I didn't want to remember my brother this way. It was bad enough I would always remember him in that damn hospital bed all bruised and battered. I didn't want to see his lifeless body and know we'd never be able to spend another moment together. He was so young and full of life; these were the memories I needed to hold onto now and always.

"Well, I most certainly need to see my baby," my mother said as she stood up.

"I will give you all a minute," the nurse said. "I'll be right outside this door. When you are ready Mrs. Buchanan I will take you to see your son."

As soon as the nurse closed the door, my mother faced me. Her eyes were bulging from her head. A vein in her forehead was prominent. She had venom in her voice as she emphasized every word. "You... Did...This! You are responsible for this! You killed your brother. It's entirely your fault. Just know his blood is on your hands."

"What are you talking about?" I asked, dumbfounded. My heart was throbbing in my chest. "I didn't kill Brody. He was hit by a drunk driver."

"That's right. He was hit by an SUV while he was on a motorcycle. He didn't have a chance in hell to survive, now did he? He had no business riding that godforsaken thing. He should never have had the bike. And he wouldn't have had it if you didn't give him the damn money to buy that death machine. He asked me for the money. I'm sure he told you I said no to him. I'm sure he told you I flat out refused to give him one red cent to use towards it. I bet you two concocted some story about why I was being unreasonable about it. I could just picture you all snickering and making fun of me. I hope you both had fun mocking me. Do you want to know why I didn't want him to have the bike?"

I didn't answer. I just nodded my head slowly.

"I didn't want him to have the motorcycle because I knew this would happen. And guess what, I was right. And now my son is dead. If it weren't for you, my son would be alive right now. You may not have driven the car that struck him, but in my eyes, you are just as responsible for his death as the drunk who hit him."

I opened my mouth to speak. I wanted to defend myself. But my mother stopped me. "Close your mouth. Don't you dare say a word to me. Anything you have to say means nothing. Not now, and maybe not ever. I need you to get out of my sight. I can't stand to look at you. You make me sick!"

"But, Mom," I begged.

"I have nothing else to say to you. I'll make arrangements for his funeral tomorrow. I have Cole's cell number. I will call him with the details, as far as I'm concerned I lost two children tonight."

CHAPTER SIXTEEN

True to her word, my mother called Cole the next morning and went over the funeral arrangements with him. Cole urged her to talk to me, but she refused.

Instead of my brother writing a best man speech for my wedding, as we had planned, I wrote a eulogy for his funeral. My mother acted as if I didn't exist. She said the bare minimum to me at the service as well as during the days that followed. But I was confident, as time passed her attitude towards me would change. After all, how could she really continue to blame me for my brother's death?

I guess I wasn't one to take a hint. During those first few weeks following Brody's death, I kept trying to call her. I desperately wanted to speak to her. After all, my brother was gone, and my father had died years before. She was the only family I had left. I needed my mom. But the more I pushed, the more she pulled away.

It was her idea to have a weekly, scheduled call. She said she needed to be emotionally prepared to speak to me. She told me it was too upsetting to just hear my voice unexpectedly. I didn't understand, but I complied. I hoped it would be a temporary arrangement. It wasn't. For twelve years, it was how we communicated. I told her about my decision to elope on one of our scheduled calls. When I found out I was pregnant, I waited until a Thursday to share the news. And since Violet was born on a Wednesday night I waited until the appropriate time the next day to inform my mother she had a granddaughter.

As I pulled into the cemetery's entrance, I was overcome with doubts. I couldn't decide if I should chance my mother's wrath or just make a U-turn and drive back home. I was so worried about how my mother would react to seeing me. Our relationship had definitely gotten better over the years, but it was far from ideal. And no matter how hard I tried I could never forget how her anger and hatred had cut me deeply. The confusion I felt by her actions never went away.

I stopped my car and opened the window. I needed some fresh air. While I contemplated what to do Sister Sledge came on the radio. As I listened to "We Are Family" I couldn't help but think Brody was sending me a sign and it made me happy. Over the years, I believed Brody sent me signs, and every time I felt his presence it was so comforting.

I parked right behind my mother's car. As I walked to where both my brother and father were buried, my heart beat so fast. In an attempt to try and control my nervous energy I slowed my pace down. As soon as I reached the gravesite, I saw my mother sitting on a small blanket next to Brody's grave.

I walked over to her and silently placed my hand on her right shoulder. She turned her head and looked up at me, with tear-filled eyes. She offered me a sad smile and stood up. In silence, she put her arms around me and hugged me incredibly tight. I hugged her back, equally as tight. As I angled my head so that it rested in the crook of her neck, I let out a loud sob. My mother sniffled as she ran her hand from the top of my head down to the middle of my back repeatedly. This gentle gesture made me cry harder. For the first time in twelve years, thanks to this embrace, I felt the maternal love I had been longing for all these years. I didn't want this moment ever to end.

Pulling back from me my mother said, "Well this is a surprise, Annabel. I didn't expect to see you."

"I didn't expect to be here either," I replied. "I don't really like to come. It's funny, but I always feel like a part of Brody is with me. When I am missing him, I like to think about all the great times we had, and sometimes I find myself talking to him when no one is around. Coming to the cemetery seems so final."

"It is final. I think that's why I like to come here so much. I like knowing I'm where he is. I feel more connected to him here than anywhere else. Maybe it's because I know he has to listen to what I say here. Let's face it he can't run away." She laughed quietly. "So why did you come then?" she asked kindly.

"I called your house a little while ago, and Walter told me you were here. It was actually his idea for me to join you," I replied.

"I'm glad you came."

I looked at her with inquisitive eyes.

"Really, I am. Come, sit with me for a while." She took my hand, and we both sat down on the blanket.

As I sat there, I felt more at peace than I had felt in a very long time. I wasn't sure what it was that made me feel so calm. I'm sure the quiet serenity of the cemetery helped, but I really think my tranquility resulted from feeling so close to my mother. For so many years I hoped I could experience this feeling, and finally I was.

Neither one of us spoke as we sat. We were both lost in our own thoughts and memories. After about an hour, my mom stood up and broke the silence. "There's a diner nearby," she said as she started walking to where our cars were parked. "Follow me there. I'll buy you lunch."

As soon as the waitress dropped off our iced teas, my mother turned to me and said, "I know I'm twelve years late in saying this, Annabel, but I'm sorry for what I said to you in the hospital. I should never have said those horrible things."

I couldn't believe I was finally getting an apology. Given how many years I had waited for this very moment, I was shocked I wasn't feeling differently right now. I should be ecstatic, but for some reason I felt sad. It was almost like I wasn't sure I even wanted her to say she was sorry anymore. So much time has passed it was almost as if the sentiment had lost it's meaning. Or maybe Cecelia was right. Maybe I didn't want to let go of my anger?

Oh, how I wished I felt differently. Guilt ate at me for still being this upset. I knew how hard it had to be for my mother to apologize finally. A huge part of me wanted to slide into the booth next to her and engulf her in my arms. I wanted to hold her tightly and sob. Tell her everything was okay, that I loved her, and I was no longer angry with her. But I couldn't bring myself to budge or say anything of the sort. Instead, I let the hurt and anger that had consumed me all this time get the better of me. I took a deep breath and sat up straight in the booth.

"You're right, Mother. You shouldn't have treated me the way you did. I still can't understand why you did. Blaming me for Brody's death has haunted me all these years."

Beatrice placed her hand across her heart and said, "I was so upset. My world came crashing down. My son, my *little boy* died. Brody had such a promising future ahead of him. He was young, handsome, and oh so smart. He deserved a chance. He deserved a future. He didn't deserve to be dead at twenty-one."

I opened a packet of artificial sweetener and poured it into my drink. I slowly stirred my iced tea with my straw. My eyes were fixed on my glass as opposed to my mother as I replied, "I know. But you weren't the only one who lost someone special the night Brody died, Mother. He wasn't just your son he was my brother too. You weren't the only one grieving. My heart was breaking too."

Beatrice took a sip of iced tea and gently wiped her mouth before speaking. "Yes, I know, Annabel. I know how much you loved your brother. You two had always been inseparable."

"We were. But you didn't answer my question, Mother. How could you have treated me the way you did? You may have lost your son, but I was your child too, not some random stranger who just happened to be standing nearby. Hell, you blamed me instead of the drunk driver who actually killed him."

"Annabel—"

I didn't give my mother a chance to speak. I had to get this out while I had the chance, after all, I've kept silent for far too long. "You know what, Mother. I've thought about that night so much over the past twelve years. I've tried so hard to give you the benefit of the doubt. I often found myself wondering how I would react if something similar happened to one of my children. I can't even fathom the thought. I can't think of anything more horrific than losing a child, and I hate that you had to experience it. So, in a way, I guess I can understand why you needed someone to take your anger and frustration out on. And I can sort of understand why that someone was me. It was easy to do. I was right there. The driver was in jail. But it was twelve years ago. For twelve years you have blamed me for my brother's death. For twelve years you have barely had a relationship with my family. It's messed up, Mother."

My mother nodded her head. "I know it is and I wish I could go back in time and do things differently."

"Do you really?" I asked in disbelief. "If you had any regrets why didn't you try to change the situation before now? After all, you've had twelve years. You never tried to repair our relationship, and you pushed me away whenever I tried. You've kept me at arm's length." I reached for my straw wrapper and played with it in an attempt to calm my nerves and temper.

My mother started to speak. "I'm—"

"No, Mother. Please let me finish. I've tried so hard to fix our relationship, and you know it."

My mother glanced away from me.

"I lost my brother, and I desperately didn't want to lose my mother too. You were all the family I had left."

I wiped a tear away. "If you recall, I kept calling you and calling you after we buried Brody. But you didn't want to speak to me. You not only brushed me off, but you were also down right nasty to me. You couldn't care less how I was coping, if I was coping. I was an emotional wreck, and you didn't give a damn."

"Annabel, that's not true," Beatrice tried to defend herself.

I took a sip of my drink. "Honestly, I really believe your goal was to make me feel worse than I already did. After all, why else would you have kept insisting I was a murderer?"

"I didn't do that," my mother said as she shook her head.

I pushed my glass to the side. "Do you have selective amnesia, Mother? You told me I killed my brother. Remember? You said it in the hospital. You said it at the funeral. You kept saying I was the one responsible for Brody's death. Who says that to their child?"

Beatrice reached into her bag for a tissue, which she used to dry her eyes. "I never should have said it. You've got to believe me if I could take it back, I would."

"Well, you can't. You could have righted the situation in the days and weeks, which followed, but you didn't. Instead, you just kept insinuating I was to blame. And the more you did, the more I started to believe you were right. The guilt I felt was overwhelming; it consumed me. I was unable to eat. Every time I tried, I threw up. I lost twenty pounds. Since I was only one hundred and fifteen pounds to start with you can just imagine what a picture of health I looked like. I was nothing but skin and bones. I couldn't sleep. As soon as I closed my eyes images of how I envisioned Brody's accident haunted me. I constantly reached for the phone. I wanted to talk to you, cry with you. Hell, I would have been happy just hearing your voice. But I couldn't. You made it crystal clear you didn't want to have anything to do with me. When morning finally came, I was exhausted and barely able to get out of bed. The thought of facing another day without my brother or mother was too much for me. I didn't want to go on. I didn't want to keep living."

"What?"

"You heard me. And I almost didn't."

My mother gasped.

A tear ran down my cheek as I slowly pulled up the sleeve of my shirt and thrust my arms in my mother's face. "Look!" I demanded. "The scars have faded, but they will never go away. I did this to myself. I tried to kill myself because of how you made me feel."

My mother put her hands on her ears. "Oh no, Annabel. I don't want to hear this and I certainly don't want to see it." Beatrice said, her voice a whisper.

"I'm sorry, but you are going to have to. You should have heard this a long time ago. But I never wanted to tell you. Not that I didn't want to upset you. I didn't want you to know because I was afraid you would either not care or be disappointed I failed."

"Annabel, you make me seem like I'm some kind of monster."

I wiped a tear with the back of my hand. "I'm not saying that, Mother. And I'm not trying to imply it either. I'm just telling you the facts. How you interpret them depends on your own conscience, I guess. If you're feeling like I am making you out to be a monster, maybe you should try to reconcile why you feel this way." I took a deep breath. "This isn't easy for me to talk about. If it's okay with you, I'd like to finish."

"Okay."

I took another sip of my drink. "It was about a month after Brody died. I didn't go to work that day, again. I spent the day staring into space crying, again. I called you, and you didn't want to talk to me, again. In fact, it was the day you came up with the brilliant idea of having a scheduled weekly telephone call with me so you could mentally prepare yourself to hear my voice. You hung up on me in fact. Do you remember?"

Her voice was quiet, "Yes, unfortunately, I do."

"As I listened to the dial tone, I cried harder. I couldn't handle the pain anymore. I had given up. I just wanted my misery to end. Looking back, if I'm completely honest with myself, I wasn't really serious about doing it. Which was why I waited until right around the time Cole was due home from work. The poor guy was so worried about me. He knew how fragile I was, but he didn't know what to do to help me." I rolled my eyes, "I was a really fun fiancé."

I took a deep breath. "Cole got home from work and he called out for me. I didn't answer. Our apartment was small so it took only seconds for him to find me in the bathroom. I was bleeding and crying hysterically. I hated myself for what I had done. I hated that I was willing to give up a life with the man I loved more than anything in the world because of the guilt and grief I felt. I hated myself. I just kept rocking and telling Cole I was sorry."

I paused as the waitress dropped off our omelets. "Cole was amazing. He didn't get frazzled. He was so calm and reacted so quickly. He wrapped towels around my arms and applied pressure. Fortunately my exterior wounds weren't too deep. Like I said, my attempt was definitely more of a cry for help." I picked up my fork and moved the home fries around on my plate.

"Cole rushed me to the hospital and they stitched me up. He then brought me to his parent's house. We stayed with them for almost two months until I was more stable. I took a leave of absence from work. Connie found me a wonderful therapist who helped me immensely. She would drive me to each and every one of my therapy sessions. When I was done, she'd try to do something fun with me afterward. She'd take me shopping, to lunch, or to a movie. I don't know what I would have done without her."

My mother was quiet. She was attentively listening to every word I said. But her face was unreadable. I had no idea what she was thinking, so I continued talking. "Connie and I became pretty much inseparable during this time. We were able to talk about everything and anything. And when I needed a good cry or a shoulder to lean on she was always there. She gave and gave of herself to me. It was an amazing feeling to have her just love me unconditionally. Don't get me wrong; Cole was wonderful too, but it wasn't the same. Cole was my fiancé. My lover. I didn't want to constantly be an emotional wreck around him. I wanted to be the old me with him. The *women* he fell in love with, not the shell of the girl I had become. Connie helped me do that. She spent countless hours comforting me and helping me cope. She helped me come to terms with the guilt you inflicted upon me. Connie showered me with love and affection. She made me feel valued. Honestly, if it weren't for the O'Conner's I would never have made it. So many years have passed, and we are just as close as we were then. There are no secrets between us."

I couldn't tell if my mother smirked at my comment, but I didn't give it much thought. I just continued with what I had to say, "I talk to Connie on the phone at least once a day. Unlike with us, it never feels obligatory on either one of our parts, Mother. The calls are spontaneous; sometimes they only last for a moment or two. Other times we can chat for hours. When

I'm worried or troubled, I know Connie will console me. When the kids do something funny, I have to call Connie immediately; I know she will find joy in what my children are doing. And when I just need a friend, she is always there. It's funny Connie may have given birth to my husband, but she became my mother in every sense of the word."

My mother started to cry, and I felt like a huge boulder was lifted off my shoulders. It was very freeing to finally express what I had gone through.

"I wish you would have told me what you did before now."

I poked my fork in my eggs and removed a piece of broccoli. I stared at it for a few seconds before putting it in my mouth. I chewed it slowly before answering. "I wish I could have too. But I didn't see the point; you made your feelings clear to me. You didn't want to have anything to do with me. And I was so tired of disappointing you. After all, you almost had your wish come true. I could have been gone, but I guess I blew that too." I buried my face in my hands.

My mother pushed her untouched plate to the side and reached across the table and grabbed my hands. She stared deep into my eyes. "Annabel, you've got to believe me, I never intended to hurt you the way I did. It's true I wanted to push you away. But I never thought my words and actions could have caused you so much pain. I should have known better. I realize that now, but I didn't then. I was blinded by my own grief and anger. I took everything out on you, and you let me. You never once yelled back at me, so I continued to take advantage. I was a terrible mother."

CHAPTER SEVENTEEN

As I pulled out of the diner's parking lot, I called Cole. "How's it going over there?"

I felt bad I left Cole unexpectedly with the children hours ago. Don't get me wrong, he loved hanging out with them, but I knew he planned to spend the day updating his portfolio and resume.

"Your daughter just slaughtered me in Monopoly and your son has created the largest Lego castle known to mankind. And now they are watching a movie." He paused, "Nicholas called me earlier."

I swallowed hard. Cole's boss doesn't usually call him on the weekend, and the last time he did it was to say he sold the firm.

"What happened?"

"Remember the new shopping center in Westchester we were bidding on?"

"Yes."

"Well, the contract was signed late last night."

"That's great news, right?"

"For the firm, yes. For me, I'm not so sure. This is the first new contract since the acquisition. Eastridge will have to decide who will head it up. If I manage the project, I can breathe easy for a while. If it gets assigned to one of their guys, well, the writing is on the wall for me. Nicholas wanted to give me the heads up so that I could start working on a project plan before they make the announcement on Monday."

"The fact that he called you today has to be a good sign, right?" I asked, hopeful.

"I don't know. It could be, or he simply fears that my days are numbered, and he wants to give me a fighting chance to get the gig. Either way, I've already started working on it."

"Do you need me to come home? My mother wanted me to stop by her house. She said she needed to show me something. But I don't have to go."

"No, do your thing. The kids can entertain themselves while I work."

"You sure?"

"Yeah, I'm positive. Anna, I've been worried. How did your mother react when you showed up at the cemetery?"

"Much better than I expected. She seemed almost happy to see me. We stayed at Brody's grave for about an hour and then we went to a diner for lunch. Cole, she apologized for how she treated me after Brody died."

"Wow!" He exclaimed. "She took a huge step in the right direction. That's wonderful. I didn't think she had it in her. How did you react?"

I took a deep breath. "Not as good as I should have. You know how hard it is for her to say she's sorry or admit that she was wrong. Well, I wasn't too appreciative. In fact, I was kind of cold. I feel bad."

"Don't beat yourself up. A lot of years have passed. You have every right to feel the way you do."

"But I was bitchy, Cole. Does that make me like her?"

"Do I really need to answer that question?"

"I guess not," I muttered. "I also told Bea about the night I tried to kill myself."

"Good for you," Cole said tenderly. I could picture him grinning from ear to ear as he spoke. He had been urging me to tell her for a very long time, but I never wanted to. It was such a difficult thing to talk about, let alone to discuss it with the person who motivated my actions. "I'm proud of you, Sweetie. It's about frigging time she found out. Did she take any ownership?"

"Sort of. I really think she felt bad. Cole, I just don't get it. She told me she acted the way she did because she was overcome with grief. I can understand she had to take her agony out on someone. I know I was an easy target, but I just can't understand how it took her twelve years to apologize. A part of me feels like it was too little too late. I can't shake the feeling there was more to her actions."

"You may be right, Anna, but I think you need to come to terms that there most likely are no more answers to get. You need to take her at her word that she was heartbroken when her son died and that is why she treated you the way she did. Things will never change between the two of you if you aren't open to it."

My mother's silver Mercedes was already in the driveway when I pulled up to her house. For an old girl, she sure did like to put the pedal to the metal. The front door was open, so I walked in.

"Annabel, is that you?" My mother's voice filled the foyer.

I pressed the intercom button so she could hear me. "Yes."

"Good. I asked Walter to go out for a while so we could be alone. I'm in my room. Come upstairs."

I took off my shoes and left them by the front door. My

mother had always been a fanatic about anyone walking with shoes on her beige carpeting. I remember once when I was a little girl we had a small gas leak and the fire department had to be called. My mother had the audacity to ask them to remove their shoes before inspecting the house. The expression on the firefighters' faces was priceless.

As I walked upstairs, I couldn't help but pause and peek in the room that used to be Brody's. It was amazing, both Brody and my bedrooms remained exactly the same as they did the last night we slept in them. I would have expected my mother to have at least changed my room into a storage space or something.

"Are you coming?" she impatiently bellowed.

"Yes," I answered and continued up yet another flight of stairs to her room, or more accurately put, her suite. My mother's bedroom was the size of a small apartment. Of course there was the sleeping area with a king sized bed overlooking the in-ground pool in the backyard. In addition, there was a humongous bathroom with heated floors, a steam shower big enough to fit five adults, and an enormous Jacuzzi tub. Her closet ran the entire length of the house and was motorized. So with the push of a button, her inventory of designer shoes and clothes would rotate preventing her from ever having to rummage through her belongings. But my favorite part was the sitting area. It had a couch, a gas fireplace, a large wall mounted television, a wet bar, and a built-in Gaggenau coffee, espresso, and cappuccino maker.

My mother was sitting on the couch sipping coffee. "Care for a cup?" She asked as she started to get up.

"Yes, but sit. I can make it." I replied as I walked over to the unit and pressed the appropriate buttons. One of these days, I need to splurge and purchase this machine for my home.

I sat down on the couch next to her. Before I took a sip of

my coffee, I asked, "So, what did you want to show me? Does it have to do with the wedding?"

"No. Not at all," Beatrice replied. Her eyes were sad, and her body was slumped. "I need to show you." She paused as if she was searching for the right word before finally saying, "me."

"What do you mean?" I asked as I put my cup down on the table.

"You're not the only one who has secrets, Annabel. I have plenty of my own as well. I want to open up to you. I want to let you see me, the real me. The woman I've kept hidden for far too many years. I've been trying hard to open up lately. I hope you can see that. Walter has been encouraging me. He has been helping me find the strength to break down the walls I have built in an attempt to protect my heart."

"Is that why you told me about Daddy?"

My mother took a sip of coffee. "Yes, it was exactly why I wanted you to know the truth about your father and me."

"Are you saying there's more?" I asked as I removed the elastic band from my wrist and put my hair up in a ponytail. Suddenly I felt hot.

Beatrice sighed deeply. "Oh, there is way more than your father's infidelities."

"Maybe I should have fixed a martini instead of coffee," I joked as I looked at my cup.

"Possibly." My mother chuckled. "I for one, most definitely should have. In fact, I think I will have one. I'm gonna need a little liquid courage." My mother got up and walked over to the bar and took out all the fixings for a cocktail. "Do you want one?" She asked as she poured a generous amount of gin into a silver shaker.

"Yes," I answered honestly, "but I think I will stick to the coffee for now."

"Suit yourself," she said as she poured the contents of the shaker into her glass. She took a sip before sitting back down.

"Back at the diner, you asked me why I said what I did to you at the hospital. I didn't lie when I said I was overcome with grief, but it was more than that. I felt like I had to push you away. I wanted to distance myself from you. It wasn't that I didn't love you. I did, and I still do. You may not believe it, but I always loved you, more than you could ever imagine, especially after the way I have behaved all these years. I lashed out at you because loving you hurt me too much. I was scared to lose you. After all, everyone I loved died tragically, and I couldn't take another hit to my heart. It was breaking, and I didn't want to risk it breaking anymore. It was selfish of me, I realize that now, and I'm sorry. I know the way I reacted wasn't rational. But given my track record, I couldn't help but feel whenever I loved completely I put him or her at risk for a catastrophe. Which makes your suicide attempt even more ironic. I thought by distancing myself from you I would manage to keep you safe. Instead, look what happened. I prompted you to try and take your own life." Beatrice paused to wipe a tear from her check.

"I don't understand what you are talking about. Yes, Brody died tragically, but Daddy didn't." As an afterthought, I added, "He died ungracefully maybe, but definitely not tragically."

"I am not talking about your father. I cared about him greatly, of course, but I didn't love him. Not in the way I loved William."

"William? Who is William?" I asked. I had never heard my mother talk about a William in my entire life.

"William was the reason I so adamantly opposed your brother buying a motorcycle. William was the first and only love of my life."

My eyes were glued on my mom. I watched as she slowly leaned over the coffee table and picked up her glass and took another sip. After she had placed her glass back on the table, she reached into a box, which was on the floor next to her, and pulled out a picture frame and handed it to me. The frame contained a black and white picture of an incredibly handsome man who appeared to be in his mid-twenties sitting on a motorcycle. He was looking off to the side. There was love in his eyes, and he was smiling wide.

"This was William Brody."

"Brody?" I asked as I wondered if I heard her right.

My mother slowly nodded her head. "Yes, I named your brother after him. Your father never knew. And he probably wouldn't have cared either. After all, by that time Mindy already won his heart anyway."

I was trying to process what she was telling me but I was having a difficult time comprehending. "William was very handsome. Did you take this picture?"

"Yes." She took the picture back and traced his face lovingly with her index finger. "He was looking at me. That's why he was smiling. We were so happy together. The time I spent with William was by far the happiest time in my life."

"What happened with you two?"

"So much." She sighed. "But before I go into everything I have to start further back. I have to talk about your grandfather."

"Alright," I answered as I took a small sip of coffee. I was so confused. My mother wasn't acting like herself at all.

"I know you think I am a cold and difficult woman, well I've got news for you. I'm a walk in the park compared to my father. The man was impossible."

My grandfather had moved to Florida before Brody and I were born. We never spent much time with him. He had extremely limited patience for children. Whenever he'd come to the house, he'd always give us a pat on the head, and then he'd go into a room with my mother and talk to her behind closed doors. I don't remember if I ever had a full conversation with him. My only true memory of him was the massive trust funds he put aside for my brother and me. I wished I had a relationship with him instead of an inheritance.

"You already know he was extremely successful. But his success came at a cost."

My grandfather was pretty much a self-made real estate tycoon. He started from nothing, but by the time he died, not counting the properties he had previously flipped, he owned twenty-five buildings all over Manhattan each one was worth a small fortune.

My mother continued. "He was the first and only person in his family to have money. Everyone else was dirt poor, but rather than remember his humble upbringing he pretended it never happened. He acted as if he had always been rich. Which I guess would have been fine if he wasn't so mean and demeaning to others. He had so much, but was he ever generous with others? No. Never. Not unless he got something out of it."

My mother paused to take a sip of her martini. "Oh, how his family used to kiss his ass. It was pathetic. They were so desperate to stay in his good graces, hoping to get any scraps he decided to throw their way. I'm sure if he lost his fortune they would have high-tailed it away from him and told him what they really thought about him. But they held their tongues just as they held on to the hope that maybe one day they'd get to share in his wealth. Now don't get me wrong. He wasn't completely horrible. He'd help them out on occasion. But when he did he made sure everyone knew about his generosity. Sometimes this ended up causing more problems for the recipient. My uncle Jack, his older brother, for instance, hit some hard times and reluctantly went to my dad for help. My father gave him the money he needed, plus a little extra. But then a couple of months later, at a family wedding, my dad took great pleasure in making sure the entire extended family knew all the gory details of my uncle's issues. I'm not going to get into what they were, but suffice it to say they were very, very personal. My uncle was mortified, betrayed, and oh so hurt. I remember sitting at the table watching tears stream down his face. It was the first time I saw a grown man cry. I will never forget that day."

"What was your mom like?" I asked. My maternal grand-mother passed away when I was about two years old, and I didn't remember anything about her. It's sad how much I didn't know about my family history. I didn't want the same thing to happen to my kids, which is why my mother's distance hurt me so much.

"In one word, broken." My mother paused and took another sip of her cocktail. "My mother was a very simple woman. When she and my dad got married, he was just starting out. Money was tight. They struggled, especially after I was born. But she said he was different then. She said he was fun and outgoing. She even described him as the life of the party. She would always talk about how happy she was in the early years. By my third birthday, his luck took a turn and he started raking in the dough. My mother always said it was the beginning of the end."

"That's hard to imagine," I said, although I had no idea why. It isn't like I ever had to struggle a day financially in my life.

"I know. It would seem that way, wouldn't it? But once he started making a little money, he got greedy and wanted more. Money was like a drug to him, and he got addicted fast. His work consumed him. It was all he ever thought about, all he ever did. He hardly spent time with my mother, or me, unless it was to advance his career. She was so isolated and lonely. It's funny how people were back then. All of her family and friends catered to my dad in the hopes of him sharing some of his fortune with them, but they shunned my mother. They were jealous of her for her fancy clothes and jewelry. They blamed her for my father's arrogance like she could control a grown man. My mother hated the wealthy society women she had to associate with when she had to accompany my father to events. She said they made her skin crawl. I remember once, my mother told me they were like vipers always out for the kill, and lethal when they strike. But my mom remained the perfect wife. She kept her feelings to herself. My mom would always be polite, but she remained detached. She hardly chatted with the other women. As time passed, she grew incredibly depressed. More days than not, she'd spend the entire day in her bedroom alone, reading. Books were her escape and companion."

"So sad," I said, as I imagined how lonely and depressed she must have been. I was also sorry my mother had to grow up in such an unhappy home.

"It was especially difficult for me. On the outside, I was the pretty rich girl. On the inside, I was an accessory to their marriage. I was something for them to parade around and show off. Maids and nannies raised me. I don't think my parents ever loved me. I desperately wanted a different life for you and Brody. I wanted to break the cycle, but I didn't, and I'm so sorry."

"You did, Mom," I said as I placed my hand on her knee and squeezed. "Sure we had help, but you spent a lot of time with us growing up. You were a good mother. You were tough, but fun. The three of us had a lot of great times together, don't you remember?"

"I do. But I was afraid you didn't." My mother once again wiped a tear away from her face. "You make me feel so much better, Annabel. Thank you. I loved you children so much. I only wanted you to be happy and feel loved."

"We were both," I said as I remembered the good times we shared. "We both knew you loved us, and we felt the same way about you."

"I hope so," my mother said quietly. "I never understood what love felt like until I met William. I was twenty-four years old at the time and working for my father, managing his buildings. I despised what I was doing. It was dreadfully boring. Did you know I always wanted to be a teacher?"

I looked her in the eyes. "No, I didn't. Why didn't you teach then?"

My mother picked up her glass but returned it to the table without taking a sip. "Because my father refused to send me to college."

"Why would he do that?"

"He said it was a waste of his money, me getting an education. Can you believe? Who says that to their child?"

I shrugged my shoulders, and my mother continued her story. "He said I should just focus my attention on finding myself a proper husband, make babies, and join a country club. He wanted me to live a life that would make him proud. I had a dream, and he tried to kill it. I wasn't going to let him, though. I went through the motions. I worked for him, but I saved every penny I earned. I was determined to eventually send myself to school. That's how badly I wanted to teach. I loved children so much."

I didn't know what to think or feel. Here my mother was declaring her love for kids, yet she barely had a relationship with my children.

"Would you ever have guessed, I wanted a huge family? I imagined having at least six children." She said with a far away look in her eyes.

"No, I didn't. If you wanted a big family, why did you only have two children?"

She took another sip of gin and replied. "I didn't."

With every passing moment, this day was getting more surreal. I felt like I was watching a bad soap opera, not sitting in my mother's bedroom.

"You and William had a baby?" I asked. Could I have a brother or sister out there somewhere I didn't know about?

My mother once again traced Williams face with her finger as she replied, "Unfortunately we never had the chance."

"Then what are you talking about? I'm so confused."

"Besides the three miscarriages I experienced, your father and I had another baby."

I stared at my mother. She wasn't making any sense. "What are you talking about? What other baby?" I asked.

She put William's picture down on the coffee table and asked, "Do you remember Scottie?"

I gasped and ran my fingers through my hair. What was my mother saying now? Yes, her martini was almost gone but she didn't seem drunk to me. Why was she talking crazy? "You mean my imaginary friend, Scottie?"

My mother buried her head in her hands and sobbed. "No Annabel, he wasn't your imaginary friend. He was your real life, flesh and blood baby brother. You were so excited when we brought him home from the hospital. You were only two and a half years old but you were over the moon. You kept calling him your baby. You were always on top of me when I was caring for him. You were cute as a button. I think you were the only toddler in creation who wanted to help change a diaper. You loved him so much."

I felt all the color drain from my face. My fingers turned to ice. "He was real? I always thought I imagined him."

"I know you did, Sweetie." My mom leaned over and kissed the top of my head. "I encouraged you to think he was make believe. I didn't want you to go through that kind of loss. I didn't want you to start your life knowing what grief and sadness was. You were too vibrant and innocent a little girl to experience so much pain. I wanted better for you."

I was crying now too. I wanted to ask her if anything in my life was really what it seemed to have been. But instead, I asked, "What happened?"

"He was a little over six months old. I put him down for a

nap and then you and I went into the den and played Chutes and Ladders. Do you remember how much you loved that game?"

I nodded my head.

"You beat me," my mom flashed me a sad smile. "When we were done playing, I brought you into the kitchen so Rosie could give you a snack. I went into Scottie's bedroom to check on him. He was napping an awfully long time. I wasn't concerned. I figured he was just tired; he was a very good sleeper, unlike you, and Brody for that matter. But as soon as I looked in his crib, I realized something was dreadfully wrong. He felt cold to my touch. He had a bluish hue around his nose and mouth. I picked him up. He wasn't moving, and he wasn't breathing either."

"Oh my God, Mommy," I said as I cried, knowing she lived every mother's worst nightmare. I inched closer to her, and she hugged me tightly.

When she broke away from the embrace, she replied, "It was devastating to lose a child to sudden infant death syndrome. I was a wreck. I didn't want to go on, I was so heartbroken, but I had no choice. I had to be strong. I had you to take care of. Such a sweet and innocent girl, you didn't understand why I was so sad but you worked so hard constantly trying to cheer me up, and you did." She patted my knee. "You kept me going. I convinced your father to try for another baby right away, but I miscarried. Three times."

"God Mom, I can't even imagine what you went through," I said honestly. My two pregnancies were perfect, just as my children appeared to be.

"With every loss of a baby, my marriage began to slip away a little bit more. If I'm honest with myself, I'm responsible for your dad seeking solace and falling in love with Mindy. I pushed him away. I blamed him for the babies. I had no patience to hear about his difficult days at work when I was dealing with constant loss. When I conceived Brody, I promised your father it would be our last attempt. If I weren't able to carry him to term, I'd give up on trying to grow our family. I kept my pregnancy a secret as long as I could. I never dared to dream I would actually give birth to a baby again. I was shocked when I did. As soon as I saw your brother's face, I was overcome with love for him, just as I was for you. When I held him in my arms the first time, I knew he was destined for greatness. I wanted him to have the life my William didn't have the chance to live. I wanted to name him after the only man I ever loved as much as him. William Brody."

My mother got up and walked to the window and stared at the backyard. I took the few minutes to try to process everything my mother just told me.

"Are you okay?" I asked as she sat back down beside me.

"This is harder than I imagined, Annabel. I didn't plan on telling you so much at once, and definitely not today," her voice cracked as she said today. "But I feel like I have to. And given what you told me over lunch, it can't wait any longer. Too much time has already passed."

CHAPTER EIGHTEEN

My mother picked up the picture frame from the coffee table and caressed the face of William once more. She looked as if she was a million miles away as she spoke. "As I was starting to tell you, I was twenty-four years old and was working for my father helping him manage his properties. My father was busy working on finding himself a suitable son-in-law. I think he was worried I was on the fast track to becoming a spinster. Oh, how terrible would that be for his reputation?" She snickered, "My dad was constantly trying to fix me up. I had no interest in the stiffs he found for me. One was more stuck up and droll than the next. It was a painful process. Who wants their father to scout out dates for them?"

"I'm so glad I didn't have to worry about you doing that," I joked.

"I would never put you through what I experienced. If you recall, I never commented or criticized anyone you dated, ever. Not even Mitch and I hated that pompous jerk."

"You did?" I asked. I was actually kind of shocked. Even though he was young and just starting out, Mitch was so ambitious and successful. He was always hobnobbing with the who's who of the New York legal scene. I always imagined he would have been my mother's ideal son-in-law.

"Yes, I did. He was a self-absorbed user. But did I ever express my opinion? No, not once! I kept my thoughts to myself. I trusted you had the good judgment to tell a gem from a dud. And you proved me right, eventually. You have no idea how thrilled I was when you finally dumped Mitch. I was so impressed with Cole from the first time I met him. It only took me five minutes with the man to realize you got yourself a good catch. He's one special guy. I'm so happy you have him in your corner, and that he makes you happy. He does make you happy, doesn't he?" She asked, totally sincere.

"So much, Mom," I said as I pictured my husband's handsome face. "He's the best thing ever to happen to me. He's everything I had dreamt of and more."

"Good, because that's what you deserve. I love how your eyes light up when you talk about him. I know I would have been the same way, even all these years later, if I had the opportunity to have made a life with my William. I guess I really need just to tell you about him already. I'm sorry I keep getting off topic. It's just one thing leads to another."

"Take your time. I don't mind how long it takes. It's nice talking to you this way." I smiled, "After all, I don't think we have ever had a conversation like this before."

"I don't think we have either. And it's probably a little overdue." My mother reached over and tucked a fly away piece of hair behind my ear.

"So, as I was saying, I worked for my dad. One of his buildings had this terrible flood because of some burst pipes. All the apartments on the first floor were badly damaged. I am sure you can imagine how upset the residents were. Well, to make matters worse, the superintendent was on vacation, and my dad had an important golf game. So his solution was to send me over to deal with the irate residents and manage the plumber."

I couldn't help it I smirked at my mom.

"It's okay, darling. You can just laugh out loud. It's comical now, but back then it was so pathetic. I don't know what I knew less about, defusing a situation like that or managing a plumber. Well, I got there right around the same time the plumber and his crew arrived. I directed them as best as I could, and then I tried to deal with the people. Annabel, you've never seen people so angry in your life. They acted like I purposely put a garden hose in their living room and turned on the faucet. Now, over forty years later, I can understand their rage. They were very poor people. Probably everything they owned was ruined, and whom did they have to deal with? Me. Some spoiled rich girl, in her fancy clothes, who knew nothing about anything and had no satisfactory answers for them. They were all yelling at me at once. They were horrible. I felt awful. I didn't know what to do."

"What did you do?" I visualized the scene.

"I tried my hardest not to cry," my mother chuckled. "Which was no easy feat, by the way. I was stammering and stuttering. One man looked like he was about to turn violent. I grew very scared. Fortunately, William appeared. He was one of the plumber's helpers and was actually on his way to the truck to grab some tools. He saw the scene unfolding, and he stopped and walked over to where I was. He quickly grabbed hold of the man's outstretched arm and took him off to the side of the lobby. He spoke to him, but I don't know what he said. I couldn't hear anything. They were too far away. When he was done speaking to the man, he walked back to the group and addressed them all. He assured them he and his boss were in the process of fixing the pipes as quickly as possible. Then he told them they should go back into their apartments and prepare a detailed list of what was damaged so I could bring it back to the building's owner who would then report the damages to his insurance company. Then, despite the fact he had never laid eyes on me before that moment, he assured them I was there to help them. It was amazing. His speech worked. Everyone went back into their apartments to compile their lists."

"He was a lifesaver, huh?" I smiled.

"He sure was. As soon as he saw the situation was under control, he went out to the truck and got the tools he needed. When he reentered the building, he didn't say a word to me. I wanted to stop him, talk to him, but I didn't know what to say. So I didn't say anything. I was so angry at myself. I kept thinking the least I could have done was say thank you to him."

"Yeah. Thanks would have been a good starter," I said as I winked at my mother. It can't imagine her ever being at a loss for words.

"I know." My mom paused and took another sip of her drink. "Fortunately William wasn't shy like I was back then. When he finished working he approached me and said it seemed like I had a rough day. He told me he wanted to buy me a beer to help me relax. He took me to this dive of a bar. I had never been in a place like it in my life. I kept thinking my father would be completely mortified if he saw me there. It was quite liberating. William and I hit it off immediately. We stayed in the bar for hours, just talking and drinking beer."

I shook my head. "I can't picture you drinking beer. I don't think I've ever seen you have one."

"You haven't. I haven't drunk one in over forty years. The taste brings back too many memories."

My mother rubbed her face before continuing. "I hated when the night ended. William seemed upset too. He begged me to hang out with him again the next night, and I did. I didn't tell my parents anything about him. I didn't want to hear their opinions, especially my father's, who by the way, was still trying to find me the perfect husband."

"Why?"

"I knew they wouldn't approve, and I was right. When my father finally found out about my relationship with William he went berserk."

"Why? Wasn't William a nice guy?"

"William was the best guy in the whole world, but he wasn't up to my father's standards." My mother rolled her eyes. "His character didn't matter to my father. He couldn't care less that William was the perfect man for me, simply because William wasn't perfect on paper. William didn't meet any of the prerequisites my father demanded." My mom began ticking them off on her fingers, "William's family was dirt poor. His father died when William was a child, and his mother cleaned houses to support William and his younger sister. William dropped out of high school to help his mother make ends meet. If his actions didn't speak volumes for his character, I don't know what does. But of course, my father couldn't see any of it. He just kept seeing how my relationship with William wouldn't advance his wealth or social status. It was sickening."

"What did you do?"

"I ignored my father as best as I could, but it wasn't easy. I kept hoping and praying he'd have a change of heart and one day he'd open his mind to the fact there was more to love than what's in your wallet. But nothing of the sort happened. The closer I got to William, the more adamant my father was I shouldn't have anything to do with him. It was horrible, especially when William and I started talking about marriage."

"What did your father do?"

"You'll love this one," my mother let out a low throaty laugh. "He threatened to cut me off and disown me if I married William."

"Huh?"

"Yes, you heard me right. You'd think William was a murderer or something. It was nuts. I told my father he could do whatever he wanted to do because I didn't care. And I meant every word. My father could take his money and shove it. I didn't want one penny of it if it meant a life without William."

"Did you tell your dad this?" I asked as I attempted to reconcile in my mind the woman, who now sat next to me with the girl she once was.

"Of course I did, but he didn't believe me. He kept telling me I'd change my mind. He raged insisting I couldn't live any other life but one of privilege. He was so wrong."

My mother bent down and picked up the cardboard box by her feet. She placed it on her lap and rummaged through it. She pulled out a small pouch. She reached inside it and pulled out a gold band with a tiny pink topaz stone and handed it to me.

"Do you remember this ring?"

I held the ring up and looked at it. Then I squeezed my left hand around it tightly as memories came flooding back to me. A tear escaped from my eye.

"Of course I do. You gave me this ring for my sixth birthday. I loved it remember? I never took it off. I wore it all the time. I felt so grown up every time I saw it on my finger."

My mother took the ring out of my hand and kissed it before placing it back in the pouch. "I remember. But I never bought you the ring. William gave it to me. It was my engagement ring."

I sat up straight. "It was?" I asked, shocked. "And you let me wear it?"

"Yes. Let's face it, I couldn't wear it anymore, so I brought it to the jewelry store and had it resized so it would fit you. Oh, Annabel, the ring meant the world to me. It gave me such pleasure to see how much you loved it too. You wore it for years until you said you outgrew it. It broke my heart when you stopped wearing the ring, but there was nothing I could do about it. So I just put it back with all my mementos from my time with William."

"I'm sorry, Mom."

"Don't be. You had no way of knowing the significance of it."

She was right, but I still felt guilty. At one point in time I loved the ring so much, why did I just discard it? Why didn't I want to save it? Was I really that spoiled?

"As I was saying, William and I got engaged. It was the most amazing day of my life. I wanted to make William as happy as he made me. And like you did with Brody, I bought William a motorcycle. I knew he always longed to have one, but he could never afford one. I used the money I saved for college to buy it as an engagement present for him. Teaching was no longer as important to me; after all, I had raising babies to look forward to. He was over the moon. Everything was so perfect for us."

"I guess your father had a change of heart."

"Hell no!" My mother said probably louder than she intended. "He remained on his high horse. He told me I could stay at his house until I married William, but if I were idiotic enough to actually go through with the wedding he and my mother would have nothing to do with me. He vowed he'd never give me another cent."

"The fact a parent could be so cruel to their child is horrible," I said.

"Yes, it was. I wanted out of my parent's house. I couldn't stand being there living with my father the hypocrite and my mother the doormat. I was determined to move out as quickly as I could. William and I found the cutest little apartment in Brooklyn." Gesturing with her hands, she clarified, "It was much, much smaller than this bedroom but it was adorable. It was all I wanted, all I needed. But I never had the chance to live there. Days after we signed the lease William was riding his motorcycle, the motorcycle I bought him. He was on his way to see me. We were meeting at a coffee shop near where I worked. As he approached the restaurant, he lost control of the bike. To this day, I still don't know exactly what happened, but I saw the entire accident. Oh Annabel, It was horrible. My strong, amazing William looked like a bloody rag doll as they lifted him on the stretcher and placed him in the ambulance. I rode with him. I held onto his hand tightly as the paramedics tried to stabilize him. I kept praying to God he'd be okay. But like your brother, he only lived a few hours after he was admitted to the hospital. I had to call his mother and tell her William, my William, her William was dead."

My mother buried her head in her hands and started sobbing.

I didn't know what to say, so I wrapped my arms around her tightly. My heart broke. Two of the people she loved most in the whole world died almost identically.

Bea freed herself from my embrace. "He was the love of my life, Annabel, and he was gone. I only had myself to blame. I couldn't stop thinking if only I didn't buy him that damn motorcycle he'd be alive. I hated myself for killing him."

"But you didn't kill him, Mother. It was an accident," I said as I rubbed my mother's back. "Just like I didn't kill Brody. His death was an accident too. Don't you see?"

"I know that now, but I didn't believe it back then. I needed someone to be responsible for taking away the love of my life, and the only person I had to blame was myself. This was why I didn't want Brody to have the damn bike. I was afraid history would repeat itself. Just the thought of him on a motorcycle made me sick to my stomach. Brody died the same way William did, and I couldn't stop blaming you for his death. It was just too similar to what happened with William and me. Does this make any sense to you?"

I thought for a moment, and while I could never fully forget how horrible my mother acted, I think I could begin to forgive her. After all these years I was finally able to understand some of her motivations and the thought processes behind them.

"Unfortunately Mother, yes it does make sense."

"I hope you mean it. But even if you don't, it does makes me feel better."

I decided to let her comment drop. Instead, I asked, "What happened after William died. How did you end up with Daddy?"

"I spent the first two weeks after William's death in my room crying continuously. My mother was somewhat sympathetic. I have to give her that. My father, however, was just as obnoxious after William died as he was before. Actually, he may have been even worse. He kept telling me I should be thankful William was gone. He told me I would have thrown my life down the drain if I married him. I couldn't stand listening to him. Eventually I came out of my room. I barely ate or slept. I was a walking zombie. Numb. I felt nothing. My father resumed his quest to find me the ideal mate, and he fixed me up with the son of someone he was trying to acquire property from, your father. I dated your dad for a very short time before we got engaged. He was a nice enough guy, but I didn't let myself love him. I couldn't let myself be vulnerable again."

My mother looked at William's picture once more. "I married a man I wasn't in love with because the man I loved was dead and buried. My father got the property he wanted for a steal. In exchange, he offered to buy me a house. And while I wanted no part of his money, I took it because I knew his money was the only thing he loved in this world." She made a sweeping gesture with her hands. "He bought us this ridiculous house. I have no idea why anyone ever would need a house this size. But I picked it out because it was the most expensive one I could find. I hoped my father would have scoffed at the cost, but he just wrote a check. And he kept writing checks, which I kept on taking. But know this Annabel, I'd have gladly done without all his money if only I could have experienced some happiness instead."

CHAPTER NINETEEN

We live our entire lives thinking we know those closest to us. But do we ever really? This question had been plaguing me all week ever since I had the heart to heart chat with my mother. It was very unsettling to find out your mother never loved your father. It was even more troubling to learn she wished she had been able to marry and make a life with another man. After all, if her wish had come true, neither my brother nor I would have ever been born. I couldn't help but wonder what type of life she and William's children would have had. I bet their childhood would have been much different than Brody's and mine. After all, they would have grown up in a house, like Cole's and mine, filled with love rather than indifference.

I was still shocked at how much I didn't know about my mother's past, and the experiences which shaped her into the woman she was now. I can't say I completely understood what made her tick, but I do think I can relate to her more than I ever had been able to before. That said, there remains one big unanswered question. Which is precisely the reason why I was not going to the bakery alone today to help her pick out a wedding cake.

As we approached the storefront, I saw my mom sitting by the counter. She was glancing at her watch. I was about ten minutes late; I knew how much tardiness annoyed her. I really wanted to arrive on time, but there was an accident on the parkway. I opened the door and a bell chimed. My mother immediately turned around. I watched her face fall as she took notice of who was with me. She didn't even attempt to disguise her disdain.

I walked towards her, and she stood up. "Hello, darling," she said as she air kissed me. "You didn't tell me you were bringing him."

Did she have to say "him" like it was a dirty word? I ignored her tone and replied, "I didn't think it would matter." Turning to my son I said, "Harley, go give your grandmother a hug."

"OKAY!" he screamed loudly and threw his arms around her waist. I know at some point he will grow up and change, but for right now, my little boy was the most affectionate child known to man. He loved everyone.

My mother didn't move. She remained rigid. She didn't make any attempt to touch my son. It hurt my heart. When Harley let go of the embrace, she looked me square in the eyes and replied, "Annabel, do you really think it's appropriate to include a child in making wedding plans?"

"We're at a bakery, Mother. I don't see how his presence makes a difference one way or another. He's just going to hang out here with us." My mother rolled her eyes as I reached into my bag and pulled out my iPad and handed it to my son. "Besides, he's going to be wrapped up in his game in a few minutes anyway."

Harley he sat down at the counter and began playing. I smiled at my son. "We'll get a snack when Grandma and I are done, Sweetie."

"Very well, Annabel. What's done is done. There's no sense in harping on it, but next time, please give me some advanced warning, will you? We really should get to work. After all, you were supposed to be here fifteen minutes ago."

"Certainly, Mother," I said as I glanced at my son, who was as predicted already lost in his game.

"Donna, we're ready," my mother called out and snapped her finger in order to get the woman's attention.

Either the lady didn't notice or mind my mother's rudeness. She greeted me warmly. "Hi, there! I was just going over some choices with your mom before you arrived. I was telling her these days we are doing two types of wedding cakes. People are opting either for traditional or non-traditional. The latter are growing in popularity. Here take a look at these pictures," she said as she handed us two large pieces of cardboard with multiple pictures of cakes on both of them. "See the ones in this portfolio are all classic looking. They are tiered round cakes. The way the cakes are decorated is different, of course, but they all have the same look and feel. The cakes on this one are more unique. Some of them resemble the old fashioned style, but if you notice the tiered cakes are square not round. And some of the others are totally unique."

"Wow! This one really stands out, Mother! I love this idea!" I said as I pointed to a cake that was comprised of four tiers of little square cakes. Each one was covered in turquoise frosting, and they all had little white bows also made out of frosting on top of them. The cakes resembled Tiffany ring boxes. On top of the fourth tier, there was a small round cake featuring yet another frosted bow.

"You've got to be kidding, it's horrible," my mother scoffed. "I'm not having a sweet sixteen party for goodness sake. I'm getting married!"

"The cake your daughter picked out is actually our most popular one, Mrs. Buchanan," Donna chimed in.

"Well, just because the rest of the world has lost their common sense doesn't mean I am going to have a ridiculous cake for my wedding. I want no part of any of these," my mother said as she thrust the modern portfolio back at Donna. "My wedding is going to be a classy affair. I want a cake that screams elegant. Here!" She tapped the portfolio with a long French manicured fingernail. "Look! This is what I am talking about," she said. Her finger was on a three-tiered round cake with decorative frosting, which resembled lace. "Isn't this perfect?" she gushed.

"It does look exactly like what you were describing."

"This is perfect. It is exactly the style I want. The decision is made!"

"I'm so glad I could help you decide," I flashed my mother a toothy grin. She didn't reply. Instead, she went over specifics with Donna. I ordered two coffees, a cup of hot chocolate, a large chocolate cupcake for Harley as well an assortment of cookies from a different woman standing behind the counter. Harley followed the tray and me to a small table in the back of the store.

We were only seated a minute or so when I felt a gentle tap on my shoulder. I looked up and saw an elderly woman. She was holding a newspaper and an empty coffee cup, which had a paper plate, folded into it. "Your son is so precious. I was sitting right there," she said as she turned and pointed to the table directly behind us. "I couldn't take my eyes off him. I don't know if I have ever seen a child enjoy dessert more. It gave me such pleasure to watch him for a few moments. Enjoy these moments, and don't blink. If you do, you will miss out on all the simple milestones. Time goes by so quickly. I know. I blinked, and now my little boy has a grandson of his own."

"I'll try not to blink, I promise," I gave her a warm smile before she walked away. I turned my attention back to my son who was now covered in frosting.

"Your son is a mess," my mother said as she approached the table. She gave Harley the once over. She used the back of her hand to wipe away imaginary cake crumbs from her chair before she sat down.

"Who cares?" The elderly woman's words still rang in my ears. "He's enjoying himself. That's all that matters."

"I guess. I just hope he doesn't enjoy himself on my suit. It's Armani you know," she said as she scrunched her face in disdain.

"Guess what Grandma!" Harley said with a mouth full of cake.

"What?" my mother asked sounding bored.

"My birthday is in two days!"

"It is, is it?" she asked. I couldn't decide if she was playing coy or really had no idea.

"Yep!" And holding up his fingers he exclaimed, "I'm gonna be six!"

"You're a big boy," my mother said. She looked as if the conversation was paining her.

"Yep! I am the biggest now than I ever was. And in two days I'm gonna get even bigger."

"True again," she replied, as she yawned. Then almost as an afterthought, she asked, "What do you want for your birthday?" I was amazed. She sort of was having a conversation with my son.

He took a big bite of cupcake and said, "Birthday cake!"

She looked at him as if he lost his mind. "Birthday cake? Really?"

"Yep! What's wrong with it? Cake's good!" To prove his point, he took another huge bite of his cupcake.

"While you are correct, your answer was not what I expected you to say." She replied as she took a dainty sip of coffee.

Harley just shrugged his shoulders. My mother reached into her Prada bag and pulled out a card shaped envelope. "Oh, that reminds me. This is for Harley's birthday."

I didn't have to open it. I already knew what the card contained: one hundred dollars in cash for me to buy him a present with and also a check for four hundred dollars for me to deposit in the bank for his future. She gave my kids the same thing for every birthday.

"Thanks, Mom. I am sure I already know what's in here, and it's very generous of you. It's too generous of you." I put the card down on the table. I couldn't bring myself to put it in my bag. "My kids don't need this amount of money for their birthday. They don't understand it. And even though I always use the money to buy them something, and tell them it is from you, they're not dumb. They see right through it. They know Cole and I picked out the presents. Just one time it would mean so much to them, and to Cole and me if you just picked something out for them and gave it to them yourself. It doesn't have to be much. You just heard Harley. All he wants for his birthday is cake. You can't go wrong with anything you buy him."

My mother shook her head. "I don't know, Annabel. What do I know about what a five-year old boy wants?"

"You just nailed the problem precisely, Mother. You don't know anything about him because you never spend any time with him. I think you said more to him today than you have in his whole life." I paused and took a deep breath, "Mom, he is such a sweet boy. Do you have any idea how sad it makes me that you won't have anything to do with him?"

My mother didn't utter a word. She just took another sip of coffee. So I continued, "Now it isn't like you have a close relationship with my daughter, but you do interact with her, a little bit. You have spent some time with her. You even played Barbie's with her once or twice. And I think you may also have French braided her hair one time too. But you never seem to have any interest in Harley. Why mother?"

Again my mother remained quiet. Her eyes darted all around the room. She looked everywhere but at me.

"Can't you answer my question?" I demanded as I banged my fist on the table causing some of my coffee to spill. I reached for a napkin to clean it up. "I'm sorry I'm getting upset, but I just don't understand why you ignore my son. Look at him."

My mother glanced in his direction.

"No, Mother. Please. Really look at him. He's a beautiful, smart, and sweet boy. He's a messy eater; I'll give you that. But he has no other faults. Joy radiates from his very being. Why can't you see it?"

My mother covered her face with her hands and let out a large sigh. "I don't want to see it. Okay. It's too painful for me to see."

"What do you mean?" I asked, completely confused.

"Look at him, Annabel. What do you see when you look at him, besides your son?"

I shrugged my shoulders, clueless of what she was getting at.

"Who does he look exactly like?"

I smiled at him. "I don't know. I guess he sort of looks a little like me."

"No. He looks exactly like your brother, and he has since the day he was born. I swear it's almost like Cole had no part in his creation."

"I can attest to the fact he did," I said with a smirk. But then her words sank in. The pieces of the puzzle were slowly fitted together. I said, "Wait a minute. Let me get this straight. You don't want to get to know your grandson because he looks like my brother? Is that right?"

"Yes," my mother said softly.

I laughed. "Don't you think you're being stupid?"

"No." My mother tried to defend herself. "Seeing him makes me miss my son too much. You had no control over how he would look, but you did select his name. Why in the world did you have to go and name him Harley? Whatever possessed you to do something like that? It's absurd! Who names their child after the manufacturer of the motorcycle that killed their brother? Thank goodness you didn't have two sons, you'd probably name the other Davidson."

I couldn't help it. I laughed. Hard. My mother gave me the stink eye.

I tried to suppress my laughter. "You know, I like it. If Cole and I ever decide to have another baby, I'll have to remember that name."

Beatrice shook her head and sighed deeply. I noticed there were tears in her eyes.

I rubbed my forehead a as realization hit me. I was no longer laughing. "I'm sorry. When I picked out his name I didn't once stop and consider your feelings. It was insensitive of me. I should have thought about how it would make you feel."

"Yes, you should have," she spat.

"I'm sorry. I know that Harley is an unconventional name, especially given the circumstances. But I found comfort in the name. After all, the names I chose for both of my children were tributes to Brody."

"What are you talking about? Your daughter is named Violet for heaven's sake."

"Yeah, I know. What were the two things Brody loved most?" I asked as I winked at my mother and pictured my brother.

My mother didn't reply. So, I answered. "Motorcycles and the Baltimore Ravens. Remember how obsessed he was with the team?"

Beatrice offered me a sad smile. I could tell she too was picturing Brody decked out in is favorite jersey. I continued speaking, "I always thought his love of the team was funny considering how all of his friends were busy rooting for the Jets or the Giants. I remember how much grief they gave him for his choice, but he didn't care. Their teasing never fazed him. Our

Brody always did beat to his own drum. He never followed others and he never cared what others thought. He practically lived in his Raven's jersey. The violet jersey."

My mother brought her hand up to her mouth and uttered, "Oh my. I didn't realize." She smiled.

"If I'm honest with myself, I can understand why being with Harley can be difficult for you. I'm sure it opens up a lot of old wounds. But don't you realize by turning your back on him, by choosing the past instead of the present, you are missing out on a wonderful future with your grandson. I know Harley isn't Brody. Brody is gone, and as much as I hate it, he's never going to come back. But Harley is here now." I smiled at my son. "He's full of life and love. I'm sure, if you'd only give him a chance, his presence and love can help fill up some of the voids in your heart."

I pushed the envelope my mother had handed me moments before back at her with my index finger. "Here take this back."

"What are you doing, Annabel?"

"I'm standing up for my children. I'm fighting so they have what I didn't have growing up. Brody and I never had a real relationship with our grandparents. I don't want the same thing to happen with my kids. I want them to be close to all their grandparents. They are already so close to Connie and Patrick. They are beginning to adore Walter. I want them to love you too." I reached for her hands and squeezed them. "Come on. Wouldn't it be wonderful if they were able to confide some of their hopes and share their accomplishments with you? Wouldn't it be great if they couldn't wait for you to come and visit? Don't you want them to cherish you?"

My mother contemplated for a moment, and then she said softly, "I guess getting to know the children better would be nice. And I think Walter would really enjoy spending more time with them too."

I took a sip of coffee, pleased with myself. "Good. Cole's

parents are coming over on Tuesday night for Harley's birthday. I'm making dinner. Please, come over with Walter at seven o'clock. Bring Harley a present, any present. And once and for all get to know your grandson. You may not think you want this but mark my words, one day you will thank me for doing this."

Her voice was barely a whisper as she replied, "Okay."

CHAPTER TWENTY

"Here, give me the plates. I'll set the table," Connie said as she grabbed the dishes from my hands. She and Patrick arrived a half hour ago. He was in the den entertaining the kids, and she was helping me prepare dinner. Cole had to work late, so he wasn't due home for at least another forty-five minutes or so.

"Are you okay?" Connie asked as she returned to the kitchen. She could always sense when I was on edge. I put the wooden spoon I was holding down and turned to face her.

"I'm just nervous. My mom and Walter should be here any minute. I pushed her into coming here tonight. I'm afraid it was a mistake. What if it's a disaster? What if she ruins Harley's birthday."

"Come here, Anna," she ordered. She pulled out a chair. "Sit down."

I did as I was told.

"You need to snap out of this already. Stop second-guessing everything you say and do when it comes to your mother. It is getting annoying already."

I twirled my hair around my finger. "But Connie—"

"Don't but Connie me. I made you a promise years ago that

I would not sugar coat anything. I've been telling it like it is for years, and I'm not about to change that now. So you listen to me and listen to me good."

"Okay."

"I've always had your best interest at heart. One of the happiest days in my life was when Cole told me he was going to marry you. I know my girls sometimes get jealous of our relationship. You know I think of you as my third daughter and not as my daughter-in-law."

"I know."

"And when you listen to me you are happier, isn't that right?"

I rolled my eyes but smiled. I didn't have to answer her; she knew the answer was yes.

"I want you to think about the last few months. You have had a wonderful opportunity, one that I honestly didn't think was possible. You've spent more time with your mother recently than you have in the past twelve years. She's really been making an effort to repair your relationship. From what you've told me, she's opened up to you. And you, in turn, have done the same. And I am thrilled you both are finally beginning to understand each other. Do you guys have a lot of work left to do? Hell yes. But you are traveling down the right road."

"I know, you're right."

"Of course I am. But Anna, have no doubts, she is controlling this reconciliation. She is the one who made the first move."

"Yeah," I snickered. "Because she needed help."

"No, Anna. She wanted your help. Let's face it; your mother is a very self-sufficient woman. She has no qualms about hiring people to do anything she needs. She could have easily found a wedding planner to assist her. But she didn't. She reached out to you."

"I didn't think of that."

Connie rolled her eyes. "Yeah, I figured as much. I know you don't trust her, and I don't blame you for walking on eggshells around her. She hurt you badly. But you really need to let go of some of your anger; it isn't doing you any good. You need to try and keep more of an open mind when it comes to her. Don't always anticipate the worst. Sure, you may end up being disappointed, but you also may find yourself pleasantly surprised. I don't know about you, but personally, I don't see the point in getting upset until there is actually something to be upset about. Today is your son's birthday. He's happy. You should be happy too. Save the worry for something worth worrying about."

"SIT DOWN AND RELAX, Babe. Here, have a little wine," Cole said to me as he handed me a glass of Napa Valley Cabernet. Then he took the dishtowel out of my hands and reached for the pot I just finished washing. "You did enough today. Let me take care of the rest of this."

"You don't have to twist my arm, though I do feel bad since you had a very long day yourself," I yawned and plopped down at the kitchen table. I took a sip of wine. "Well tonight was a success, don't you think?"

"I've got to admit when you told me you had invited your mother and Walter over tonight I had my doubts about how the night would play out. I kept remembering my birthday dinner all those years ago. What a debacle that was. But I saw a different side of Beatrice tonight."

"I know! I told you she has been acting strangely. I really think Walter is responsible, don't you? He's definitely been a good influence on her. It's so funny; I was talking to some of the girls at work today about the wedding. Almost all of them couldn't stand the guys their mother's remarried. It seemed like they resented the men and as a result their relationships with their mothers have suffered. I feel completely opposite. I wish Beatrice had met Walter years ago. I'm so happy she found a guy like him."

Cole nodded his head.

I continued speaking, "I've got to be honest, I still don't fully understand what he saw in her, but I am glad he is part of her life."

Cole chuckled. "I know what you mean. I guess there are just some things we will never understand."

"True. You know what else? I'm happy. I feel like I am finally getting to know her. It sucks that it has taken so long for us to get to this point, but I am glad I'm finally starting to have a relationship with her again. I just hope it isn't too late for the kids."

"I know. But I think you should be hopeful. Did you see your son with her tonight? He didn't leave her alone for a moment after she gave him his birthday present. Beatrice really outdid herself with the train set. Harley was in heaven."

I smiled as I remembered how happy my son was all night long. "Very true. But Cole, don't forget your mom was there as well. I bet she was entertaining the kids."

"I don't think so," Cole said as he put the last pot away in the cabinet. He walked over to the kitchen table and poured himself a glass of wine before he sat down next to me. "I was in the den with them. My mom was definitely taking a back seat in the entertainment department. In fact, she spent most of the time talking to my dad, Walter, and me. It was all your mother doing the playing."

"Really? I find it hard to imagine, but I am happy it happened. What about Violet?" I asked before I took another sip of wine.

"First off, she was madly in love with the Alex and Ani bracelets your mom brought her. I bet you didn't think Bea would pick up something for her too."

I didn't answer.

"She was playing with your mom and Harley too. It was actually really wonderful to watch."

"You know what shocked me the most?"

"Harley eating all of his broccoli?" Cole joked.

"No, although that was odd. What I found so interesting was how our mothers hit it off. They seemed to have so much to talk about. Didn't you find it strange?"

"I don't know. I didn't give it any thought," Cole said as he rubbed his head. "But now since you mention it, it was pretty peculiar. But then again, my mom can talk to anyone about anything."

"Yeah, I know. I have gone shopping with her remember? She stands in line for five minutes and manages to find out the entire life story of everyone near her. It's crazy!"

Cole chuckled. "Yeah, I know. But she has never gotten your mother to warm up to her. No matter how hard she or Dad tried. Beatrice has always been so cold and distant around my parents. I don't think they ever spoke more than five words to each other before. And tonight, they were pretty chummy."

"Bizarre," I said again as I tried to stifle a yawn. Man, I longed for the days when I was able to stay up all night long.

"Speaking of strange, how weird was it Beatrice agreed to go with my mom to help out at Harley's school on Friday?"

"She did what?" I almost spit out my wine. "Where have I been all night? I missed everything."

"Well, when you cook up a feast like you did tonight you are bound to miss out on a few things," Cole joked. "But seriously, you heard me. Beatrice is going to Harley's school on Friday with my mom."

"I don't believe it, especially since her wedding is the following weekend. I would think she'd be petrified of catching a sniffle. After all, could you imagine how catastrophic it would be if she had an irritated nose on her big day?"

"Her coming down with something she picked up at our kid's school would be a calamity of ginormous proportions!" Cole said as he laughed. "But seriously, in less than two weeks your mom's going to be married again." Cole reached across the table and squeezed my hand. "Now since you aren't going to be swamped with wedding preparations, what are you going to do with all your free time?"

Free time? The thought sounded heavenly. These past few months had been a whirlwind. I had no clue how I had been able to handle it all. But rather than say any of this I gave my husband a salacious smile and said, "I'm sure I can think of something else to do with my time."

"That's what I was hoping for. But seriously, you've spent a lot of time with your mother planning this wedding. Between selecting flowers, cake, invitations, photographers, caterers, and bands, you have been busy at least one day a weekend for almost three months. I bet it will be strange for you when the wedding is over."

"Yeah. It will be odd. I've got to admit, I really had fun being involved in all the plans. Although for the life of me I have no idea why my mother had me tag along. It wasn't like she ever listened to my opinion. Whatever I suggested, she picked out the opposite. I'm still shocked Violet and I were allowed to select our own dresses."

"Well, the wedding isn't here yet. Beatrice still has time to change her mind doesn't she?" Cole asked.

I laughed.

Cole reached for the bottle of wine and topped off our glasses. "Something has been bothering me. Since you are so involved with planning this event, do you ever regret our decision?"

I took a sip of wine. "You mean us eloping?"

"Yeah," Cole answered softly as he nodded his head.

I looked up to the ceiling before I answered. "Kind of. I

don't know. I've got mixed feelings. I loved our wedding don't get me wrong. It was so romantic and intimate on the beach. But it definitely wasn't the wedding I dreamt of. I remember when I was a little girl every game of house I played included me walking down the aisle. I was a bride for three Halloweens. For as far back as I could remember I always dreamt of having a huge wedding. But I realized long before we eloped a wedding doesn't make a marriage. I wanted a marriage. I wanted to share every day and night of my life with my best friend, the man who even after all these years continues to make me weak in the knees with just one look, the guy who knows how to make me laugh even when I want to cry, and whose kisses feel like home. And that's what I was lucky enough to get." A tear fell down my cheek.

Cole reached across the table and gently wiped the tear away. "We still would have had all of that if we had a big wedding with all our friends and family, Anna."

"I know. But the time wasn't right. I wasn't in the right emotional place. Fantasies change. Dreams change. And people change too. But one thing I wouldn't change is my life with you." I got up from my chair and sat down on my husband's lap. I let my kiss tell him just how much I loved him.

CHAPTER TWENTY-ONE

I swear it was intimidation by dehydration!

The weather was unseasonably warm for June. It was the perfect day to hang out on a beach with a good book. Unfortunately, I had to travel from Long Island to Manhattan with four of my co-workers. Once we reached the city we then had to hop on the subway and head all the way uptown. By the time we reached John McGrevor's office we were all sweltering and in desperate need of a shower.

It was no surprise he had us waiting for him in his conference room for forty-five minutes. Once he finally graced us with his presence, he began to berate us, and he hasn't let up one bit since he walked into the room. His verbal attack would have been less painful if he had offered us a glass of water, like the one he kept sipping from. But he hadn't. It was crystal clear his lack of manners was intentional.

I often wondered what made people tick. How could someone so successful be so clueless as to how to treat people? Didn't he realize you got more out of people by being fair and kind than being heartless and cruel?

It was Cecelia's, turn on the hot seat. As she defended her team's actions and decisions, in an attempt to stay calm, I jotted down some items I needed to pick up later today at the grocery store. I had to give Cecelia credit. She wasn't letting him fluster her. I could only hope when it was my turn to face his wrath I would be able to handle it just as well as she seemed to be doing.

While I was great at coming up with witty retorts way after the fact, usually when I was in the shower the next morning, I was never quick on my feet. I was petrified that McGrevor was going to rip me to shreds. My one saving grace was I knew Cecelia would have my back if things got really bad. Cee was the opposite of me. I like to avoid conflict at all costs. Cecelia, on the other hand, met challenges head on. She never held back her opinions despite how uncomfortable they may be to express. I often wished I were more like her. She had been encouraging me to speak up more often, and when I reluctantly listened to her, I felt great. Unfortunately, I don't follow her advice anywhere nearly as much as I should. I really don't know why I always let my insecurities get the better of me.

Even though my iPhone was on silent, the sound of the vibration was loud enough to divert everyone's attention to me. I glanced down and muttered, "crap," under my breath. Out loud I said, "Excuse me." I got up and walked over to the doorway.

"You're not seriously interrupting a meeting with me, your client, to go and answer your mobile phone, are you?" McGrevor asked in an indignant tone.

I flashed him an ice-cold stare. "I'm sorry, but yes, I am."

I walked out of the room and closed the conference door behind me before pressing the answer button.

"Hello, Mrs. O'Conner. This is Kathy, the nurse at Violet's school. I'm sorry to have to call you, but I wasn't able to reach your mother-in-law. Violet had an accident today."

My stomach flipped and bile filled my throat "What

happened? Is she okay?" I asked as I hoped for the best and braced myself for the worst.

"During lunch, she and her friends were goofing around on the monkey bars. Jamie dared Violet to do a flip. Unfortunately, when she tried she slipped and landed on her arm. I'm not a doctor, but I think it may be broken."

I rubbed my hand across my face. "Oh no! Is she in pain?"

"Yes, she is. Can you or someone come pick her up?"

Crap! Connie and Patrick were in Atlantic City. They went yesterday and were going to be staying there until tomorrow afternoon. They went every spring to celebrate their anniversary. Of all the days for me to be in the city! I hardly ever had to go to my client's offices. Usually our clients came to us. I sighed deeply. "I'm actually in Manhattan," I replied. "It may take me a while to get there."

"Okay. Come when you can. She will be fine. She's calming down, and I'll keep her with me until you get here." Despite the nurse's attempt to comfort me I felt terrible.

As soon as I disconnected the call with the nurse I dialed Cole's number and filled him in on the situation. I glanced at my watch as I spoke to him. "If I leave now, and I have no idea how I'm going to be able to get out of here easily mind you, it will take me at least two hours to reach the school, assuming I don't have to wait for any trains. God, I hate for her to be sitting there in pain for such a long amount of time. I also feel terrible I have to bail on this meeting. It's actually going worse than I expected. My team needs me for support." As soon as the words came out of my mouth, I wanted to kick myself. I ran my fingers through my hair. "What's wrong with me? What am I saying? I'm such a terrible mother, aren't I?"

"No. You are honest, Anna," Cole tried to comfort me. "You take your job seriously, and there is nothing wrong with that. In fact, it's the very reason why you are so good at it. I know how hard you, and everyone else, have been working on this account." He paused and sighed. "Do you want me to go?"

I opened my mouth to say yes out of reflex. But I didn't dare utter the words.

"No. You can't go. There's too much going on at your firm right now. You can't be running out. Yesterday you found out that you were selected to head up the new shopping center. You need to stay I'll go. After all, we don't have any other choice. Your mom's away."

Cole was quiet for a moment, and then he said, "But your mom isn't."

"What? You want me to call my mother and ask her to go and get Violet? Have you lost your mind?"

"She is Violet's grandmother, isn't she?" he replied, sarcastically.

"Yes, but she is far from grandmotherly," I spat back.

"Anna, you really aren't being fair. Believe me, I'm far from the president of the Beatrice Buchanan fan club, but your mother has really been trying to make an attempt to repair your relationship. She's been working on getting to know the kids better too. My mom kept on raving about how wonderful she was at Harley's school last Friday. You need to cut her some slack. I bet she'll help you out. She may even appreciate the opportunity."

"Yeah right," I snarled as I started to pace. John McGrevor's employees stared at me, but I didn't care. "I'm sure that won't be the case." A huge part of me wanted to punch my husband in the throat.

"There's only one way to find out," he snickered.

In a small voice, I asked, "What happens if she won't go?" I sighed deeply. "I'd hate to ask for help only to have her to turn me down. I don't think I could forgive her if she didn't go and get Violet. If I don't ask her, I'll never know what she'd do." Sheepishly I continued, "And if I don't know then I won't have to be disappointed or angry." Suddenly I remembered my conversation with Connie.

"Anna, you know I love you, but you are being ridiculous. Grow up and stop walking on eggshells around your mother. She's not perfect, but neither are you. Relationships are a two-way street, and I'm sure some of her actions were reactions to yours."

I didn't answer. I bit my lip. The truth hurt.

When I didn't respond Cole continued, "You need to stop living your life in fear of angering other people. Really, what is the worst thing that will happen if you ask? Come on, even if Beatrice doesn't go, I bet Walter would go in a second. Call her, and then call me back."

He didn't wait for me to reply. He hung up the phone. I hated to admit, it but he had a point. I glanced back at the conference room. Even though the door was closed, I could hear the voices inside were growing louder. I had no doubts; the conversation clearly was becoming more heated with every passing second.

I didn't think. I just dialed. My mother answered her cell phone on the second ring. "Hello, darling! I am surprised you called, but I am thrilled. I have the best news!" She gushed. "I just got off the phone with the banquet manager at the club. Remember I was worried they wouldn't be able to order enough lobsters in time for the wedding. I don't know why I didn't think to have them on the menu sooner, but—"

"Mom, I am sorry to cut you off, but I have a problem."

With a tone that signified she was upset with the interruption, she asked, "What is it?" Then in a muffled tone she said, "Honey, be a plum and go see if they have these in an eight and a half?"

When I thought her attention was focused a bit more on me than designer pumps she was lusting after I stated, "I'm in the city at a meeting with an impossible client. Cole's at work too.

Connie and Patrick are out of town, and the school nurse just called. She thinks Violet broke her arm."

"Oh no! That's terrible."

I paused for a second. "If I leave now, which will be quite difficult, it'll take me about two hours to get to the school. Is there any way you can go get her and stay with her until Cole or I can get home and arrange to take her to the doctor?"

Very calmly my mother replied, "No."

I felt like someone sucker punched me. My worst fear was confirmed. My heart pounded in my chest, and I felt my face flush. "What do you mean no? What are you doing that's so important you can't put on hold for a couple of hours to help your granddaughter and me out? Is Nordstrom's having their semi-annual sale? Do you really need another pair of shoes so badly? Never mind. Don't answer. It doesn't matter. I never ask you for anything, ever. And the one time I'm desperate enough to put my fears aside and work up the courage to ask you for help you say *no*?" Tears streamed down my face as I spoke. "I guess Walter is with you and it was him you asked to fetch your shoes. Can you put him on the phone, please? I need to speak to him. Maybe he won't be too self-centered to help me."

"Well, that was quite harsh, Annabel, don't you think? But it wasn't completely unwarranted," my mother scolded. "I really wish you would've let me finish speaking before you assumed the worst of me and jumped down my throat. I don't want to get into a fight with you, so I'm going to forget you said what you did. I can tell you are stressed and under pressure. But to clarify, what I was going to say, if you had only given me the chance to speak, was no I wouldn't just get her and wait. I am not going to pick Violet up and sit around with her at your house or mine until you or Cole got home from work. That would be insane. There is no need for the child to wait around for you two, especially if she is in pain. I'm going to call my friend Miriam. Her son is a very successful orthopedist, you know. She owes me a lot of favors. I'll have her call her son and arrange for him to squeeze us in. In fact, I will make sure he takes us as quickly as possible. Then I will pick up Violet from school and take her to his office."

"You... will?" I asked, dumbfounded, as I wiped a tear from my face.

"Yes. And while I hate Violet is hurt, I'm very happy you reached out to me for help. It's nice to know I can be there for you. Listen, I've no idea how long Walter and I will be at the doctor's office, so there is no reason why you or Cole have to kill yourselves to get home quickly. Finish up your meeting. Don't worry about Violet. She'll be in good hands."

For the first time in more years than I could remember, I said, "I love you, Mommy," before hanging up the phone.

I then called the nurse to let her know my mother was coming. Violet was supposed to go to her friend's house after school for a play date. I texted the mother to let her know the plan had changed. And then to Cole I sent:

B & W are getting V and bringing her to the Dr. I hate it when you are right!

INSTANTLY HE REPLIED:

Tough! Speaking of tough, you are tougher than you think. Act that way!

I TOOK a deep breath and opened the conference room door. I walked back in feeling determined, invigorated, and hopeful.

With venom in his voice, John McGrevor stared at me and bellowed, "Finally, you grace us once again with your presence. Anna, I really find it utterly rude and disrespectful you had the audacity to exit a meeting, with me! I am paying your firm to perform a service for me. I expect your full attention. Instead, what do I get? You walked out of this room to conduct a personal conversation! I can't believe the level of disrespect. I hope you had a nice chat. Well if your actions don't speak volumes about how you approach your work, I don't know what does." He paused to take a sip of water. "Given how this entire experience with your firm has been to date, I can't really say I am surprised."

All the adrenaline that had been pumping through my veins finally caught up with me, as did my husband's text. I think for the first time in months I saw clearly. I finally understood what Cole, Cecelia, and Connie have been trying to tell me. I was my own worst enemy. And I was also a lot like my mother. I had lived far too much of my life scared. I had allowed myself to be crippled by my fear of being hurt or rejected. I've tried to bury my feelings and bite my tongue as a self-preservation method, but it didn't make me happy. Instead, it made me angry and bitter. When I finally did speak my mind, I always felt better. I didn't want to make the same mistakes my mother had made. I didn't want to wake up one morning and wish I had acted differently.

I didn't plan my words. I just spoke from my heart. "With all due respect, John, I find your attitude a big part of our problem here. Yes, I had to excuse myself for a few minutes while I attended to a personal matter. You see, unlike you, I have my priorities in check. My child's school called to tell me they think she broke her arm. I made arrangements for someone else to pick her up and bring her to the doctor so I could complete this meeting and support my team. I'm staying here despite the fact the only place I want to be right now is with my child. I know you are unhappy with how things have gone with my firm and I'm sorry. We're only human, and although we try, we are not perfect nor will we ever be. I'm sure we have made mistakes along the way, but you have made some as well. You have been obnoxious and downright disrespectful to each and every person assigned to your account from day one. You have berated us over and over again. We should have completed this project months ago but we were unable to because every time you approved a concept three days later you changed your mind. Needless to say we are losing money on this account. But we are willing to see it through to completion, despite everything. That, John, is how we approach our work. But if you'd rather us just part ways now and leave, we can arrange that as well. The way I see it, the ball is in your court. You tell us what you want to do and we'll be more than happy to oblige you."

His eyes bulged. "Who do you think you are? No one speaks to me in such a manner."

"Well, that's probably part of the problem, someone certainly should have a long time ago," Cecelia chimed in as she squeezed my leg under the table.

"This is unbelievable! I'm not paying you people to be insulted!"

"We're not trying to insult you, John," I clarified.

He rolled his eyes in response.

"If you feel like we are, then I truly am sorry." I flashed him what I hoped would appear to be a sincere smile. "We were simply trying to explain there have been pain points on both sides since this project began. Where do you want to go from here?" I asked pointedly as I closed my notebook and picked up my briefcase. "Do you want to move forward or just part ways? It's your choice. We're fine either way."

He cleared his throat, and then took another sip of water before he answered. "You're really not giving me much choice, now are you, Anna? After all, I've invested a lot of time and money with your company. For me to start over from square one with another firm would be ludicrous. I don't have the time nor do I want to throw more money down the drain. I need to get this project over and done with already. So, I guess we'll just finish."

"Okay, fine. But from here on out the rules of this game are going to change. From this moment forward, we're going to need you to treat us with respect. Do you think you can manage that, John?"

He didn't utter a word. He stared at me for a few seconds, and slowly he tilted his head ever so slightly to show his compliance.

"Splendid," I said smugly. I pointed to the pitcher of ice water sitting in front of him, "You can start now by offering us a glass of water."

CHAPTER TWENTY-TWO

"**W**hat's wrong with you? You can't possibly be serious! You're not getting your nails polished in yellow!" Beatrice barked, as we stood in front of the enormous wall of nail polish shades.

My mother had gone to this salon for more years then I could count. I wouldn't be surprised if she was one of their very first customers. I remembered as a little girl always accompanying her, usually with one or two of my girlfriends by my side. I loved getting my nails done as a child in wild, bright colors, and now, all these years later, I still did.

My mother changed her longstanding Thursday morning appointment and insisted Violet and I came with her for a manicure and pedicure the day before the wedding. I took off from work and picked Violet up from school early.

I winked at my daughter. "Why not? I think this shade would go perfectly with my dress and my new tan." I answered, as I opened the bottle of the Essie polish and applied a thin coat to my pinky nail in an attempt to get a better gauge of the exact shade. Violet thrust down the neon pink polish she held in her good arm and focused her attention on both of us.

"Don't be preposterous, Annabel. You can wear your far out

colors any other day of the year, but not for my wedding. Don't you want a nice, clean French manicure instead?"

"Not particularly. You know I like vibrant hues. How about this aqua?" I asked as I smirked at Violet.

Beatrice sighed deeply. "I don't think so. I don't like it any better than the yellow. What are you trying to do? Drive me batty before my big day? Must you always be so difficult?"

"Mom, please! Is this really necessary? It's only nail polish colors after all!" Violet said with quite a bit of sass as she rolled her eyes at me. "Do you really have to give Grandma more stress than she already has? She is getting married tomorrow remember? It's her day, not yours. Can't you just try to roll with the punches for once and make her happy?" My mother leaned down and kissed my daughter's head.

There was nothing like being scolded by your child, especially when you knew she was right. Ever since my mom picked Violet up from school and brought her to the doctor's office to treat her broken arm, Violet had developed a newfound love and respect for her grandmother. I was so thankful I listened to Cole and asked my mother for help. I just wished it didn't take me so long to have done it. Maybe if I reached out to my mother sooner, my kids would have known they could count on her also.

"Fine," I said with a smile. "I can argue with one of you ladies but not both of you at the same time." I picked up a pretty, but pale, shade of mauve. "Will this work?"

"Finally, you've come to your senses. Thank you," my mother replied as she picked up a sparkly shade of pale pink. "What do you think about this one, Violet? I think it would look marvelous with your dress."

"I love it, Grandma!" Violet said as she nodded her head. Then the three of us were ushered to the back of the salon. We had our pedicures first. Violet sat next to me, and Beatrice sat across from us. We all were pretty much silent, lost in our own worlds. Violet was busy playing a game on her iPad, my mother was thumbing through a Vogue magazine, which she had pulled out of her gigantic Fendi bag, and I caught up on work emails. Even though I took the day off, I couldn't stop myself from checking to make sure everything was under control. I gasped when I read the latest email from John McGrevor. Not only was he polite, he also complimented my team on the new concepts we submitted to him late last night.

Once our toes were finished, we were then ushered to the manicure stations. We sat in a line. I was at the middle station, and Violet was on the end closest to the window with her cast arm propped up on two pillows. I expected her to be gazing outside, but instead she kept her eyes closed as her fingernails were filed. If she wasn't bopping her head to the Taylor Swift song playing on the radio, I would have thought that she was taking a nap. She probably was just trying to tune out the conversation my mom and I were having. I wish I could be so lucky.

For what felt like the fiftieth time in the last two days my mother was going over the agenda for tomorrow to make sure I had it all down pat. The wedding was to take place at eight o'clock at night. The dresses and tuxedos were going to be delivered to the country club in the late afternoon, so we didn't have to travel with them or dress in advance for our arrival. Beatrice wanted to avoid as many wrinkles as possible. She was taking a leap of faith and was allowing me to be in charge of getting my and Violet's hair styled. This was a small miracle. I had to swear to her on Cole's life we would be finished by four o'clock in the afternoon, at the latest. I also had to promise her I would make sure Violet wore a button down shirt to the salon to avoid any possible snafus come dressing time. And I also vowed that Violet would stay indoors afterward to prevent any possible wind damage.

Beatrice was then sending a limousine to pick me up at five

o'clock and another one to pick up my family an hour later. Although it should only take forty-five minutes for me to reach the country club, she wanted to allow for a little extra time just in case of traffic. Upon my arrival, my mom and I were supposed to do a full walk-through of the club to make sure everything was exactly as *she* wanted. I really didn't understand the purpose. If the napkins were the wrong shade what could really be done at that point? After all, the guests would soon be arriving. But there was no talking reason with my mother, so I didn't try. I just agreed to all of her requests. It was much easier that way.

I glanced down at my nails. Although the color wasn't my usual style, I was happy with how they came out. My mom was right. They would look better with my dress than the yellow I originally selected. I hated it when she was right.

The manicurists moved like precision swimmers. Practically in unison two of them grabbed my mom's and my pocketbooks while Violet's picked up her knapsack and escorted us all to the drying station, which was located at the front of the salon. As soon as we sat down, Beatrice exclaimed, "Oh my! I almost forgot, Annabel! Make sure to tell Connie and Patrick to arrive a little bit earlier than the invitation called for. I thought it would be nice if we included them in a picture or two, don't you think since they are the children's grandparents as well?"

I nodded my head and smiled. "Yes, I do, Mother," I answered. "Actually it would mean a lot to me."

My mom didn't comment further about my in-laws. Instead she asked, "Now do we have to go over any of this again? Are you sure you have it all straight, Annabel? Timing will be everything tomorrow."

"I think I've got it all committed to memory," I replied with what I hoped was a straight face. I couldn't help but wonder how many more times Beatrice planned to repeat the same thing to me over the next twenty-four hours.

"Even I've got it Grandma!" Violet answered. "And I've been trying not to listen to you. It's not rocket science, ya know. Mommy's smart. She can keep it straight." Then she turned to the girl who did her nails. "Can I please have a ten minute massage?" For emphasis, she first looked at her broken arm and then she turned to face my mother and me before adding, "You have no idea how stressed I've been!"

CHAPTER TWENTY-THREE

There was something so relaxing about being in the back seat of a limousine, alone. Or, maybe it was just the fact I was alone that I felt so relaxed. Regardless, I was relishing in the silence. When the car came to pick me up, I fully intended to go over the toast I wrote for Walter and my mother a few more times. But I just couldn't bring myself to do it. I already had my speech committed to memory. I definitely didn't need any more practice. Besides, if I recited it one more time, it would sound forced, and that wasn't what I wanted.

Uncharacteristically, I turned my phone off as well. I didn't want any distractions. Instead, I opted to just watch the scenery. Somehow, staring at the other cars and trees was mesmerizing me. I was extremely content. Today went smoother than I had anticipated. I was shocked; Beatrice only called me two times to make sure I had everything under control. She seemed much calmer than I expected. I can only pray she will manage to stay this way.

As the limo exited the parkway butterflies filled my stomach. I had no idea why I started to feel nervous, but I did. I took a few deep breaths to try and calm myself down; I closed my eyes. When I opened them, we were already at the club's complex.

The Glen Maple Country Club was definitely off the beaten path, by design. You could drive past the entrance five times before spotting the small white sign advertising the club's existence. There was a hidden driveway, which led to a long, winding maple tree lined road. It was the most exclusive country club in Long Island, and my parents were two of the founding members. Brody and I both had our first birthday parties here. So many holidays were celebrated in the massive dining room surrounded by my parent's closest acquaintances. My brother and I both learned how to swim in the enormous pool out back when we were toddlers. And we both took golf lessons here as well. I hated the sport and was awful at it. At first, Beatrice refused to let me quit. She was an avid player, and she wanted me to follow in her footsteps. But eventually, my lack of talent was an embarrassment to her. She really hoped Brody's experience would have differed from mine, but it was practically the same. Fortunately for him, I paved the way. All he had to do was ask her to stop the lessons, and she let him.

While I hated the sport, I always loved the look and the feel of the golf course. The grass was always so green and lush. The peaks and valleys offered so much definition, and the trees and flowers were always perfect. I had assumed the ceremony would take place outside on the course overlooking one of the many man-made lakes. However, when I suggested this to my mother, she scoffed as if I suggested she get married on Mars.

The limousine came to a stop outside the clubhouse's entrance. I grabbed the bag where I had packed the shoes Violet and I were going to wear, and said to myself "It's show time." The driver opened the door for me. I paused for a moment and stared at the massive brick building and thought of my brother. God, I wish he was here today, but in my heart ,I knew he was with us in spirit.

I walked up the marble staircase and opened the heavy wood door. As soon as I entered the building, I practically crashed into Walter. He looked like a nervous wreck. His hair looked like his hands had attacked it. He was pacing and muttering to himself while shaking his head from side to side. I prayed he wasn't having second thoughts about tying the knot.

"Anna!" Walter exclaimed. His eyes lit up when he saw me and he rushed over and engulfed me in a huge hug. "Thank goodness you are finally here. I didn't know what to do."

"Walter, what are you talking about? Is something wrong?" Even though I haven't known Walter for very long, I've never seen him act this way. I would never have pegged him for a man who'd get so flustered.

He snorted. "Something wrong? No! Everything is wrong!" He ran his hands through his thick white hair. "Your mother is having a meltdown. She is a complete and utter mess. I don't know what to do. Every time I try to calm her down, she freaks out more. I've never seen her behave this way. She is totally beside herself. She actually just kicked me out of," he paused to make air quotes, "the bridal suite. She told me to leave her alone and not come back until you were with me. So that's what I've been doing. I've been waiting for you, and pacing. I really wish I didn't quit smoking twenty-five years ago. I'd kill for a cigarette right about now! See how rattled the woman has made me?"

I've seen Beatrice in panic mode many times so I didn't envy Walter. "Oh no. How long have you guys been here?" I asked as I glanced at my watch. Fortunately, for once in my life I was right on time.

"Too long, that's for damn sure. She was too antsy to stay at home, so she insisted we come here earlier than planned. It was the worst decision ever!" Walter took hold of my hand and started walking fast. "Come on. I'll bring you to her and then I am going to find the bartender and have myself a nice stiff drink, or two!"

Walter practically dragged me down the long corridor towards the winding staircase. Thankfully he released his grip as we walked up the staircase. He took the stairs two at a time. Clearly, he was in a hurry. I found it difficult to keep up with him. He stopped in front of one of the card room entrances. He knocked on the closed door, which I guessed correctly was temporarily transformed into the bridal suite. He didn't wait for a reply. He opened the door but didn't walk inside. He gave me a gentle shove into the room, and called out, "Beatrice, your daughter is here." To me, he said in a barely audible voice, "Good luck." Then he turned around, and pretty much ran down the hallway.

My mother was sitting in a tall, red velvet wingback chair. Her back was to the door, and her head was tilted down. I rushed over to her and knelt down. "Mother! What's wrong? You're crying."

My mom opened her arms and engulfed me in a hug. She kissed the top of my head. "Thank God you are here, Annabel. This is a disaster, darling! For months, we've worked so hard for this day, and now nothing has turned out right. All our work was for nothing!" Tears streamed down her face.

I wasn't used to my mother losing her composure so easily. This reaction was completely out of character for her. Usually, she got angry, not sad.

"What are you talking about, Mother? Walter said you were upset, but I figured he was exaggerating. What could possibly be so wrong to make you cry on your wedding day?"

She stood up and straightened the gray pencil skirt she was wearing smoothing it down with her hands. Then she dabbed her eyes with a tissue. "I don't even know where to start. Come with me, and I'll show you. It's probably best you see the disaster firsthand."

I followed my mother down the corridor and back down the stairs. I caught a glimpse of Walter sitting at the front bar. He wasn't alone. There were a few other men sitting on the opposite end, who based on their attire just finished a few rounds of golf. Walter wasn't interacting with them, nor was he watching the baseball game that was playing on the big flat screen television right in front of him. Instead, he was typing frantically into his iPhone. It didn't look like he had touched his martini, but he did looked a bit more relaxed than he did when I first arrived. I prayed he wasn't going to change his mind about this wedding.

My mother didn't even glance at Walter. Instead she walked briskly in the direction of the small banquet room where the ceremony was to be held. I struggled to keep up with her. When we reached the room, I noticed the door was closed. "Go on. Open the door, Annabel." She snickered.

I reached over and tried to turn the knob. When it didn't budge, I tried to push the door. Finally, I gave it a pull with all my might. I turned and faced her. "I can't. It's locked."

"Yes. I know," she said as she shook her head in disbelief and dismay. "It's locked because last night... Oh, I can't even believe this." She placed her hand on her forehead. "You remember the layout of the club right?"

"Of course I do. We used to come here several times a week, after all."

"Right." My mother glanced up at the ceiling. "Well, you remember how the locker rooms are upstairs right above this banquet hall, right?"

"Yes," I said slowly, still confused.

"Last night one of the pipes in the showers burst. Apparently, this happened after everyone left for the evening, so water was leaking down all night long and caused massive damage in this room." Screeching, she continued, "Parts of the ceiling collapsed!"

I gasped, "What?"

"You heard me. The room is a disaster! When I first saw it, I thought I was going to have a coronary. Even Walter lost his cool. But did I get a phone call from the club this morning when they discovered this? No! Not even a courtesy call!" Her voice grew louder with every sentence. "Am I some poor soul who found this place in the Yellow Pages? No! I've been a member of this club for more years than I can count and they didn't even have the decency to call me as soon as they realized what happened. It's inexcusable! I mean really, Annabel, I was planning on getting married in this room, not arranging a mahjong game!"

"This doesn't sound right," I said as I bit my lower lip. "Are you trying to tell me Tommy didn't call you?"

My mother started to nervously tap her foot. "Yes. That's exactly what I'm saying. He waited until Walter and I arrived to spring this news on us. Tommy has managed this club for twenty-five years. And during the entire time I've been nothing but good to him and his children. I am not just talking financially, mind you. Although I've been extremely generous to him over the years." My mother pointed at her chest. "Did you know when his daughter graduated college it was me who was responsible for her getting her first job? I called in some favors. The poor kid would have had such a difficult time of it if she had to do it on her own. Don't get me wrong, she was very bright, but she never applied herself. And this is the thanks I get!" She outstretched her hands.

I looked around. I hoped to see Tommy but he was nowhere in sight. "I don't understand this," I said softly. "This doesn't sound like him at all. What did he say? Why didn't he let you know right away?" My mind spun in circles as I threw out questions.

My mother rubbed her eyes. "He gave me some cock and

bull story that he thought he'd be able to have the room repaired in time for the ceremony."

"What?" I asked again as I looked at her like she lost her mind.

"You heard me." She started tapping her foot harder against the oak wood floor as she spoke. "How he had the audacity to say that to me, I will never know. Does he think I was born yesterday? I've had enough work done at the house over the years to know a room this size, with this much damage, couldn't possibly be repaired in one day. And besides, even if by some miracle he was able to pull it off, how could he have thought I would want to exchange my vows with Walter while inhaling paint fumes?"

I didn't know what to say to comfort her so I kept silent. I simply squeezed her arm instead. There was no point dwelling on the predicament; we couldn't change it. We did, however, have to move forward, and we had to act quickly. After all, the guests would be arriving soon.

I looked my mother in the eye and said, "So, the cocktail hour is in the other small banquet room, and reception is in the main dining room. Did you decide to have the ceremony downstairs? I know it wouldn't be your first choice of location, but it does offer a nice view of the pool and tennis courts."

My mother leaned against the closed door. She spat out, "I didn't decide to have the ceremony anywhere."

"What do you mean?" I glanced down at my watch. "There isn't much time left to make a decision. They'll have to set up the area quickly. Before we know it, everyone will start showing up."

She placed her hands on her hips and shook her head from side to side. "It's already set. Good old Tommy took care of the decision for me, as well." She exhaled deeply. "Come on. I'll show you."

I followed my mom down the long hallway to a large glass

door, which led out to the golf course. She opened the door slowly and stepped outside. I followed her down the stone pathway. "Look at this!" She said with venom in her voice. "He arranged for us to get married outside, on the golf course! What was he thinking? I thought I made myself perfectly clear to him I wanted the ceremony to be inside. Do I not speak English?"

I bit my bottom lip again as I contemplated a reply. I knew she was livid at the change, and I knew she was vehemently opposed to getting married outdoors, but Tommy did a fabulous job. The setup was beyond beautiful, and it was exactly what I had originally envisioned.

I smiled. "Mother, I know you didn't want this but just look at it."

My mother rolled her eyes as she pursed her lips.

"No, Mother. Really look at it." I demanded as I spun her around. "You couldn't ask for a more picturesque location to get married, well unless you dashed off to a Caribbean island or something." As soon as those words were out of my mouth, I instantly regretting making the reference to my own wedding. Fortunately, my mother didn't mind or seem to notice so I continued. "It's a beautiful day. There is barely a breeze and practically no humidity. You don't have to worry about your hair getting messed up. Your guests will be incredibly comfortable sitting outside on this magnificent course with their eyes glued on you and Walter."

Beatrice stared at me, but she seemed to be growing ever so slightly calmer. I took advantage and kept talking. "Look at all the attention to detail! Tommy might not have handled the situation properly, but he did put a lot of thought and care into this setup. Look," I said as I pointed. "They lined up the chairs in a semi-circle. No matter where anyone sits, they'll have an unobstructed view of the altar. That wouldn't have been possible to do if the ceremony was indoors." I clutched my mother's arm. "Please, don't let this minor deterrent ruin your special day."

Very sarcastically she replied, "Oh, don't be silly, dear. I am not this upset simply because of the change in location."

I glared at her.

"Oh, Annabel, this is just the beginning. There's more," she said bitterly. With that she turned around and started marching back towards the club's entrance. I followed her in silence. I couldn't imagine what else she could be referring to and I wasn't sure I wanted to know.

She stopped in front of the heavy wood door, which led into the main dining room. She opened the door, and I followed her inside. "Look at the tables, Annabel." She demanded.

I did as I was told and I gasped.

The tables looked exquisite, just as I anticipated they would. In the center of each and every one, there was a small round bowl that was filled with either cut white tulips or mini calla lilies as opposed to the monstrous arrangement my mother ordered.

"Oh, Mother." I couldn't help it. A nervous giggle escaped my lips. "The florist must have made a mistake with the order. They sent what I wanted you to get and not what you actually chose."

Beatrice buried her head in her hands. "I know. I don't know how they could have done this. I thought I made my wishes crystal clear. What more could I have done, made the arrangements myself?" Her nervous foot taping began again. "I don't understand how they could have screwed up like this. They've been in business forever. They have an amazing repu-tation. And yet, somehow my order was completely wrong! I called them up as soon as I saw this. I went ballistic. I was going to demand they rectify the situation immediately and bring the arrangements I ordered."

"Would it even be possible?" I asked trying to be practical. "Do they have that amount of flowers just laying around? Also wouldn't they have to order the vases?"

"We'll never know. They were closed when I called." She exhaled deeply. "But don't worry. I left some message for them. My vocabulary put a truck driver to shame."

"No wonder Walter is busy drowning his sorrows," I said. I couldn't help it, a small chuckle escaped my lips. If looks could kill I would certainly be dead by now.

"You think this is funny?" My mother asked, as her eyes bulged out of her head. I've never seen her so irate in my life.

"Sorry. I didn't mean to laugh, really." I bit my lower lip in an attempt to stop giggling. "Honestly, though, I think you need to lighten up a little. This is still your big day. Enjoy it. I'm sure everything else will be perfect."

"You think?" My mother snarled as she folded her arms in front of her chest.

I smiled. "Yes, mother. I do."

"Oh goodie. I'm so glad you have such faith," she said sarcastically. "Care to see the cake?" Then she stomped towards the back of the dining room.

I was afraid to follow her, but what other choice did I have? On a small table, which was covered with calla lilies, sat the wedding cake. It wasn't the classic three-tiered round cake with decorative frosting that resembled lace my mother had so carefully ordered. Instead, it was the cake I had fallen in love with at the bakery, the one with the four tiers of little square cakes covered with turquoise frosting and white frosted bows on top which resembled Tiffany ring boxes.

I bit my bottom lip so hard that I drew blood.

"Do you see this?" Beatrice put her hands firmly on her hips. "Annabel, they did exactly what the florist did. I don't even understand how this is possible. How could they both have screwed up? Seriously, I thought I made myself perfectly clear at the bakery. Didn't I?"

There was no point in my answering. My mother didn't seem to expect me to. She started walking around the cake.

Looking at it from all angles, she started to flare her hands. She was totally losing whatever cool she had managed to hold onto. "How many times did I say that afternoon I wanted a classic cake? Clearly, that ditz, Donna, paid no attention to anything I said. This isn't what I ordered. Look at it!" She pointed at the cake, "It looks like I'm having a sweet sixteen party and not a wedding. I will be a laughing stock!"

"Come on. It's not so terrible Mother. I think the cake looks beautiful. And more importantly, I'm sure it will taste delicious."

"Oh who cares about taste? You know my friends. They are all on perpetual diets! They won't even taste the cake! I knew I should have just ordered fruit plates!"

"Did you call the bakery? They may have time to fix it," I asked as I looked at my watch. "After all, the cake wouldn't be served until the end of the night. This could be rectified, I'm sure."

"Walter said the same thing. In fact, he insisted on placing the call. I think he was afraid of what I would say to them given how livid I was."

"And?" I asked, hopeful.

"They were closed too! So I'm stuck with this!" A tear fell down her cheek. I wiped it away with my finger.

"Okay, so there were a couple of hiccups today," I said. "But please, try not to get so upset."

My mother glared at me in response.

I ignored her and continued. "Yes, things didn't work out quite the way you had wanted them to. But really, does life ever go according to plan? You of all people should know it never does. Life is just as much about the journey as it is the destination. I know you're upset and disappointed. And you have every right to be. I am not discounting your feelings. You and I have put a lot of time and effort into planning this wedding. And I know you wanted everything to be perfect. And yes, there have been some issues and errors today."

"Some?" my mother interrupted.

"Okay, yeah. There've been a lot of mishaps, but in the long run, does any of it really matter? When you look back on this day will you really be thinking about the cake or the flowers not being what you had ordered? Or will you remember today as one of the best days of your life because you began a new chapter with the man you love?"

Beatrice sighed deeply and shrugged her shoulders.

CHAPTER TWENTY-FOUR

"Ms. Buchanan," a pretty, young girl with a long bouncing blonde ponytail, dressed in a tuxedo, called out to my mother. I was thrilled for the interruption. No matter how hard I tried I wasn't making much headway in my attempt to calm my mother down. I longed to be at the bar with Walter. I could totally use a drink, or four, right about now.

"Yes?" Beatrice replied as she turned around and faced the young girl.

"Tommy wanted me find you and let you know that the dresses and tuxedos arrived a little while ago. They're hanging in the appropriate rooms. I already let your fiancé know."

"Thank you, dear," my mother said with no enthusiasm.

"You're so welcome!" The girl flashed my mom a super bright smile. "Oh, and the woman who's going to do your makeup is also here. When you are all dressed and ready, just buzz down to the front desk and someone will escort her up."

"Alright," my mom replied, before turning her back on the girl.

"Ugh! I almost forgot," the girl said as she smacked her forehead for emphasis. "I also just dropped off a bottle of champagne in your room. Tommy thought given the circumstances, you may want to sip on some while you get ready."

"Thank you. How very thoughtful of him," I said to the girl.

"Pfft," my mother muttered. "Champagne is the very least he could do after everything that happened here. Dear, you didn't say, and after today's turn of events, I know I shouldn't assume anything anymore. Can you please be a plum and make sure the champagne Tommy had you deliver is on the house. I don't want to find it on my bill later tonight. I'm not in the mood to have to pay for another gift if you know what I mean."

"Um, yeah. Of course," the girl stammered and walked away, with her head down.

I took my mother's hand. "Come on Mother. Let's get dressed. I'm sure once you slip on the beautiful Chanel dress you bought you'll feel one hundred percent better."

"Well, I certainly can't feel worse, now can I? Fine." She sighed. "Let's go."

As I walked with my mother towards the staircase, I peeked by the bar expecting to spot Walter again, but he wasn't there. I couldn't decide if it was a good sign or a bad one. I hope he didn't split. When we reached the top of the stairs, I glanced once again at my watch. Cole and the kids should be on their way by now. I really wanted to text him and fill him in on the debacle this day had quickly become, but I decided against it. He'd soon experience it first hand. What was the point in ruining a good limo trip for him and the kids?

My mother opened up the door to the suite and stepped inside. Even though we were only gone for about an hour or so, the room was completely transformed. A dressing area was created with pale pink fabric. Two oval shape full-length mirrors in wooden stands were brought in and positioned adjacent to the dressing area. In addition, there was a garment rack on the other side of the dressing area, which held three dresses, each one wrapped in a protective bag. A long wood table was also added to the room, and it was already covered with the entire makeup essentials we would soon need. Two bouquets of flowers were sitting on the table as well as the basket of white rose petals Violet would scatter down the aisle. Harley was going to hold the basket for her due to her broken arm. Some additional chairs were also brought in and placed throughout the room. Finally, in the center of the room, on a small round wooden table, was the promised bottle of champagne. It was chilling in a silver bucket of ice. There were four crystal flutes placed alongside it.

"I'll get dressed first. You can open the champagne," my mother announced as she made her way towards the garment rack. She flipped the two large dresses and picked up the one which was tagged 'Beatrice.'

"Almost show time," I muttered to myself as I angled the champagne bottle away from my face and the glasses. The bottle opened with a pop, and a drizzle of foam ran down the side. I used one of the white linen napkins, which was placed on the tray to wipe up the liquid. I poured champagne in one glass. I was just about to fill the other when my mother screamed.

"What's wrong? Are you okay?" I jumped up and yelled back in reply. The side door sprung open and Walter emerged from the adjoining room. He looked exquisite, in his black tuxedo.

"Beatrice. Are you okay?" he asked, concerned.

My mother didn't say a word, but slowly she pulled back the pink fabric curtain and revealed herself.

I didn't know what to say, or what to do. I just stood there, staring at her. I couldn't utter a word. Walter didn't say anything either. Seconds passed, although it felt more like minutes. My mother was also quiet, and she didn't take her eyes off me. Finally, I broke the silence. "That... that... Isn't the... the... dress you... you... ordered." I stuttered. "What's going on? How could they have sent you the wrong dress?"

"You got me. I sure can't figure it out." She replied as she walked towards the full-length mirror and gazed at her reflection in disgust.

"It's not even similar," I remarked remembering the stunning cream colored beaded Chanel dress she had modeled for Violet and me at the boutique. "It isn't even white or cream. It's wine!"

She turned around to face Walter and me. "I know!" she answered looking distraught.

"It actually looks like it's the same shade my dress is."

"Again, I know." She snickered. "I really don't understand what is happening. Nothing is going right. We've worked so hard for months, for nothing." She sat down in one of the large chairs and buried her head in her hands. Once again, she started to sob.

Walter knelt down beside her and placed his hand on her thigh and squeezed it tenderly. "It's okay, Bea. You look beautiful. And you really don't have to wear white you know." He laughed. "After all, it's not like it's your first time."

My mother punched him in the arm. "Really? Thank you for that information. This day is quickly turning into a disaster. Do you think your little comment made me feel better? I swear you're no better than she is. Neither one of you is helping."

Sheepishly, with a boyish grin, he said, "Sorry."

I knelt down next to them. "Mom, Walter does have a point. You do look beautiful in the dress. You wanted this wedding to make a statement, didn't you? You sashaying down the aisle in that outfit will have everyone talking for months!"

"Ugh! Precisely what I'm afraid of! Annabel, I want them talking for the right reasons. Not because I'm dressed like a fool."

"But you're not, Mom," I tried to reassure her. She really did look beautiful in the dress. It was tea length with a gathered waist, three- quarter length sleeves and a round neck in a beautiful shade of marsala.

"Whatever. I give up," she said as she waived her hands in the air. "I'm done. Just go put on your dress, Annabel." Then she turned and faced Walter. He gently stroked her cheek. I made my way to the garment rack and grabbed the other large bag, the one with my name on it. I entered the makeshift dressing room. As I took off my sneakers, I said a silent prayer the bag didn't contain a polka dotted or leopard printed dress. I didn't think my mom could take much more of this. I really felt bad for her.

As I slipped out of my jeans and removed the zippered sweatshirt I was wearing, I heard Beatrice and Walter whispering, but I couldn't make out what they were saying.

I slowly unzipped the bag and pulled the dress out. Then I gasped.

"Is everything okay in there, darling?" my mother asked, sounding oddly calm and smug.

"Um, I'm not sure," I answered honestly as I slipped into a dress that clearly wasn't what I ordered either. The style was similar, though. It was an A-line, form fitting dress, with a long flared bottom which reached my ankles. But instead of it being one-shouldered, like the one we bought, this one had a sweetheart neck. But the largest difference was the color. It wasn't wine, like the dress I had picked out and the one my mother was now wearing. It was white!

I slowly peeled back the pink fabric and emerged from the makeshift dressing room. My mom and Walter were no longer sitting off to the side looking distraught. Instead, they were standing right in front of me, and both of them had huge smiles on their faces.

My eyes bounced back and forth between my mom and

Walter. I couldn't comprehend what was happening. I had so many questions.

"What's going on? Why are you looking at me like that? What's happening here?" I asked. I didn't allow either one of them to answer a question before I tossed out another one. With every question I asked, my voice got louder and louder.

"Do you really not have a clue, darling?" My mother asked as she smirked at me.

"No," I answered honestly. "I really don't," I whispered.

My mom gazed into Walter's green eyes. He nodded, and then he reached into his back pocket and pulled out his iPhone. "Stand together ladies and smile. I want to take a picture of the bride and her mother."

My jaw dropped. "What?" I asked, as Walter snapped the shot.

CHAPTER TWENTY-FIVE

I took a large gulp of the champagne Walter had poured for me. The bubbles made my nose tickle, but I didn't pay any attention. "Can one of you please explain what is going on? I'm so confused."

Walter glanced at his Rolex watch. "Beatrice, I will allow you to do the honors. I should go downstairs now. Cole and the O'Conner's should be arriving soon. I want to be able to greet them when they get here and get them all squared away." He put his own glass of champagne down. "Oh, and I'll also send up the makeup artist so she can make you ladies even more beautiful than you already are."

He picked up his flute again and finished off his drink. Then he leaned over and gave me a big hug. "I said it before, but it deserves repeating. You look beautiful, Anna. I'm so happy to be part of this special day. You will allow me the honor of walking you down the aisle, won't you?"

Despite my confusion, I quickly answered, "Yes. Of course." Then he was gone.

"Mom, can you please tell me what is happening here?" I asked. "I really am so confused. What's all this talk about me being the bride and Walter walking me down the aisle? Today is your wedding, not mine." I pointed at my gold wedding band I wore on my finger for effect. "I am already married, remember?"

Bea got up and walked across the room to where her designer handbag was placed. She carried the bag back to where I was sitting. She sat down next to me once more and rummaged through her purse. She pulled out a thick square envelope and handed it to me. "This may help explain things a little more," she said.

I held it in my hand for a second. It looked so familiar. I slid open the seal and pulled out an invitation. It was the style I had liked the most when we went shopping. I've never been so confused in my life. I read the printed words as I prayed for clarity...

COLE AND ANNABEL
ARE RENEWING THEIR VOWS...

BUT THEY JUST DON'T KNOW IT... YET

MISS VIOLET & MASTER HARLEY O'CONNER
ALONG WITH THEIR GRANDPARENTS
HOPE YOU WILL JOIN THEM IN THE CELEBRATION OF
LOVE...

SATURDAY JUNE 15th - 8:00PM
GLEN MAPLE COUNTRY CLUB
Remember...
SHHH... it's a SURPRISE!

. . .

"WHAT DOES THIS MEAN? This isn't the invitation you picked out," I said as I handed it back to my mother.

"I know," Beatrice smirked at me. "It's the invitation you picked out. The same way the flowers and the cake are exactly what you wanted. Even the location of the ceremony is outside just like you desired. You planned every single aspect of this wedding, Annabel. You just didn't know it."

Before I could answer there was a knock on the door. "Come in," my mother answered in a singsong voice. The makeup artist walked in. She was about twenty-two years old, with long copper colored hair, which fell down to her waist. Her right arm was covered with tattoos, and she was gorgeous. The best part was she didn't try to make small talk. She moved whatever she needed over to where we sat. She began working on me first as my mind raced.

"So there wasn't really a flood?" I questioned.

"Nope," Beatrice laughed. "But you have to admit it was a brilliant idea, wasn't it? I can't take credit for it, though," she chuckled. "Walter thought that one up on his very own. He's a sneaky man! I simply had to convince you there was a flood. He didn't think I had it in me. But I certainly proved him wrong! I did a good job of acting, didn't I?"

"Yeah. I would never have guessed you were capable of such a performance. But then again, there is a lot about you I didn't know." I paused and peered into her gray eyes, "Well until recently that is."

My mom's eyes were sad. She reached for my hand and squeezed it. "I know, and I am glad we are changing that."

"Me too. We've got a lot of years to make up for." The artist angled my chin to the right and continued working. A harsh realization struck me. "So you and Walter aren't really going to get married today?" I asked.

My mother smirked at me and shook her head. "No. We aren't."

"Were you ever engaged?" I asked, disappointed.

My mother laughed. "No, we were never engaged. You renewing your vows to Cole has always been my plan, and my plan worked perfectly!" My mother extended her left hand and looked at the Paraiba Tourmaline with pink sapphires ring on her ring finger. "But Walter did really buy me this beautiful ring. Oh, Annabel, you look so distraught. Don't fret. Walter and I are extremely committed to each other. He's the best thing to have happened to me in a very long time, maybe even ever. But at our age neither one of us sees the point in getting married. We're just going to live together. If anything happens to change our minds, with respect to marriage, we'll cross that bridge when the time comes. But for right now, today is your day. You are going to declare your love for your husband in front of all your friends and family. You are finally going to have the wedding you spent your childhood dreaming about. The wedding you missed out on having because of my bitterness and insensitivity."

"My friends and family?" I questioned as the makeup artist angled my chin the opposite direction.

"Oh yes. Did you think you were going to walk out on the fairway only to be surrounded by my friends? Ha! Yes, there will be a few of my friends here, of course. How could I not invite the ladies? They would never let me live it down if I excluded them. And, besides, if the girls didn't insist on dragging me on that cruise I would never have met Walter in the first place. So in a way they are responsible for today as well." She paused briefly, "But don't worry, except for a select few, all the guests will be the people who matter most to you and Cole."

"Really?"

My mother nodded.

"How did you manage that?" I asked. It wasn't like my mom socialized with my friends or family. I never confided stories about them to her.

"It was easy, I had a lot of assistance," my mother flashed a knowing smile my way. She counted off on her fingers, "Connie, Cecelia, and both your sisters-in-law. They all helped me."

"They did? How? You don't even know Cecelia?"

Except for when I received promotions, my mother never took any interest in my career. I think she only paid attention to my advancements because it gave her something to brag about to her friends. And while Cecelia and my friendship extended outside of our office I didn't talk about her with my mother.

"Close your eyes, please," the makeup artist requested. I did as I was told, and she started to curl my eyelashes.

"I probably should start at the beginning, shouldn't I?"

In unison, the makeup artist and I answered, "Yes." I guess she wasn't so quiet after all.

My mom arched an eyebrow at the young girl who immediately glanced downward, looking embarrassed. She began to apply mascara on my left eyelashes.

"Well, to start off, Walter and I didn't quite meet the way I told you. I believe I probably already mentioned although the cruise line had a reputation for impeccable service, I never saw it. Not once! They were so slow. I was at the pool with the girls, but I might as well have been there alone. They were all sleeping or reading, and I didn't feel like doing either. I was bored out of my mind. I decided to go to the bar and have a cocktail. When I got there, it was fairly empty. There were only a few people sitting there, and they all had drinks in front of them. They only had one bartender on duty, and he was busy shooting the breeze with a pretty young thing. Now, I am no prude. He had every right to flirt with her, but not when he had customers waiting."

The artist started applying mascara on my other eye's

lashes, as my mom continued. "I tried to get his attention. When I snapped my fingers, he looked right at me. He knew I was waiting for him. But he didn't care. He made it clear I was on his pay no mind list. Well, I'm sure you can imagine how his disrespect made me feel. I started clicking my nails on the bar while tapping my foot. I wanted to express my displeasure while trying to control my tongue. After all, I was on vacation. Then, I heard a loud sigh. I turned around and realized it came from a man who was standing next to me."

"Walter?" I asked as the artist began applying eyeshadow on my lid.

"Yes." My mother nodded her head. "While I didn't know how long he was waiting there, I figured he had to be as frustrated as I was. So, when the bartender finally sauntered over to take my order I gave him a piece of my mind. I expressed my displeasure in his service, and I told him the man standing next to me was just as upset as I was." She paused for a moment and bit her lower lip. "You know how I can get, you've seen me in action before. Well, this was a choice performance if there ever was. I was loud, and I was rude. It would have been bad enough if I spoke for myself, but like I said, I spoke for Walter too."

I clenched my hands. Even though I only knew Walter for a short period of time, I knew he would never approve of such an approach. He was gentle and kind. He was soft spoken and a true gentleman. I bet his sigh was because he was frustrated with my mother's actions not the bartender's lack of attention.

"What did Walter do?"

"Besides look like he wanted to kill me?" Beatrice chuckled as the makeup artist began working on her face. "He reached into his pocket and handed the man two twenties. He apologized for my outburst. He also explained that he never met me before and I certainly didn't speak for him. He told him to prepare the same drink he was making me for him to keep things easy. Then he turned to me." My mother clutched my hand as she continued. "Oh, Annabel. There was such hatred in his voice. He glared at me. He said 'I shouldn't even be wasting one second of my time on you lady. You don't deserve it. You sure are a piece of work.' He gestured towards the ocean and said, 'You are here, on this phenomenal ship. You should be enjoying yourself. But you can't, can you? You're a cold, miserable woman. It's clear by the way you just treated that poor boy that the only way you know how to make yourself feel good is by making everyone else around you miserable too. It's pathetic. The poor kid is a bartender on a cruise ship, not a cardiac surgeon. So, he was flirting with a girl instead of being at the ready to shake up a martini for you. Where is the calamity, lady? No one's life was at stake if we waited for another minute or two for a beverage. But you sure acted as if it was.' He then finished up by asking how I would feel if someone spoke to me, or better yet my son, the way I had just spoken to the bartender."

Beatrice sighed deeply and crossed her legs at the ankles. "No one has ever spoken to me that way. I was shocked, mostly because I knew in my heart he was right. I've been so miserable for so long, longer than I cared to remember. I didn't intend for it to happen but a tear rolled down my face. I tried to turn my head so he wouldn't see it."

"Did he notice?"

"Yes, he sure did. And then he apologized. He told me he was out of line stooping down to my level. He said he had no right to talk to me the way he did. But I told him I was glad he did. I said I needed someone to come along and wake me up. Then I asked him if he'd sit with me while we had our drinks. He said yes."

"I'm shocked."

"He later told me he only agreed to join me because he felt guilty for telling me off. I made sure to explain to him I cried because his words hit a nerve. And then, probably because I thought I would never see him again, I started telling him my story. And once I started, I just couldn't stop. He was listening so intently as if he cared. I told him about everything, everything I kept buried deep inside me for all these years. I told him about my father and William. I told him about your dad and Mindy. I told him about you and Brody. And I told him what I said to you the night our Brody died."

I was dumbfounded. "You opened up to a complete stranger on a ship?" I said as I stared at her.

Her eyes were closed as the makeup artist applied eye shadow. "I know. It was totally out of character. Unlike your mother-in-law, I don't share my life story easily. I don't know what came over me that day. There was just something about him, which made me feel comfortable enough to do it. And I was glad I did. He saw what I never allowed myself to see."

"Which was?"

"The fact I had lost both my children the night Brody died. As we sipped our martinis, he told me while I couldn't change what happened with my son, I did have time to repair my relationship with my daughter. I knew he was right. I felt terrible I had managed to turn him into my therapist, so I asked him if he'd like to join me for a drink after dinner. I expected him to say no, but he surprised me again with another yes. And well, as they say, the rest is history. Everything else I told you about our time on the ship was true."

I got up and walked to the window and looked outside. I lingered there only for a moment before returning to the chair next to my mother. "Okay, so you explained how you and Walter really met, but that doesn't explain this wedding business or how you knew who to invite."

The artist started applying more blush to my mother's cheeks as she answered, "True. So Walter and I began to spend more and more time together. As we did I started to feel an array of emotions, which had been lacking in my life for so long. The biggest one was happiness. Before spending time with Walter, I don't remember the last time I was truly happy. Walter made me laugh. He made me feel comfortable and cared for. He reminded me of William in a lot of ways. I was able to let my guard down around him. I loved it. We spent hours and hours talking about our pasts. He knew how hard it was for me to have lost Brody. After all, he lost his own daughter. He kept encouraging me to reach out to you, to make things right. I didn't know how to do it, or what to say. I couldn't picture myself just calling you up on the phone one Thursday and saying hey, Annabel, I am sorry for being such a bitchy mother these past few years, let's get close. That approach would never have flown. I wanted to rebuild our relationship slowly, organically." She paused, "Also I wasn't sure you would want to spend time with me."

"Makes sense."

"Walter and I actually did discuss marriage. And during the conversation, this idea hit me. Brody died, and our relationship fell apart right around the time you and Cole were first engaged. I couldn't think of a better way to try to make up for the past than to go back to the past, so to speak. I've regretted the fact I had no involvement in your wedding. I also felt terrible you abandoned your dreams because of my actions. I realized if you and I planned a wedding we'd be forced to spend time with each other, allowing us both the opportunity to get to know one another again. I also knew you'd never go along with it if I told you I wanted to throw you a vow renewal ceremony and reception. So instead I came up with *Plan Bea*," my mother smirked at her pun. "I pretended I was getting married, and asked you to help me. I knew you'd go along with it. After all, you would have felt guilty to have said no to me."

"Boy, you sure have me pegged." I reached over and squeezed her knee. "We really did get to know each other so much better during these last three months."

"I'm smarter than I look," Beatrice joked. "I also knew you'd tell Connie about the wedding as soon as you found out about it."

"Which I did. Well, I actually waited until the next morning to make the phone call," I clarified.

"I also knew Connie would feel the need to call and congratulate me, even though I've barely been civil towards her over the years."

"Um, bitchy towards her would be a more accurate description, don't you think."

"Yes." My mother took a deep breath. "Fortunately for me, she's a very kind and forgiving woman. This is hard for me to say, Annabel, but I am very thankful to her. These past years, she's been the mother you deserved rather than the mother you had, the mother I was."

"Mom, don't say that," I said. Although her words were true, I hated to hear her say them out loud.

"Annabel, it's the truth. You know it, and I know it. But the past is the past. The future I intend to change." She smiled.

"I know. Wait. She did call you." I suddenly remembered my mother mentioning the conversation.

"Of course, she did, probably as soon as you hung up with her. When we spoke I filled her in on my plan."

"Connie knew about this?" Shock filled my voice.

And as if on cue there was a knock on the door. "Come in," my mother and I answered in unison. Connie walked in, holding Violet's hand. Violet was already in her dress. I guess the bag here with her name on it was empty. Connie was wearing the exact dress my mom was wearing. Behind Connie were her daughters, Shannon and Denise. My friend Cecelia picked up the rear. All three women were wearing the wine one shouldered dress that I had picked out for myself the day I went shopping with my mother.

My eyes darted around at each of them. Connie dropped

Violet's hand and embraced my mom. "We did it, Bea!" She exclaimed triumphantly. "Walter showed us the picture. Her expression was priceless!"

"I know! Oh, Connie, I wish you could have been here to see her first hand. She had no clue! Your timing is perfect. I was just telling Annabel about when we first spoke." My mother confided.

Then turning to me, my mom continued as all the girls sat down. Cecelia reached for the champagne bottle and poured a glass for Connie. Violet sat down on one of the big chairs, and the makeup artist went to work on her face.

"When I called Connie she loved the idea," my mother said as she patted Connie's leg. "She couldn't wait to help me orchestrate everything. She and Cecelia compiled the guest list." My mom smiled at Cecelia. "She told me who your best friend was, and gave me Cecelia's phone number. Finally, she arranged for the all the girls to meet me at the store and get fitted for their dresses. And speaking of dresses, ladies, you all look lovely!" Everyone smiled back at my mom.

"So you guys all knew about this, and didn't tell me?" I looked around at the women I cared about most in the world, as I pretended to be angry.

"And ruin a surprise?" Denise asked as she winked at my mother.

"We'd never do that!" Shannon chimed in.

"Oh, it's so much fun keeping secrets from you Anna Banana!" Cecelia added.

"Speaking of secrets, did Cole know?"

"No," Connie answered. "He had no idea. But he knows now. Your mother arranged for the limo that picked him and the kids up to swing by my house first. He was shocked to see us in the car," Connie gave Beatrice a conspiring grin. "On our way here I filled him in on the plan. He loved the idea and can't wait to marry you again."

"It's almost show time." My mom said as she glanced at her watch. "Before we pose for the photographer and walk you down the aisle, I just want to tell you what your wedding present is."

"There's more?" I asked, shocked. Although I needed nothing else at this moment, I was curious as to what my mother had up her sleeve. She was on a roll, and I was sure her present wouldn't disappoint.

"Yes. I've arranged a second honeymoon for you and Cole. You're going to return to St. Kitts and stay in the same hotel where you were married, except this time you will be staying in one of their suites. The room is to die for!" she gushed.

"When?" I asked as my mind raced. Although I would love nothing more than to jet off to the Caribbean tomorrow, neither Cole nor I could just pick up and leave on a moment's notice.

"Don't look so petrified, dear." My mother shook her head. "I know that you will need to arrange everything at work first." My mother flashed Cecelia a knowing smile before continuing. "You actually don't leave until the first week in September. However, tonight and tomorrow night you and Cole will be staying in the city. I've booked you a room at The Parker Meridian. First, you will have breakfast at Norma's." My mouth watered as I thought of all the decadent breakfasts they serve. What they could do with waffles and pancakes was amazing. I doubted I would have the willpower to pass up the Nutella packed flapjacks.

As I decided to forget about my diet, my mother continued, "I left the day open, so you can do whatever you like." Beatrice winked at me. "But I did make early dinner reservations for you at I Trulli. After dinner, I got you first-row tickets for a Broadway show."

I wrapped my arms around my mother and held her tight.

"Wow, thank you so much. I can't believe you did all this for me."

When the embrace ended, I engulfed Connie in my arms. "And thank you so much for watching the kids this weekend."

"Don't thank me, Anna. Patrick and I aren't watching them," Connie replied with a chuckle.

"You're not? I just assumed—"

My mother cut me off. "They have other grandparents, you know," Bea chided. "Other grandparents who love them, both of them."

CHAPTER TWENTY-SIX

As the photographer snapped what I prayed would be the last picture, Tommy, the country club's manager, approached us. "Excuse me, everyone," he said. "The guests are all here, and they've already taken their seats outside. We need to begin the ceremony soon if we want to stay on our schedule." He glanced at his watch for emphasis.

"We'll begin the procession in a moment." My mother replied as she touched her hair with her hands and made sure it was firmly in place.

Tommy turned around and began to walk out of the room, but Walter stopped him. "Tommy, I'm assuming that Judge Emerson arrived although I would have thought he'd stop by to see us before the ceremony."

Tommy looked around the room nervously, "Um. I don't know. I assumed he was one of the gentlemen here."

Walter glanced down at his watch and shook his head and pursed his lips. He turned to my mother and whispered softly, "He hasn't answered any of my texts. He better not have chickened out." If I weren't standing right next to Walter, I wouldn't have heard him. What did the judge have to be afraid of?

Walter had insisted from early on, according to my mom,

that one of his legal cronies would officiate the ceremony. I thought it was such a sweet gesture, but now, knowing my mother and Walter never intended to get legally married I didn't understand why he made such a fuss. After all, Cole and I were just renewing our vows. Anyone could have done the honors, even Tommy, although he had his hands full this evening with my mother.

As if he read my mind, Cecelia's husband, Bryce, chimed in, "Don't look so worried, Walter. What's the worst? If the judge doesn't show up, I can always officiate. Let's face it. The ceremony is really just for show anyway. And after all the chick flicks Cecelia has made me watch over the years I would probably do a kick ass job!"

Cecelia gently punched her husband in the arm. "You are very funny especially since I think you like those movies even more than I do." Then she turned to me and whispered, "You'd die if you knew how many times he made me watch *Pretty Woman* with him."

I laughed, and Bryce smiled at Cecelia with such love in his eyes. It was crystal clear he totally adored her.

"Thanks, Bryce," Walter replied. "You're very kind. Hopefully, we won't have to take you up on your offer. I can't believe he isn't here."

An incredibly handsome man appeared at the doorway and called out. "I'm here old man!" He kept talking as he approached us. "You never give me any credit. Just because I arrive late for lunch doesn't mean I can't be prompt when I want to be."

I heard a gasp.

Before embracing the man in a huge hug Walter scolded, "Prompt would have brought you here fifteen minutes ago, Keith!"

"Are you okay?" I asked Cecelia, as I grabbed ahold of her arm.

She moistened her lips with her tongue. "Of course I am, why?" She asked as she wrung her hands.

"All the color just drained out of your face."

Bryce turned his attention to his wife and put his hand on her forehead. "Sweetie, Anna's right. You don't look so hot. Are you feeling okay?"

"Of course I am." She took a deep breath. "Don't be silly you two. I just remembered something I forgot to do at work, and I got a little nervous, I'm fine. Really, I am. Stop staring at me like that, please."

Although I turned my focus on Keith Emerson I kept stealing glances in Cecelia's direction. The judge was completely the opposite of what I had pictured Walter's friend to look like. I expected him to be about Walter's age. Instead, he appeared to be closer to mine. He wore an Armani black pinstriped suit with a stunning multi-colored striped tie. He had dark brown hair, which was sprinkled with a few grays, ice-blue eyes, and chiseled features. I glanced at my sister-in-law's expressions, and I instantly knew I wasn't the only one who noticed his good looks.

"Good to see you again, Beatrice," Keith said before giving my mother an air kiss. Although he turned to face me, I couldn't help but think his eyes were focused on Cecelia who was standing beside me.

"Hi! You must be Anna." He then looked to my left, "and Cole?" he asked. We both nodded. "Wally told me all about you guys. Thanks for letting me be a part of your special day."

"We really appreciate you doing this, Keith," Cole answered. Then, he began to introduce the judge to everyone. As my husband rattled off everyone's names, I noticed Cecelia was chewing the cuticles of her perfectly manicured nails. Her emerald green eyes were fixed on the judge as she backed away from the group. Cole introduced her last, "Finally this is our dear friend, Cecelia."

"Hello, Cecelia," Keith said slowly. He appeared to be studying her. Their eyes locked for a few seconds. She looked even more nervous than she did before as she twirled a long strand of red hair around her index finger.

He was grinning at her. She gave him a closed mouth smile in return before whispering, "Hi." She coughed twice before she turned her back to him and focused her attention on fixing her husband's perfect tie.

"Are we done with introductions?" My mother asked in a very business-like tone. "You all heard Tommy. We have a schedule to keep." She clapped her hands, for emphasis. "Come on. We have guests waiting and a wedding to put on! Now Keith, you, scoot. Get outside under the canopy. Everyone else, let's line up and head over to the fairway. I certainly hope everyone remembers the order we are walking down the aisle."

Walter patted Keith, on the back and the judge walked out of the room. When he reached the doorway, he paused for a second and turned around. When his eyes met Cecelia's he smiled. She looked at her shoes in response.

Beatrice reached down and grabbed my children's hands and escorted them out of the room. Everyone followed her, but Cole and I hung back for a moment. He leaned down and gave me a tender kiss.

"When my mom told me what Beatrice had in mind, I was shocked, but I was thrilled too. I'm so happy to get to marry you again, Beautiful. You're the best thing ever to happen to me and I love you more than words can ever express."

"I love you too Cole," I replied as I stroked his cheek. "And you know what the best part of this wedding is?"

He cocked an eyebrow at me.

"We can enjoy every second of it. We won't have any pre-wedding jitters. We already know we found our happily ever after."

COLE and I met up with our family and friends outside on the golf course. Beatrice had everyone gathered slightly off to the side from where our guests sat. She clearly took charge of the situation because everyone was lined up perfectly and ready to go. With a nod of her head, the cellist and the flute player began to play a classical song, which I think was written by Bach, although I did fail music history in high school.

Cole walked down the aisle first with his parents.

Tears filled my eyes as I saw my little boy take the basket of rose petals from Walter's hands so that he could hold them for his big sister. With her cast, Violet couldn't handle holding the basket and dropping the petals. But together they made a wonderful team and were able to accomplish the task perfectly. I loved how close they were. In so many ways they reminded me of Brody and myself. I looked up at the sky and blew a kiss upward. I wanted to send love to my little brother who I missed terribly. I had no doubt in my mind he was looking down on us right now. I felt his presence and his love so strongly. A large part of me knew he was finally able to rest in peace knowing my relationship with our mother was repaired. He would have hated what went on between us all these years.

Cole's sisters and their husbands walked down the aisle next. Then Cecelia and Bryce walked down. She still seemed off to me. She walked stiffly; she appeared so tense. I wondered what was bothering her. She seemed perfectly fine until the judge entered the room. After he had arrived, her entire mood and demeanor changed. Bryce kissed his wife when they reached the altar. He turned to the right to stand by the men, and she walked to the left.

I hated to see Cecelia upset. I hoped I would be able to get her to open up to me after the ceremony, but I doubted it. Even though she has always been there for me, I knew she found it difficult to share her innermost troubles and fears. It's funny she had such an outgoing personality, yet she was also extremely private. She kept her feelings very close to her heart.

My mother turned to me, squeezed my hand and asked, "Are you ready, darling?"

I smiled wide. "Completely."

Walter turned to me. "Thank you for letting me escort you down the aisle. I've spent so many years wondering what my little girl would have been like had she had the opportunity to grow up. I'd like to imagine she'd have turned out exactly like you, Anna." He kissed me.

A tear rolled down my cheek. My mom reached over and wiped it away. "Stop that now, Walter. You're making her cry. What is the matter with you? We can't have her mascara run!"

I laughed. My mom knew exactly how to end a sentimental moment. I kissed Walter. "I always wanted a dad like you too, you know."

He beamed at me, and we began to walk down the aisle. I was in shock as I looked from side to side. Every row was filled with family and friends from every aspect of my life. I couldn't believe my mom was able to pull this off. Also, I couldn't stop wondering how much time she must have spent with Connie, my sisters-in-law, and Cecelia to have accomplished this.

When we approached the altar, I handed my bouquet of flowers to my mother and then I reached for my husband's hand. I turned to the right and faced Cole.

"Family and friends," Judge Emerson began in his deep, clear voice. "Thank you so much for joining Annabel and Cole on this exquisite evening. As we stand here on this vast golf course, under the twinkling stars, I can't help but think of all the beauty there is in this world. To me, however, there is nothing more beautiful than finding everlasting love. Love isn't easy. It takes a lot of effort. Many times the endeavor is hard, and people give up prematurely, which is heartbreaking to me.

Because then, they miss out on the joy and happiness only true love brings." He paused and glanced to my left.

Returning his gaze to my husband and me he continued, "Annabel and Cole know the meaning of true love. Like all couples, they have experienced difficult times." The judge looked toward my left again.

I knew I should have been focused on his words, and the sentiment he was trying to convey, but I wasn't. I was too curious as to why he kept turning to my left.

"Annabel and Cole laugh often, and hard. They celebrate life, not just on special occasions because they make every day a special occasion. They are each other's best friend and true-life partners. Together they are one."

A tear rolled down my face and Cole wiped it away.

The judge yet again glanced to my left before leading Cole and me in our vows.

When the judge instructed Cole to kiss me, let's just say Cole didn't need to be told twice. It was funny; Cole and I have been through so much together. But just like our first kiss as husband and wife, so many years ago on the beach in St. Kitts, I felt so much more than his tender lips on mine. I not only felt his deep and unwavering love for me, I felt the hope and promise in our future. I knew no matter what life threw our way, with him by my side everything would always be all right. To me, his arms were home.

CHAPTER TWENTY-SEVEN

C ole and I finally had a moment alone as we stood outside the dining room's closed door. All of our guests were already inside waiting for our grand entrance. I was cherishing the peace and quiet. My head was spinning even though I only had two glasses of champagne. The cocktail hour breezed by in a whirlwind. It felt more like fifteen seconds as Cole and I worked the room, hugging and kissing everyone in attendance. I still couldn't believe my mother was able to pull this off. Some of the people here Cole and I haven't seen in years. But I shouldn't be surprised. I should know by now when Beatrice puts her mind to something there is no stopping her.

I took advantage of being alone with Cole to ask him a question that had been on my mind the entire night. "What do you think was going on with Cecelia and the judge?"

"What do you mean?" Cole asked, confused.

"Really? You didn't notice anything between them?" I shook my head in disbelief. "Cecelia's entire mood changed as soon as he walked in the room. In fact, when he spoke for the first time she turned as white as a ghost."

Cole stared blankly at me, so I continued. "And him! Did

you notice how he couldn't take his eyes off of her? He was blatantly staring at her when you introduced them."

"Nope, I didn't notice anything," Cole answered as he adjusted his bow tie.

I cocked my head to the side and arched my eyebrow as I asked, "What about during the ceremony, didn't you see? He kept glancing in her direction?"

"Don't you think you are being a little melodramatic?" Cole asked as he rolled his eyes. "I think you've been watching way too many made for TV movies. The judge was focused on us, not her."

"Cole, come on. Please! Think about it. He was constantly turning and looking towards my left during the entire ceremony. Why would he do that? I don't think he was gazing longingly at my mother, do you? I'm sure he was looking at Cecelia." I paused and took a deep breath before continuing. "It was strange. Sometimes I really felt like he was speaking to her and not us."

Cole ran his fingers through his thick black hair. He didn't answer right away. "Do you really think so?"

"Yes," I practically yelled.

Cole shrugged his shoulders, "So maybe they know each other." He was clearly not concerned or even intrigued.

"That's the thing," I said exasperatedly. "I managed to get Cecelia alone during the cocktail hour, and I point blank asked her if she knew the judge."

"What did she say?"

"She didn't answer me right away, Cole. When she finally spoke, she said she'd never met him before today. But she wasn't looking me in the eyes. I know she was lying."

Cole sighed and looked frustrated. "Anna, you're acting crazy. Why would she do that? You're her best friend."

"I don't know, Cole. But I told her I didn't believe her."

"You did."

"Yeah, I did. She looked so upset and sad. Cole, she didn't deny lying. She told me tonight's my night and she's not having this conversation with me today. Something is going on, and I'm worried about her. I don't understand any of this. Why was Walter so insistent about Keith conducting the ceremony? Why was he so concerned when the judge was late? And why did she lie to me?"

"Anna, you know I love you but sweetheart, I really think you are blowing everything out of proportion. A lot has happened today, and your imagination is running wild. Let it go. Let's just enjoy tonight. Please."

I opened my mouth to speak but I didn't have the chance because Tommy, the country club's manager, suddenly appeared at our side. "It's show time guys. They're ready for you. The band is going to announce you now." He opened the heavy wood door as the singer of the band shouted, "Ladies and gentleman put your hands together for Mr. and Mrs. Cole O'Conner!"

All of the guests stood up and cheered. Cole grabbed my hand and held it high above my head. We walked into the dining room and then around the dance floor.

The singer's soulful voice filled the room announcing our first dance.

"Oh my God," I whispered to Cole when he wrapped his arm around me, and we started to dance. "My mother called me at work to ask me about wedding songs a while back. This was the first one I mentioned to her." Realization hit me, "Oh my God. She really was listening to me."

"Anna, I think she's been paying attention to you all along. But you were unable to see it, and she was afraid to show it."

"I think you're right," I looked around the room and saw so much love. Violet was dancing with Harley. Patrick was holding Connie close. Walter was giving my mother a kiss while Cole's sister, Denise, dragged her husband onto the dance floor.

There was one person however who didn't look happy, the judge. He was nervously tapping his foot while blatantly staring at Cecelia who was dancing with her husband. As Bryce spun her around, her eyes met the judge's, and they locked for a moment. Cecelia buried her head in her husband's neck and nuzzled it. The action wasn't lost on Keith. He stood up and threw his napkin down on the table. I couldn't take my eyes off of him. I thought he was going to storm out of the room, but instead he just walked over to the bar. As he waited for his drink, he continued to blatantly gawk at my best friend.

The song changed, and all I wanted to do was head over to the bar where Keith was still standing, holding what looked like a glass of scotch. It was crystal clear that Cecelia wasn't going to enlighten me as to their relationship tonight. My husband already thought my imagination was running wild. So there was no way I could tell him what I just saw. He'd think I had completely lost my mind. As far as I could tell, my only hope of finding out what was going on with Keith and Cecelia was to speak to the good judge myself.

Before I could move from my spot on the dance floor Walter approached us. He tapped Cole on the shoulder and asked, "Can I cut in?"

"Of course," Cole replied, with a smile. He gave me a kiss on the cheek and patted Walter's back as he walked away.

As I danced with Walter, I watched Cole approach Violet. He took her good hand and brought her to the center of the dance floor. She was grinning wide as she moved to the music with her daddy.

"Anna, I meant everything I said to you earlier," Walter whispered into my ear as he held me close. "I can only wish if my daughter had lived she would have turned out to be half the woman you are. I'm really happy to have had the opportunity to get to know you, and I'm thrilled to have you as part of my life. I'm sure your mother told you, it was me who encouraged her to reach out to you to try and rebuild your relationship. I really prayed reconciliation would be possible, but I wasn't really sure it could be. When Beatrice told me her plan I was skeptical. Actually, I thought she was insane. I didn't understand why she just didn't apologize to you. But we both know Beatrice. She never does anything the simple way."

"You can say that again," I said with a chuckle.

"I really wondered if you would go along with her little plan. I wouldn't have blamed you if you didn't. In fact, if I was in your shoes I don't know what I would have done. To be honest, I don't think I would have juggled all my obligations around to help a woman who treated me the way she had treated you all these years, just to help her plan a wedding. But you did. You didn't think you just acted. You wanted to make her happy even though she has probably made you so miserable for such a long time. But Anna, finally, the past is the past."

"I know," I said as a tear ran down my face. "I'm excited for the future, Walter." I kissed him on the cheek. "And I'm thankful you're a brave man. Or should I say a crazy man for giving Beatrice a chance."

"Yeah, I am probably completely off my rocker," Walter replied, with a grin.

He spun me around. I glanced across the room where my son sat with his cousins and Cecelia's twins. I watched my mom approach Harley. She leaned down so she was at his height. She whispered something in his ear. Harley nodded, stood up, and took her hand. Together they walked onto the dance floor. My mom picked my little boy up, and she began to sway to the music with him. Harley nestled his head in his grandmother's neck, and tears fell freely from my eyes.

"Walter, can I ask you something?"

He nodded his head, "Of course."

"Would it be alright if I called you Dad?"

A tear rolled down his face.

I gave him a kiss on the cheek before leaving him on the dance floor. I walked over to where my mother was still dancing with my son. He was giggling, and she glowed. I put my arm around her waist, and she looked into my eyes and smiled.

She kissed my son. "Watch out, Anna, this one here's really going to be a heartbreaker."

"He's a charmer, for sure."

My mother brushed a tear away from her eye. "I was so mad at you at the bakery. You know, when you confronted me about Harley. I know that couldn't have been easy for you to do. But darling, I'm so glad you did it. And I'm glad that Walter insisted we went to your house for his birthday dinner. Truth be told I almost chickened out. But you were right about everything. I was being foolish and juvenile. If I'm honest with myself, I always wanted to be a part of his life. I just needed to open my heart to him and get to know him."

"Yeah, just like I needed to get to know you, Mom."

SNEAK PEA - PLAN CEE
CHAPTER ONE - CECELIA

I THOUGHT I WAS GOING to die. I didn't have to turn around. I already knew it was him. Despite years of desperately trying to forget, I'd recognize his deep throaty voice anywhere. Although, I never imagined, even in my wildest dreams, I would actually hear it again.

"I'm here old man!" He called out in a joking tone, one that I remembered all too well. I bit my lower lip hard as memories assaulted me. I didn't trust myself to glance in his direction, nor did I know if I wanted to. Since his voice was growing louder, I assumed he was walking over to where I stood. The room which only moments ago felt so large and spacious now seemed close in around me.

I found it difficult to swallow as he continued to speak.

"You never give me any credit." He quipped. "Just because I arrive late for lunch doesn't mean I can't be prompt when I want to be."

Walter's eyes lit up and he smiled wide. Only moments before he was worried the judge wouldn't show up to officiate the wedding ceremony, but now he looked so happy. I took a deep breath. I tried desperately to calm myself down. I knew I was being irrational. I didn't sleep well last night. Clearly, my imagination was playing tricks on me. Yes! I was overreacting. I had to be wrong. It couldn't really be him.

And then, I remembered something Walter said innocently only a few moments ago. He used the judge's last name. He said it was Emerson. My knees wobbled. I wanted to scream. There was no use in trying to convince myself the voice belonged to another man any longer.

I focused my attention on Walter as I tried to control my frantically beating heart. The older gentleman tried to look serious as he halfheartedly scolded his friend, "Prompt would have brought you here fifteen minutes ago, Keith!"

I gasped.

Before Walter engulfed him in a hug, I saw his face. He was older, of course. But he was just as good looking, as he was when I saw him last, twenty years ago. He was dressed in an Armani black pinstriped suit with a stunning multi-colored stripped tie. His dark brown hair was sprinkled with some grays. I felt faint as I realized even though there was some creases on his brow and around his aquamarine eyes, he was even more handsome now. How was that even possible, I wondered?

"Cecelia, are you okay?" my best friend, Anna, asked as she grabbed hold of my arm with much more force than was necessary.

I moistened my lips with my tongue. I was afraid of what my voice would sound like when I spoke. I felt like I was on the verge of tears. "Of course I am." I lied as I wrung my hands. "Why?"

"All the color drained out of your face." she replied, concerned.

My husband, Bryce, turned his attention to me. He wrapped his arm around my waist. "Sweetie, Anna's right. You don't look so good. Are you feeling okay?"

· · ·

"YEAH. I'M FINE." I said before taking another deep breath. I forced a smile for good measure, which unfortunately was a futile attempt. Both of them glared at me in response. It was clear from the expression on their faces neither one of them believed me.

I tried to sound more enthusiastic this time. "Of course I am." She took a deep breath. "Don't be silly you two. I just remembered something I forgot to do at work and I got a little nervous, I'm fine. Really, I am. Stop staring at me like that, please."

Neither one of them took their eyes off me. I don't think they even blinked. Don't get me wrong. I knew they meant well, and I knew they both loved me, but neither one of them was helping me right now. Why couldn't they simply take my words at face value? Why couldn't they just let me be?

Frustrated, I snapped, "Enough! Stop staring at me like that. I said I was fine, I'm fine!"

Anna dropped my arm like a hot potato and pursed her lips. She didn't take her eyes off me though. But instead of looking concerned, she looked sad and hurt. I felt terrible.

What was wrong with me? I shouldn't be taking my irritation and frustration out on her, especially today. She should be enjoying herself right now. After all, she spent the last three months working like a mad woman trying to make her mother, Beatrice's, wedding to Walter perfect. I didn't want to ruin today for her. She should be happy today. She should be laughing and smiling, not be worried about me. I blinked away fresh tears, which desperately threatened to escape.

I flashed my friend a small smile, and said softly. "I'm sorry."

"Love you," Anna whispered to me before she returned her attention to her mother, Walter, and Keith. She made a point to glance in my direction every chance she got. Subtly isn't one of her strong suits. It was funny, I was sure my husband bought my story about remembering something troubling at work. I'm actually a little surprised he didn't whip out his iPhone from his tuxedo jacket's pocket and hand it over to me so I could fire off an email to myself with my recollection's troubling tidbit so I didn't forget it again. My friend on the other hand, I was sure, saw right though my lies. Even though we have only known each other for ten years, our bond was so deep. There was no doubt in my mind, the first chance Anna had, she would be grilling me about the judge. I prayed the wedding would keep her busy enough so I didn't have to answer any questions tonight. I wasn't ready to discuss him or the past.

Cole, Anna's husband handled the introductions. I chewed on the cuticles of my freshly manicured nails. I tried to put my best game face on as Cole innocently said, "And finally this is our dear friend, Cecelia."

My stomach did a summersault. I worried what Keith would say or do.

Thankfully, all he said was "Hello, Cecelia." I got off lucky. I hoped. Sure, his words were harmless, but the way he was looking at me was anything but. I felt like he was studying me, trying to gauge my reaction. Fortunately since the last time I saw him, I had gotten really good at keeping my true feelings all bottled up.

I wanted to glance away and look anywhere except at him. But I simply couldn't help myself. Being this close to him after all this time was too much for me to ignore. Against my better judgment, I looked deeply into his ice-blue eyes. Keith returned my stare and our eyes locked. Memories bombarded me, which I tried unsuccessfully to block out of my mind. He was grinning at me. He looked like a little boy who was up to no good. And in that instant I realized his appearance here tonight couldn't possibly have been a coincidence. He planned this!

What was I doing, I wondered as I twirled a long strand of strawberry blond hair around my index finger. I coughed, twice. It was a nervous reaction. I couldn't look at him anymore. I turned away and faced my husband. I busied myself by fixing his perfect tie. Bryce didn't seem to mind or care.

"Are we done with introductions?" Beatrice asked in a very business like tone. "We have a schedule to keep, you know." She clapped her hands, for emphasis. "Come on, everyone. We've got guests waiting and a wedding to put on! Now Keith, you, scoot. Get outside under the canopy. Everyone else, let's line up and head over to the fairway. I certainly hope everyone remembers the order we are walking down the aisle. Let's get going."

Walter patted Keith on the back. When Keith reached the doorway he paused and turned around. His eyes found mine. He arched his eyebrows and he smiled. I, in return, looked down at my shoes and prayed no one else noticed his actions.

I was so thankful the ceremony was going to be held outside, because I really needed some fresh air and a stiff drink.

Keep Reading

HEROES WITH HEAT AND HEART

If you love steamy romance, and helping a good cause, you need to download Heroes with Heat and Heart Volume 2 - including one by me, download it here for only $0.99

100% of the proceeds goes to the Grassroots Wildland Firefighters organization!

ACKNOWLEDGMENTS

Thank you for reading Plan Bea. I hope you enjoyed it as much as I loved writing it. Most days I still don't believe I've written two books. It's a surreal feeling to accomplish your dream. But my dream is only a reality because I had so much help along the way...

Mom, thank you for being not only my mother, but also my dad, and my best friend. I wouldn't be half the person I am without your love and guidance.

Marc, thank you for being my biggest cheerleader, even though it often puts you in the hot seat. You're a good man enduring hours of conversations about my "imaginary friends." Oh, I finally realized how to get you to read...I have to just keep writing books!

Carl, Paul, and Hannah, thank you for being such cuties. The stories your mom shared about you shaped Violet, Harley and young Brody. Tania, thank you for your friendship and for being my "mommy expert" I know I bombarded you with questions. Les and Bobbi, I loved watching your second chance romance unfold. You guys got me thinking about the power of love and were my inspiration for this book. Tasha, thank you for helping me pick the perfect bag for the cover.

Samantha March, words can't express how much I appreciate everything you do each and every day. I'm so honored to have you in my corner! Over the last year or so, you've become a dear friend. I'm sorry for constantly blasting you rapid-fire emails daily at 5:30 AM.

Samantha Ettinger, AKA editor extraordinaire, I don't know what I would have done without you! Thank you so much for all your hard work! Your suggestions and insights were amazing, and I learned so much from you. You shaped Plan Bea into the best possible book it could be.

Greg Simanson, you are a genius! Saying that you created a cover of my dreams would be an understatement. Especially since you did it for me twice! Every time I look them, it takes my breath away...

Meredith Schorr, thank you so much for being an awesome friend. I don't know what I would've done without you. You've talked me off the ledge more times than I can count and have been an incredible sounding board. I love how we can chat about everything and anything.

Thank you to all the book bloggers out there. You guys are the best! I know you work so hard just for the love of books. Your praise and constructive criticism means so much to me as does your friendships. I love you all.

If you enjoyed Plan Bea it would mean the world to me if you left a short review on any retailers website and/or Goodreads. I love to chat and stay connected to readers. You can find me on Twitter @feelingbeachie, or on Facebook. My blog is Feeling Beachie or email me (hilarygrossmanauthor@ gmail.com). To find out about new releases (including Plan Cee) join my mailing list HERE.

XOXO,
    Hilary

ABOUT THE AUTHOR

Hilary Grossman is a recovering corporate executive. She spends her mornings and weekends hanging out with her "characters." She has an unhealthy addiction to denim and high heel shoes. She's been known to walk into walls and fall up stairs. She only eats spicy foods and is obsessed with her cat, Lucy. She loves to find humor in everyday life. She likens life to a game of dodge ball - she tries to keep many balls in the air before they smack her in the face.

If you haven't already signed up to join Hilary's newsletter, please do so... Some really exciting projects are coming up!

www.ingramcontent.com/pod-product-compliance
Lightning Source LLC
Chambersburg PA
CBHW071130200626
46817CB00018B/2559